Love Rehab 2

Kia Smith

Contents

Synopsis

Pain was what she *knew. Rising like a phoenix* is what she **did.**

After all that childhood trauma, Desiraè Thomas's life is finally good.

She's made peace with her past.
Her relationship with her Mom is better than ever.
She's starting a business.
She and Dre are moving towards marriage and baby carriages.
She has a great group of friends.
And finally, she's able to breathe again.

Life is good... until tragedy strikes again, and she's back in the place where it all started.

While she isn't quite who she used to be, Desirae isn't quite sure of who she is anymore, once faced with her new normal.

The scariest thing about life is change, but what's even scarier than that is staying the same.

When old ghosts come back to haunt her and her back is once again against the wall, Desiraè once again has some important decisions to make, making sure that no one else, but most importantly, she — doesn't get hurt in the process.

Will her old habits die hard? Or will she fight like hell to rise above it all, in a way that only she can?

For Your Listening Pleasure

If you like to listen to music while you read, check out the playlists below by scanning with your phone.

<u>Apple</u>

<u>Spotify</u>

Dedication

to the little girls who grew into big girls, still trying to figure this life and love shit out.

Author's Note

Hey y'allllll!

Welcome back if you're familiar with me, or welcome to the party if you're new here. Writing this was a fun process for me and I hope you enjoy this layered story as much as I do.

In order to understand who our FMC Desiraè is, stop here and go read **Love Rehab.** Though it *technically* didn't end on a cliffhanger, it gives important context on who she once was and all the things she overcomes. This story picks up about three years after her 21st birthday. I decided to write part two because I think we all deserve to know what life looks like after experiencing so much trauma.

Speaking of trauma, I do want to give you a trigger warning of what you may see here. Taking care of yourself should always be your first priority, so if this fiction story is too much for you, consider reading other things in my catalog.

Trigger warnings:

Explicit language + sex scenes (they be cussin' and fuckin')

Violence (people be getting beat the fuck up and unalived)

Mention of pregnancy loss

Death

Abuse (emotional, mental)

Suicide ideation

Grief

P.S. - Remember, this is a work of fiction. It is easy to say what you would do when you aren't in the situation. So, some things may seem far fetched or unrealistic, but that's the point of fiction, duh! Lol. So not too much on my girl, okay?

Happy Reading! Happy Healing

XOXO,

Kia

Prologue

"*I fuck with you shorty, and I always will,*" *LaShawn called out to me as he kept his eyes on the road.*

"I know you don't have a reason to fuck with me ever again, but I had to let you know because even when I was fucked up, I still had a lot of love for you. I just didn't know how to show it. I'm a changed man now. I know you don't ever want to get back together, and I honor that. But if you ever needed a friend, a nigga to pull up on you, to support whatever you got going on. Just know, all you need to do is make one call, and I'm there."

I was pissed. Pissed that I somehow found myself in LaShawn's presence again. It had been years. Pissed that he was offering this unprovoked apology. Pissed that a teensy part of me believed him even though I knew damn well that I shouldn't. First loves were strange like that. I may have been young as hell loving him, but I knew it was authentic and true. But his decisions tainted me and almost helped send me into an early grave.

I was a grown-ass woman now, with my own life, my own career, and a man of my own. I didn't want to hear or need an apology from LaShawn.

Or did I?

Otherwise, why did I find myself in his car, driving all over the East Side of Chicago in a snowstorm? For a bitch that has her own shit going on, I sure easily found my way back to him.

He made a sharp left on 76th and Stony Island, almost losing control. The snow was coming down in buckets, and the city had yet to disperse the ice trucks. Shit was a mess and yet, I was more afraid of being seen in this car with Shawn than I was about getting into an accident due to all the black ice that hid in the crevices of the busy Chicago streets.

I remained in my head, grateful that the music was blasting and that the heat was on until he broke the silence.

"Aye yo Rae? You not gone say shit?" he asked in a slightly agitated voice. I turned my head towards him and looked him over. He was 29 now and gone were his long braids in intricate designs. He now rocked a wavy fade. Gone were his too-big jeans and overly flashy jewelry. He put some weight on him, more muscle than anything. His baby face was now covered in a full beard. Grown-ass man Shawn was fine as hell, but the sensation between my legs that I used to feel for him was non-existent.

I had grown up too. I wasn't the same little girl he used to make a fool out of and I definitely was not the young adult who was so hurt that I chased anything familiar so I could feel **something.**

My whole life had changed. My whole mindset was different. My life was peaceful now and not filled with chaos. I zoned out for a minute, thinking about the parallels between our lives and just how different shit was now.

Shawn interrupted my thoughts. "Rae? So you just not gone say shit at all?" he repeated, visibly exasperated as he cut his eyes over at me and then focused back on the road.

"I'm not sure what you want me to say, boy. I mean... I been moved on and I'm good. You have your life, and I have mine... I don't hold no ill feelings towards you, G. We just ain't gotta be friends either."

"The fuck you mean we ain't gotta be friends?" he exclaimed. He seemed shocked that I didn't want his olive branch of friendship, but after five plus years, what exactly did I need it for? Especially now?

"Why do you want to be friends with me? Like, explain it to me like I'm five, because the shit simply doesn't make sense. Why would I want to be friends with someone who traumatized me so deeply? How am I to trust you? What would your wife say about that? What would my man have to say about that??? Like, you wanting to be "friends" makes sense to you?" I shot back.

Shawn did this thing where he bit the inside of his jaw before he said something harsh.

"Fuck that nigga! I had you first!" he barked. Shawn was losing his cool, and I just couldn't believe it.

"Not too much on my man because I still owe you and the bitch you married an ass whooping," I said in an unbothered tone. I wasn't yelling or raising my voice at this nigga because he simply wasn't mine to do that with anymore.

"Not too much on my man," he mocked me, scoffing and shaking his head. I damn near saw smoke coming out his ears. He was so mad, and I was perplexed as to why. I worked hard to contain my anger and learn how to talk to people better and actually listen. But I knew bullshit when I heard it and my patience was wearing thin.

Throwing my head back, I cackled for a good two minutes. He was so used to having his way with me that his eyes and ears couldn't fathom the woman

I was in front of him. His mindset reminded me of Peter Pan: Just a nigga who wouldn't grow up and I hated that for him.

"LaShawn, look. We can cut this short. I don't even know why I'm here, but you and I both know that I shouldn't be. I don't have the energy to go back and forth with anybody, let alone YOU. I don't owe you shit. And I don't have to be your friend. Now, take me back to my car before it gets ugly," I snapped.

Shawn kept driving, swerving in and out of traffic up I-57 and I felt myself gripping the passenger side door just to calm my nerves. I hated snow. I hated driving in it. And I hated how other people drove in it. It pissed me off.

"And you can slow the fuck down too!" I exclaimed. Though I worked hard to not curse people out anymore, that fire still lived inside of me and I was okay with that.

Shawn kept ignoring me, pushing his new Range Rover up to 100mph. At that moment, I instantly regretted getting into this car with him. At his big ass age, he was still reckless and that blew me.

"Look Desiraè, I know I fucked up with you. And I can't go back and change that. All I can say is that I'm sorry. I want to be a part of your life in any way that I can. Fuck yo lame ass nigga. Fuck my wife too if I'm being real."

I rolled my eyes all the way to heaven and then looked down at my phone screen. The picture on it was of me, Dre, and my family at a cookout we had over the summer.

"I hear you LaShawn, but the answer is no. Now take me back to my c-," my words got caught in my throat because instantly, the Range jerked forward and we slid all over the icy intersection while drivers beeped and yelled obscenities at us. LaShawn lost control of the wheel and next thing I

know, a bright light shined in the window as a huge semi truck came speeding down our way, without seeing us.

LaShawn tightly gripped the steering wheel to regain control, but the damage was already done. We flew head first into that semi. I felt the impact on my forehead first, as shards of glass cut me in my face as I went through it. I couldn't even turn to Shawn and see if he was okay but I felt my entire body jerk forward and instantly, everything went black.

Chapter One

Desiraè

I bolted out of my sleep, drenched in sweat. For months now, I had been having the same dream about LaShawn and I every night. I didn't know why, because it had been over five years since we saw each other, but I did peep that he followed me on Instagram the other day. I wasn't following him back though. I preferred to leave the past in the past, because I worked way too hard to have a stable future. At twenty-four now, I was doing my best to balance it all: being a girlfriend to Dre, a good daughter, a good big sister, a good employee, a good friend, a good culinary student, and an aspiring entrepreneur.

My days were sometimes hectic. I went from work to class at night, to being at home with Dre and still trying to make time to hang out with my girls and my family. I didn't have time to entertain anything LaShawn was talking about, but for some reason, he just couldn't stay out of my dreams. I looked over to my left in our queen sized bed, and watched Dre sleep like a damn bear. Some nights he would feel me jolt awake and console me after I told him I was having a bad dream, but on most nights he was a heavy sleeper due to his own rigorous work schedule.

Working in tech, Dre was a Senior Analyst and the youngest at his company. His weeks fluctuated between working almost ten hour days and traveling for different conferences and business meetings. I was super proud of him and everything he did to better himself. He came a long way from that kid in foster care, but it was always in him – not on him. When Dre wanted something, he didn't stop until he got it. Once he got it, he then went back and accomplished more. It was inspiring to say the least.

Not to mention, he was a damn good boyfriend to me. We started off rocky in our younger years, but with the help of Dr. Love, we were now more solid than ever. I ain't no love expert, but I learned that being vulnerable and how to properly communicate could transform a relationship. We really were growing up together and sometimes I would be in disbelief at how much we've changed over the years. I loved him and Dre sure as hell loved him some me. I never wanted for anything, he was faithful, the sex was good, and he supported me in all things I wanted to do. Most girls my age were dealing with what they considered "hell" in the dating world, I was just glad we finally got our shit together. We were young and in love, and I wouldn't have had it any other way.

Snapping out of my daze, I grabbed my phone and checked the time. 4:44AM illuminated the screen and I sighed. I kept waking up frequently around that same time whether I dreamed about LaShawn or not. Taking the initiative to have some time to myself before my busy day started, I opened my notes app and wrote out my daily gratitude list. While scrolling through Instagram one day, I came across a video of this girl who said at the start of every morning, write 3-5 things you were grateful for to set the tone for the week. These days, it was a bit easier for me to have gratitude because I truly *was* thankful for everything. So the first thing I did almost every morning was that list.

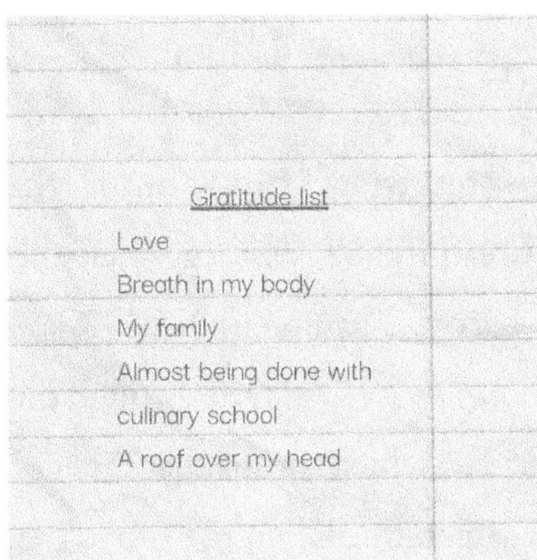

And that concluded my list. Dre was still asleep, so I decided to get some breakfast going. Slipping on my black Skims dupe dress from Amazon and a pair of red fuzzy slippers, I walked across our hardwood floors to the kitchen. About a year earlier, Dre and I moved in together to a two bedroom, two bathroom apartment in the Redwood area of Bloomington. Though I sometimes thought about moving back home to Chicago or a bigger city, Bloomington became home. My mom and siblings were here. My friends. Dre. And even Dr. Love. I was now a head-chef-in-training at Ruthie's Steakhouse, a more upscale restaurant in the town. I decided to go to culinary school to enhance my cooking skills. I was naturally good at it, but I still had dreams of opening my own restaurant and naming it after my grandmother, Earline. My eyes watered a little thinking about my Gramz. I missed her everyday and still felt a twinge of guilt for leaving her at her most vulnerable moment. I had gotten better at forgiving myself since then but the reality of her never coming back still stung.

And it always would.

***

Opening our stainless steel fridge, I took out all the ingredients for our breakfast of brioche bread french toast, eggs benedict, strawberry-mango smoothies, and duck bacon. Turning on the HK speakers in the kitchen, the sounds of *Love Ballad by LTD* played through them while I got started on our meal. It was Friday, which meant that Dre got to work from home today, but he still woke up in the morning to go to the gym in our complex. I was working a later shift at the restaurant today because I had class in a few hours. I was only a month away from graduating from culinary school and I was excited. The two year program was rigorous and often made me question myself, but I had a great support system. At any moment, I could call on my girls, my mama, or my man and they'd fill me up. With that in mind, I kept going and perfected my craft both inside and outside of school. I started researching where to start when it came to opening a restaurant and all the information was overwhelming. But the first thing I did was obtain my LLC and trademark the name of the restaurant. Dre helped me get both and supported me on many nights that I would stay up late researching locations, designing menus, and looking at grants that I wanted to apply to. Dre made a nice salary with his job and I knew my mom would throw me some money too, but the truth was, grants were where it was at. Why use money from a bank or borrow from loved ones when I could get free money? My friend Angie, who was a writer and editor for Bloomington's Daily News, helped me write up my mission statement and helped me apply for grants. My friend Bri, worked in marketing and she designed my logo and set up Instagram and Facebook pages for me. Even though the restaurant was just a dream so far, Bri figured I better lock the pages down now so that would be one last thing for me to worry about.

It was all so overwhelming, but I wanted this *badly*. I thought back to my troubled past and smirked and shook my head. I think my younger self would be proud of me, even if we didn't think we'd make it this far. In a lot of ways, I knew life was still just beginning for me, but I didn't want to discredit any of my hard work that I put in.

My thoughts were interrupted by the sounds of Dre's size 11 feet that lightly thumped across the hardwood floors as he walked into the kitchen. I was over the stove flipping the brioche bread in the skillet when he walked right up behind me and rubbed on my booty while planting soft kisses on my neck.

"Morning bae," he said sleepily. It was now 5:55AM and he wanted to eat before he got ready for the gym that opened at 6AM.

"Good morning baby," I replied, giving him a quick peck before turning back to the French toast.

"How you sleep?" I asked, putting the finished food on our plates before starting the eggs and smoothies.

"I always sleep good when I'm next to you," he replied.

I smirked. Dre hated when I got outta bed before at least cuddling and kissing on him but if he had it his way, he'd be waking up to my mouth on him every morning. I didn't always feel like doing that, and with these crazy dreams I've been having plus my job and school schedule, I wasn't as well rested as I should have been. Me and my girls often talked about the audacity of men who expected women to be super freaks 24/7 after working and going to school and bleeding once a month.

Now, no shade to the women who were able to muster up that extra energy, but I knew that I wasn't one of them. At least, not all the time. But I tried my best for Dre, because I knew how important sexual connection was for him. Snapping out of my thoughts, I grabbed our plates and set them on the kitchen table. Dre smiled sleepily at me, before taking a forkful and stuffing everything in his mouth. I snickered. Dre stood tall at 6'1 and was 180 pounds of all muscle. The boy inhaled all my meals up like I didn't feed us damn near everyday.

"This is good as fuck, Bae!" he wolfed his food down with excitement in his voice. His approval made me smile. I made every meal with love and I loved hearing his satisfaction. Since I was in school, Dre became sort of my test dummy while I tried new foods with him. I introduced him to a lot of different things over the years food wise and he appreciated it. We came a long way from those pizza puffs from BaBa's and a three piece wing dinner from Pete's.

I watched Dre savor the last bit of duck bacon and then hastily jump out his chair so he could get to the gym. But before he walked out the kitchen, he cupped my face.

"You the best chef in the world, Bae. I'm so proud of you," he said and kissed the top of my forehead, the bridge of my nose, and then finally my lips. He was so sweet to me and knew all the right things to say. I got warm on the inside and smiled at him in a daze.

While cleaning the kitchen, I looked at the clock—it was barely 7:30 a.m. It felt like I'd been up all day, and I was ready to lie back down but I still had to shower and get ready for school and work. I put my phone on the charger and hopped into the shower, lathering myself in the shea butter and mango scented Dove, Honey Pot Co feminine wash, and Naturium shower wash. I took my shower ritual very seriously, which wasn't complete without a Champagne Toast candle, a towel getting toasted in the towel warmer, and my old school tunes playing. My friends and family often called me an "Old Lady" because my taste in music centered around 70's, 80's, and 90's music. It's not that I didn't know any of the newer songs out, I just didn't care for them too much.

Once I showered, I checked my phone and noticed that my mama called me ten minutes earlier. Calling her back and placing it on speaker, I lathered up in lotion, deodorant, and baby oil gel before deciding on my outfit for the day.

"Hey Ma!" I yelled from the closet.

"Hey baby. I just called to hear your voice. You good?" she asked.

"I'm okay. I had that weird dream again last night..." I let my voice trailing off. My mama was the only one who knew about the dreams.

"Same scenario?"

"Yeah. It's weird. I know he follows me on Instagram, but I literally don't know why. I barely post on there as is, and I'm def not trying to talk to his ass," I huffed.

The outfit of the day would be some Fashion Nova jeans, My school shirt, and some Crocs lined with fur on the inside. They were the comfiest pair of shoes I owned. My hair was done in some shoulder length faux locs in a light and dark brown color. Since I worked around food both at school and at work, I had to keep my hair and nails short.

"Yeah… stay as far away as you can from that Rae. He can look but remember, if he reaches out, which he likely will, you don't owe him anything."

"You ain't gotta tell me twice. I don't want nothing to do with that man for real. If Dre knew he was following me on there, I'd never hear the end of it" I said, shaking my head.

LaShawn and I's history would forever be a sore spot with me and Dre. Even though we've grown a *lot* from the situation, there were certain times that he would be brought up in minor arguments. After these many years, I learned to let Dre talk his shit because he was entitled to feel how he feels just like I was entitled to move on from it. Something I've learned over the years is that men never really get over their egos being bruised or feelings getting hurt. That's why it's so many men out here at their very big ages dogging women out, all because some lil girl in second grade didn't want to be their Valentine or whatever.

Sometimes, it felt like Dre put me on such a high pedestal that it seemed insane to him that I would make a mistake like that. Even though I was young as hell and was grieving. But sometimes, it's less about the "why" you did something and more about the action itself.

I respected it.

I held space for him.

And I let that shit go.

The way I see it, no one ever put a gun to Dre's head and forced him to be with me. I firmly believed that love was a choice. By choosing to love me, he chose to deal with my bullshit too because regardless of what he thought – I wasn't perfect. And I didn't want to be. It was a struggle at times, but we pushed through it the best we could.

Me and Ma finished chatting on the phone and I was dressed and on my way out the door when Dre was coming back in from the gym.

Giving him a quick hug and kiss, I sprinted down the hall towards the stairs leading to our parking lot and hopped in the car. My school was only fifteen minutes away from my crib, but I liked to get there a bit early to find parking. Finally finding a spot, I walked into the building that I called home for the last two years.

I couldn't believe that I was about to be a certified chef in just four short weeks. It was a surreal moment for me. I knew Gramz would be so proud of me, and for once, I was proud of myself too. Coming where I came from and going through what I had, I didn't know too many people who stayed committed to their dreams. Being the only Black woman in my cohort was another thing. From day one, I was immediately aware of the differences between me and my classmates.

Being around majority white people was a culture shock for me, considering that I was around mostly Black people my whole life. Most days I didn't mind it but over the years I had a few incidents where I had to check both instructors and classmates about their assumptions concerning Black people and food. I cried and complained many nights to my circle about the lack of diversity and how much of an outsider I felt, but they all encouraged me to keep pushing no matter what. The world would always assume and be prejudiced towards Black people, especially Black women. ***Push back, boss up, and move on*** was the mantra I adopted to get me through the difficult days.

Those long days and nights in school and working full time were starting to pay off and I was anxious to start my next chapter. Before I locked my phone in my bookbag, I opened Instagram and took my Chef of The Day picture and posted it to my story. Moments later, hearts started popping up. I wasn't super big on social media but I did like to share my school journey. I then went over to my DMs and replied to the funny videos my friends and Dre sent me and then saw that I had a few DMs in my message request. I knew that most of it would be those annoying spam pages but my heart almost stopped seeing his name in there and a message.

Should I open it?

Nah, I shouldn't.

But no harm in opening it. He will only know if you saw it if you reply. And yo mama said you don't owe him anything.

Looking at the clock, I had five minutes to get into my classroom. Clicking on the name, it said:

KingShawn.071

I'm proud of you shorty.

A simple message. Coming from a person that I shared nothing with anymore besides history, yet for some reason it made me smile a little bit. Just a little though. I almost double-tapped it wanting to acknowledge that I saw it but decided not to. Like my mama said, I don't owe him anything. I was actually surprised to see him on Instagram, since he never liked social media in the past.

Pushing LaShawn in the back of my mind, I focused on my four hour class. Today, we were tasked with making a few popular French dishes. After washing our hands and putting on our aprons, my classmates and I worked diligently on not fucking up. Our professor, Jeniffer LaBreaux was a world renowned chef from New Orleans who has let food take her all over the world. She's appeared on the Food Network multiple times and has cooked for everyone from President Obama to Beyoncé. She was no nonsense as hell and I admired the fuck out of her. There weren't too many Black people who were in this space and she didn't know it, but Chef LaBreaux was my role model. Needless to say, I worked my ass off in this class and it was my hardest one. Some days class literally felt like an episode of the Food Network show, *Chopped* and it stressed me the hell out.

While my dream was to move back to Chicago and open up a restaurant, I knew I wanted Mz. Earline's Kitchen to be more than typical soul food. Nothing wrong with regular soul food, but ever since being in school, I knew there were ways to elevate it to a potential never seen before. I wanted quality food and quality experiences in my restaurant. I wanted it to be a community staple *and* a place that people from all over couldn't resist. Those days of helping Gramz sell dinners out her back window near the deep freezer would come in handy, I just knew it. I just had to graduate, finish stacking, and then scope out a place to even house my restaurant. It's a lot, but once I'm locked in on something, there's no stopping until the goal is met.

"Chef Thomas! Excellent call on the dash of lemon herb with the meats," Chef LaBreaux called out.

She was walking around, silently observing and tasting a few of our concoctions. We were graded on a number of things. Taste, presentation, technique, and execution to name a few. In this industry, you had to have thick skin and an open mind. While not cocky by any means, I knew what I knew when it came to seasoning and presentation. I could take the blandest dish and make it flavorful and pretty. Four hours later, the Causolette, the Coq A Vin, and the lemon crepes were all finished. I was so hot that I decided to take a water and air break during our intermission. Reaching for my purse, I checked my phone for any messages or missed calls. Aside from messages in the group chat, nothing was out of the ordinary, aside from another message from Shawn.

I knitted my brows together and sighed. This nigga was still something else I see.

KingShawn.071

I don't really do nunna this internet shit. HML when you free. 773-994-0317.

I felt my eyes rolling to heaven again. This nigga still had the same number and still expected me to just drop things and call him as if we were cool like that. Careful not to double tap, I screenshotted the message and sent it to my mama.

Now he wants me to call him

You better not!

She didn't have to tell me twice. I sincerely had no intention of doing that, but wondered if I should even say something to Dre. We didn't have any secrets between us, but due to this topic being so sensitive, I didn't want to create an argument over something so trivial. I locked my phone and put it back in my locker before heading back to class, and mentally prepared myself for work in the next couple hours. As class wrapped up with the assignment for the next class given out, Chef LaBreaux called for me to stay behind.

My stomach dropped to my knees.

Was I fucking up? Was I failing horribly? Was I—

"Chef Thomas, I wanted to commend you for the work you've been doing in my class this semester," Chef LaBreaux cut in, halting my thoughts.

I gave her a warm smile and rejoiced on the inside.

"Thank you, I appreciate the challenge this class gives me."

Chef LaBreaux smirked as she looked me over. I held her gaze, hoping I didn't look as nervous as I felt because if there was one thing I couldn't do, it was control my facial expressions.

"I don't say this often, so believe me when I say, you are well on your way to becoming an excellent chef one day. Tell me, what are your plans after you graduate next month?"

I exhaled slightly, realizing that I had been holding my breath for a while.

"I plan to finish out my head-chef-in-training at Ruthie's by the end of this year. Then, work that for a couple of years or so until I save enough to open my very own restaurant one day. I'm naming it after my late grandmother and it will serve elevated soul food options." I spoke nervously. I didn't share my dream with anyone outside of my immediate friends and family.

Chef LaBreaux offered me a warm smile and nodded her head before clapping her hands.

"That's amazing to hear! If you ever need help figuring out what's next for you in life chef-wise, don't hesitate to reach out. It's not many of us"—she said, pointing to the color of our skin—"in the culinary world. And more than anything, I like being a resource to young women with ambition and talent like yourself. My only regret is not saying something to you sooner."

I smiled nervously. Today was taking the most pleasant turn. That's how I knew I couldn't worry about my past when the future was knocking.

"I know you have to get to Ruthie's soon but I'll leave you with this: once a week, let's meet so we can discuss your restaurant idea. I know plenty of people in the space who would love to give insight. As a matter of fact, we could even host a guest speaker and do a Q&A!" she squealed, writing it down on her sticky note.

My mind was blown. Someone I admired from afar was willing to sit down and meet with me. How lucky, I mean blessed, was I? I couldn't wait to get home and tell everybody. After promising to meet after class next week, I scurried to my car so I could head to work.

I wasn't sure what God was up to, but it seemed to align with what I wanted for myself. I zoomed through traffic, the thoughts of LaShawn contacting me and if I should tell Dre pushed to the back of my mind.

The past didn't matter when your future was so bright.

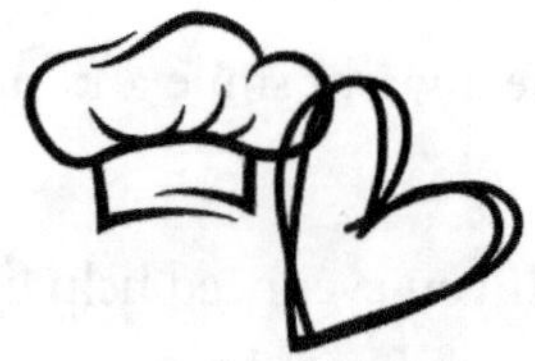

Chapter Two

Desiraè

Dre was not what I considered the most romantic nigga. He wasn't a total fuck up, but he just wasn't spontaneous or good at planning things all the time, whereas me, I could plan a special moment between us in my sleep. Being in the food industry, there was always a new restaurant I wanted to try, a new place I wanted to go, and some new environment I wanted to see, though we didn't do much traveling these days.

Dre was simple. He liked his job. He liked going to the gym. He liked being at home with me or with my family. He enjoyed playing video games, watching movies, and would survive on pizza and noodles if he could. His idea of romance was cuddling on the couch, offering me a massage, and then somehow, slipping between my legs before the night was over.

We were different, but we worked. Early in our relationship, I wanted more effort from him, which he tried to give. We did weekly dates, took road trips, caught a couple flights, and had deep conversations with one another.

After we got settled into our careers, connecting with each other got a bit challenging. While our sex life didn't lack, sometimes it felt like the romance did.

But when you work over 40 hours a week, live together, go to school, and still have to be present with others—tell me, where do you work up the extra energy to be romantic?

***

So imagine my surprise when I opened my front door, and saw red and white rose petals leading from the living room, to the kitchen and then to our bedroom. 90's slow jams filled the air and a bucket filled with ice chilled two bottles of wine from Cooper's Hawk. Small, Champagne Toast scented candles lined the table and the mantelpiece and I smelled lamb chops cooking. Following my nose, I found Dre shirtless in the kitchen with a pair of Adidas track pants on. On his back he had our anniversary date in cursive and on his chest, was a heart with my initials in the middle. He wanted to get his favorite picture of me tatted on the other side of his chest, but I talked him out of it years ago. I didn't need all that, especially since I didn't have his name or anything related to us tatted yet.

While his back was turned, I silently walked up behind him, giving him a hug around his waist and just breathed in his scent. He always smelled like the shea butter and vanilla scented Dove and his signature YSL cologne. His skin was smooth and I could tell that he'd been in my Zee Naturals body butter because his tats glistened under the kitchen lights. He towered over me and picked up weight over the years but kept it solid in the gym. My nigga was fine as fuck.

"What's all this baby?" I queried. He flipped a lamb chop in the skillet and then turned to face me. He kissed me once on my forehead, once on the bridge of my nose, and once on the lips before answering.

"Honestly, Bae... we both work hard. Especially you. I just wanted to show a little appreciation for my shorty. Can I do that?"

I stared into his big brown eyes and nodded. He kissed me on the lips again, deeper this time and let his hands roam my body. I melted. Dre's touch was my favorite and I loved the feel of his hands all over me. He rubbed my shoulders, then my lower back and then cupped both my cheeks in his hand and slipped his tongue in my mouth, where I matched his energy. A soft moan escaped my lips and I stood on my tip toes to deepen the kiss even more. We kissed like long lost lovers finally reuniting. We kissed like we wanted to swallow each other whole. We kissed like two people who would take each other right in the kitchen if we wanted to.

Until, he abruptly stopped the kiss and looked me in the eyes.

"Now, the first thing I want you to do is go to the bathroom and wash the day off you. I ran you a bath, lit the candles, and there is a glass of wine in there waiting for you. Imma finish these lamb chops and then come in there and bathe you."

"You acting totally different. If you wanna marry me boy, just say that," I smirked.

Dre matched my smirk, but said nothing and smacked me on my ass as I walked away. In the bathroom, I stripped down and got a good look at myself in the mirror. Though only 5'5, my legs were long and my grown woman weight finally came in. I sprouted over the years from skinny, to slim thick, to thick as hell, to now nicely shaped. My booty was heart shaped and my boobs grew to a nice double d size and managed to stay perky. I'd always had hips and though my stomach wasn't as flat and toned like it used to be, it was soft and graced my frame perfectly. Outside of my school and work uniforms, my body was banging, okay? A few stretch marks here and there but I still felt immaculate most days. The bathtub was filled to the brim with warm water and had a few bubbles in it, just the way I liked it. Before sinking in, I grabbed my wine glass full of Romance Red and eased my way in.

I needed this. Though the day at the restaurant was long, it was a good day. A few customers asked to thank the chef, and the head chef sent me out since I was training. Hearing people gush about how good the food was made my heart warm. That's how I knew pursuing a career in this field was the right choice. Gramz used to tell me all the time that cooking for others is an act of love. I kept that in mind every time I got in front of an oven or stove. Even if I didn't know who I was cooking for, I wanted them to feel the love in it.

Dre quietly slipped in the bathroom and just watched me for a second. H.E.R.'s *Comfortable* played softly on the Alexa speakers and I turned to match his stare.

"Thank you so much baby. I really needed this," I murmured.

Dre nodded and then kneeled to reach me in the tub. Grabbing a washcloth, he ran the same shea butter and vanilla scented Dove body wash he used, a mango scented body wash, and the Naturium body oil gel all over my skin. Starting with my shoulders, the sudsy combination made its way down my thighs, calf muscles, balls of my feet, and then finally my toes.

He then drained the tub and turned on the shower so I could rinse off. Pulling a fresh towel out the towel warmer, he wrapped it around my body and then picked me up bridal style and walked the short distance to our bedroom. Laying me gently in the middle of the bed, I let the towel fall slowly from around me as we locked eyes.

I rolled my eyes playfully. "Boyyy... you staring like you ain't seen these titties fifty billion times."

He laughed and grabbed the coconut oil. "It never gets old. I love what I see." Pouring the oil on his hands, he motioned for me to spread out.

His hands glided over my feet first, massaging them and kissing each toe. He then slowly worked his way up my calves and kneaded the muscles in them, working out the kinks and aches of being on my feet all day with deliberate pressure.

"Mmmmmm. Right *there*!" Soft moans began to escape my lips, turning the temperature in the room up a notch. His hands moved up to my thighs, fingers ever so slightly brushing my lower lips and I felt myself getting aroused. He tapped my thigh twice and told me to lay on my stomach.

Laying flat, Dre kissed me from the back of my ankle, up the back of my calf muscles, to the back of my thighs, and each cheek. I was *dripping* at this point. Dre's hands glided on each check, applying just the right amount of pressure and then leaned up to kiss me up my spine, my shoulders, and my neck. Then he descended, until his face was planted between my thighs and tongue was right where I wanted, no *needed* it to be: the opening of my pussy. Dre knew I was a sucker for his tongue, especially from the back. I sucked in a breath and leaned up on my elbows a bit, peeking over my shoulder. Dre had a handful of my ass cheek in his hand, and blew his warm breath on my mound, teasing me.

"Pretty ass pussy" he murmured.

"Put it in yo' mouth then," my voice was just above a whisper.

I felt so relaxed.

The bath, the candles, the meal I didn't have to cook, the massage.

And I didn't have to nag him about it. That was all a woman could ask for.

Dre's tongue plunged deep into my pussy and I immediately felt my orgasm rising. I rained down on him, soaking everything underneath us as he worked his tongue to spell his full first, middle, and last name. My back was now slightly arched as he lapped up all my juices like he was a thirsty dog on a scorching Chicago day. Gently, he spread me wider, latching on my clit. Next thing I know, he abruptly stops, and I whine.

"Babyyyyy, I was so close!" I panted, looking over my shoulder.

"Oh I'm not finished with you yet baby..." he says, taking off his wife beater and his sweats, dick standing straight up.

"Turn back around for me baby" he says. So I obliged, thinking that he was about to penetrate me but to my surprise, I heard a vibrating noise instead. I try to turn my head to look over my shoulder again, but he nudged my face the other way, eyes facing the headboard.

"Mind yo business, baby. I got you."

I arch my back again, and feel him move the vibrating toy between my folds.

Stars.

That's what I saw.

Like Shaq and Kobe, Dre and whatever toy he had on me tag teamed me for many minutes. Placing the toy on my clit, while lapping up all my juices, my screams and moans bounced off the walls in our bedroom and I'm sure my neighbors knew that Dre was the culprit.

And then he switched from his tongue to his index finger, then his middle finger, going in and out of me while the toy on my clit sounded like she was at the barbershop.

If I died today, I would die a happy woman.

I lost track of time, but then Dre flipped me on my back and pushed my knees up to my ears, and that's when I saw what I knew was now the rose toy on my clit. I was shaking like a salt shaker, shaking harder than Shakira and Beyoncè put together from my back to back orgasms. I reached up and grabbed his face, shoving my tongue down his throat and grabbed his super hard dick in my hand and positioned it at my opening, soaking the tip, while sucking on his bottom lip.

I needed him in me like I needed air to breathe.

Dre pushed inside and let out a *"fuckkkkkk"* which was music to my ears. Like yeah nigga, welcome to my water park.

Pumping in and out slowly at first, he looked me in the eyes, full of adoration. I matched his stare as I felt myself creaming on his dick, liquid dripping out of me and soaking everything underneath us even more. I wrapped my legs around his waist, trying to merge our bodies and souls if I could.

Dre leaned closer to my face, kissing my forehead, my nose, and my lips repeatedly, as if he was entranced. Leaning in my ear, he kept telling me how good I made him feel, how tight and wet I was, how at home he felt in my pussy.

"You so tight baby...why you got this tight ass pussy? Tight and wet baby... you gone drown me every time... I feel so at home in my pussy...you make a nigga feel *so good*" he leaned in my ear and talked me through my third or fourth orgasm of the night.

The feeling was mutual. I was *home*.

I *loved* his dick and loved that he was incorporating something new into the bedroom with the toy. Breakfast in bed with head coming right up, he just didn't know.

"Have my baby Rae-Rae" he moaned, completely ruining the mood if I was being honest. I moaned to refrain from answering. Tightened my pussy muscles and all, just to distract him but all that did was make him ask even more.

"I wanna put a baby in my baby, can I do that? I need three up outta you, shit maybe even five" he grunted, pumping in and out of me.

"Good ass, wet ass, tight ass pussy!"

I felt myself about to lose focus.

It's not that I didn't want to have Dre's kids. It's not that I didn't want to have kids, *ever.* It's just that after experiencing so much child loss when I was younger, on top of trying to finish culinary school, and establish my restaurant, I just didn't see how kids would fit into my life's equation right now. And the crazy part is that Dre *knew* this. This wasn't his first time asking, and it wasn't his first time trying to convince me during sex.

And who the fuck was finna have five kids?! Not I, said the cat.

"Rae baby, you gone have my baby? I wanna nut in you…" he begged in my ear.

I shook my head. I was on birth control, the Nexplanon implant to be exact, but I *hated* getting nutted in. I didn't want to take even an inch of a chance because with my luck and how fertile I used to be, even the most powerful birth control probably didn't stand a chance. He was pissed that I even got on this type of birth control, claiming it would be poisonous to my body. But I explained to him that if we weren't going to use condoms, then it was no point in playing Russian Roulette on me being pregnant or not every time we had sex. When you experienced all that I did, at some point I had to stop making my body a martyr and took the necessary precautions to protect myself from pregnancy. What the girls be saying? My body, my choice.

"No baby, pull out *please*" I begged, feeling his dick throb in me, a warning sign that he was close. I was feeling myself get turned off and drying up a little, my mind too focused on the bullshit he asked me and the ghosts of my past popping up, reminding me that I never got to enjoy motherhood.

"Rae, I'm finna – " and he pulls out, releasing himself on my stomach and thighs.

He fell on the opposite end of the bed, visibly tired and I took that as a chance to run to the bathroom to rinse off. I took my time in there, and came out to Dre taking a little cat nap. I walked quietly to my side of the bed, and started pulling the sheets off to take to the washer and dryer. If it was another thing I hated, it was sleeping in the wet spot. Shortly after, Dre stirred from his nap, hopped up, and walked to the bathroom. Hearing the water turn on, I walked out the room and into the kitchen to pour myself a glass of wine. My brain was in overdrive, and I knew Dre would want to talk about this before he went back to sleep. I just didn't want to. I knew it would end in the same manner every time. Pouring myself another glass, I smelled Dre's freshly showered scent before I saw him enter the kitchen.

"Rae."

I turned around and glanced at him in the doorway, him now adorning a pair of boxers and no shirt. I couldn't quite place the look on his face but the heaviness of the pending conversation lingered between us. We share a stare, neither of us wanting to be the one to break the ice, but knowing that one of us has to.

Moments pass, and I turn to pour him a glass of wine, handing it to him but he shakes his head, declining it.

"You know I love you right?" he finally asks, breaking the heavy silence. I nodded.

"Then why don't you want to have my baby? We've been together all this time, and every time I bring the situation up, you never want to at least hear me out. I'm not him, Desiraè."

I slightly cocked my head to the side and slowly sipped from my glass, trying like hell to push down the annoyance that I'm sure is all over my face. Sometimes, I hate when I'm right. I also hate when I have to repeat myself. But regardless, this conversation needed to be had.

Again.

Blowing out a deep breath, I squared my shoulders and sat my glass on the counter.

"DeAndre. I *know* you're not him. And trust me, I'm not comparing you to him in any type of way. My decision to not have children right now is rooted in me wanting to make some of *my* dreams come true and establish the restaurant. I have a couple more months of culinary school left and pretty soon I'll start taking catering orders. Tell me, where does a child fit into all that? You have your career that you've established, and I just want to establish mine. In the next few years, I want to have enough money saved to buy a space and begin building out the restaurant. I think kids are cool, but I just don't want to have any right now. What aren't you understanding about that?" I say, keeping my tone even and praying that my voice didn't elevate.

I ain't perfect, but I've really been working on not yelling and cursing whenever me and Dre bump heads. Dr. Love would be proud of me right now. What bothered me was the fact that Dre really thinks in his big ass head that me not wanting to be barefoot and pregnant *right now* means that I am comparing him to LaShawn of all people when those are two completely different niggas.

Getting pregnant and experiencing miscarriage after miscarriage all while being abandoned and abused in the process didn't exactly make me want to be the poster child for motherhood, but I knew that some women were different. In the past, I gave my all to a man and lost myself in the process, so I've spent the last few years rebuilding and exploring what pouring into myself looks like. So no, I didn't think that Dre would do me like LaShawn, but I was not willing to compromise on my goals and dreams just to appease him. I am only twenty-four, I would like to think that I have my whole life ahead of me to have some kids.

"So, you mean to tell me that yo' past miscarriages ain't making you hesitant? I know you Desiraè, you like to hide yo' feelings behind shit. The thing is, you don't even *have to* work. I make enough money to take care of you, me, *and* a baby or two. I could buy you two or three restaurants. I could make sure you have a nanny, a cleaning lady, and whatever the hell else you want. Just give me a family. I didn't come from one Rae-Rae, you did! I just want to feel like all I went through and all I have now isn't in vain. I want to know what it feels like to hear a lil boy running around with half our faces, depending on me and you for the rest of their lives. I wanna teach a lil girl who looks exactly like you with my demeanor, what it looks like to be treated right and loved properly, cuz I love her mama so much that we created life. And you let old shit, very irrelevant shit stop us from progressing."

To say I was shocked would be a lie.

This conversation always went like this. I'd explain how I wanted to focus on my dreams and my career, and Dre would throw back in my face everything that I endured – yet call it irrelevant at the same time – and only hone in on what *he* wanted. To hell with what I just said.

Every day, I thanked God that I was on birth control because fucking with Dre, I'd *stay* pregnant.

I let out a humorless laugh, shaking my head and got ready to walk past him. He tugged on my arm, pissing me off even further.

"So now I'm a joke to you? Desiraè, talk to me."

I looked down at him holding my arm and back up at him, gritting my teeth. "Dre, find you something safe to do and let my arm go."

"That's yo' problem now, you always want to walk away and shut down when we gotta discuss your shortcomings. And I'm supposed to just be okay with the shit because I'm the man right? It's fuck how I feel right? You gone deprive me of a family right?! You selfish as fuck, Desiraè!" he let my arm go and stalked toward the bedroom.

See, what Dre didn't understand was that I was actually sparing him. I'd like to think that my *hit you in your mouth first and cuss you out later* days were over. I respected Dre, I really did. And, I *do* love him.

But I was *tired*. Of him *choosing* not to understand me, the slick comments, and his lingering animosity towards me and the things I experienced when I was a fuckin' teenager. I was tired of coddling his feelings on this matter. It wasn't my fault that he grew up in foster care and didn't have a family. And the lonely void that he feels from that, probably could not be filled with children. And selfish? I scoffed at that. I never got a chance to only think about myself, my wants, my needs, and my dreams. If being locked in makes me selfish, then so be it.

***

I made my way to the bedroom to find Dre in our closet, packing a gym bag. I thought that was strange, because the gym in our complex closed at 10pm and by now, it was close to midnight. Silently, I watched him stuff some days worth of clothing in his bag.

"DeAndre, cut the shit *please*. Where are you going?" I asked, not caring to check my tone.

He ignored me.

"DeAndre...." I felt a level three crash out coming and I would've hated to turn this house upside down because he wanted to be childish and ignore me.

I was met with silence again. So, I did what any sane person would do, I grabbed his raggedy ass duffle bag, walked to our balcony, and tossed his shit over.

"Yo! What the fuck is wrong with you?!" he yelled. I smirked. At least now he was speaking to me.

"You ignored me. You know how I feel about that," I shrugged.

Dre let out an exasperated sigh and ran his hand over his waves and beard, looking like he wanted to knock me between the dresser and the headboard. How we went from such a great night full of cum to one ending in chaos was beyond me, but hey, stranger things have happened in my life.

I walked over to my side of the bed and turned the covers back, sliding into the warm sheets that just got out the dryer. Dre walked out the room without saying a word, and moments later, I heard the front door slam and the alarm activated.

I grabbed my phone and went right to his name to check his location, but that bastard turned it off on me. I scoffed, and let out another humorless laugh. I thought about hitting up my girls or even my mom but it was late, and I needed to sit with this for a moment. I was tired, but I wasn't sure if I wanted to break up with him. Compared to our arguments in the past, this one was pretty mild and no one got hurt.... At least physically.

What *was* different though, was that he never packed a bag and tried to leave like this. *This* was new. He never turned his location off on me, no matter how mad he got. *That* was unsettling. Usually when we argued about this topic, he would go to the gym, go for a drive, or go for a walk. He's *never* done this before.

And I didn't quite know what to do with myself.

Do I call his phone seventy million times until it either dies or he answers?

Do I get in my car and pull up to the places I know he would be at?

Do I text him repeatedly?

I'm not well-versed in crazy bitch antics anymore. I'd mellowed out over the years, choosing to implement what I learned in therapy. Seems like all those skills were being laughed at though.

Biting the inside of my jaw, I grabbed my phone again and opened up our text message thread.

> When you're done being mad, understand that I no longer want to talk about this.

I erased that message. It was too prim, too proper, and not at all what I was truly feeling. So, I started over.

> Don't let the sun beat you home.

And pressed send. Imagine my surprise when the message went green. I furrowed my brows, not believing what was in front of me. *This nigga blocked me,* I chuckled to myself. That was also new. He's never done that before either.

Guess I really pissed him off.

I grabbed my phone again, going over to Instagram and yup, I was blocked there too. I just couldn't believe it. Closing my eyes, I counted to ten before I did something stupid. But this was just too much new shit at once.

Leaving the crib.

Packing a bag.

Blocking me from your phone and Instagram.

I was in the mood to file a Missing Persons report on his ass. And don't you judge me... I said I mellowed out over the years, I never said I was completely incapable of going insane.

I open my Instagram app again and see I have another message request from the bane of my existence.

KingShawn.071

> When you gone call me Lady Rae?

I scoffed and tossed my phone on the nightstand. Audacity from niggas was at an all-time high tonight, and I was over it.

I looked at the clock and it was nearing 3AM and I knew my alarm would be going off in a couple hours because I had yet another long day of school then work. I was pissed, yet eerily calm at the same time. I ran the conversation we had before Dre left and the only thing I wished I did differently was curse his ass the fuck out.

Dre has *never* not come home.

As I tried to force myself to go to sleep, I said a silent prayer for his dumb ass and prayed that wherever he was, he was safe. Things were changing between us and while that's normal between all couples, this felt like the beginning of the end.

Chapter Three

Desiraè

It had been three days since me and Dre's argument and he still hadn't brought his ass home. He still had me blocked on everything, and I still couldn't wrap my mind around any of it. So, I called up Dr. Love for an impromptu emergency session and that's how I found myself laid out on her couch, ready to bare my soul, because I was about two seconds from going up to his job and causing a scene.

Over the years, Love Rehab expanded. They now had three locations and even offered virtual services for people who didn't live in Bloomington. They incorporated art therapy, in-patient therapy, and dance therapy built into their curriculum. Even the rehab center looked different with some cosmetic upgrades. Dr. Love gained more notoriety, having been seen on TV with Oprah, Dr. Phil, Tamron Hall, and even Good Morning America. People from all over wanted to come and heal their broken minds and broken hearts and Dr. Love had the most diverse team of therapists under her employment. She didn't counsel much anymore due to her traveling a lot, but she made special exceptions for clients she held near and dear, and I happened to be one of them.

I was grateful. Though I didn't go to therapy much anymore, I had to call her because I wasn't quite ready to share what was happening with me and Dre with my friends and family yet. Not that we portrayed ourselves as the perfect couple, but we weathered plenty of storms in private, and liked to keep people out of our business. Dr. Love was different though, she had seen us from the beginning and was our anchor when it came to keeping us on the right track. We sat on her couch plenty of times over the years for both individual and couples counseling, learning ways to communicate with each other and move forward with forgiveness.

I thought we were fine. And we were, until it came to this baby thing.

"Do you think DeAndre could be jealous of you, Desiraè?" Doc asked, looking at me with the softest brown eyes I've ever seen.

I jolted up and vehemently shook my head.

"Jealous for what? He literally saw where I came from and how hard I worked to get where I am. And I'm still not where I wanna be –"

"Yet, you've come a long way," Doc gently cut me off.

I nodded. "Yes, but I don't see why that would make him jealous. All I do is go to class, go to work, and be with him, my friends, and family. He's on his way to making six figures, he has me, and I would think he's pretty content with his life. He says he wants to take care of me so I won't have to work and could buy me a restaurant, but I don't want that. I want to do this for myself. And I never said that I didn't want to have his kids or kids ever, just... not right now."

"Well, as we've discussed in the past, DeAndre has struggled a bit with a savior complex. He met you and fell in love with you when you were in a *very* vulnerable state. You gaining independence by pursuing your dreams and creating the life you want in spite of a very shaky foundation, could possibly scare him. Aside from his own difficult feelings surrounding his lack of family due to him growing up in foster care, he could also be feeling like when you become all that you desire to be, you won't need him anymore. And that is how jealousy takes root. And, not projecting here at all – but in some cases, men want to get women pregnant to control them."

I was stunned. I had heard and seen examples in the media about men being jealous of their partners but never in this lifetime did I think it would happen to me.

Rubbing my temples, I sighed and just stared at Doc for a moment.

"I'm not sure what to say," I admitted.

"You're not doing anything wrong, Desiraè. It is perfectly fine for you to pursue your dreams and decide not to bring children into this world. Remember, you can only control yourself. You went through a lot when you were younger and grew from it. No one should punish you for that."

I felt a lump in my throat forming and that familiar, dull ache in the pit of my stomach.

"Then why does it feel like I *am* being punished, Doc? He hasn't been home in three days. He won't answer my calls or my texts. I feel like I am doing something wrong by standing firm in my boundaries and I'm not gon' lie, this shit doesn't feel good. He knows how I feel about being ignored. And he's doing it anyway because I didn't give him the answer he wanted in regards to a topic that I've expressed myself on a plethora of times."

Tears fell from my eyes and I didn't even bother to wipe them. Therapy was one of the few places I allowed myself to become completely undone, because I was for sure that *this* was a safe space.

Doc remained silent, letting me cry and handing me Kleenex as I got it all out. After about ten minutes, I dried my eyes, though I didn't feel completely better.

"So, what do you think I should do? Should I break up with him?" I asked. I was feeling like that old LeToya Luckett song again, torn in between the two. The battle between my head and my heart.

Doc smirked, and pushed her oversized red glasses up the bridge of her nose.

"You know that's not what I'm here for. I don't tell you what to do. You have to stop and ask yourself some questions in regard to this situation, because only *you* can assess what you *will* and *won't* tolerate in your connections," she said gently.

"You have to decide, is love enough? Are you being heard? Are you being treated with kindness, even when you and him don't see eye to eye? Are you okay with being ignored? Are you okay with being left uncertain? Whatever your answer is, you will have to accept it and move forward on it however you see fit. And remember this: Just because a connection is better than what you're used to, doesn't mean that it's the best and *only* connection for you."

Dr. Love stopped talking and looked at me, her warm brown eyes twinkling. I appreciated her therapy style because as gentle as she was, she was extremely forthcoming and often helped me put things in perspective without blatantly telling me what to do.

I nodded, and looked at the clock. Our time was up but it was well spent.

"I see our time is up but please, Desiraè. Don't hesitate to call me if you need me. Take care of yourself, okay?"

I stood, smoothed imaginary wrinkles from my pants and walked over to give her a hug. She smelled of fresh linen and expensive, flowery and vanilla scented perfume. Her hug was reassuring, and I knew that eventually, I would be okay. Throwing my shades on, I walked out of her office and out the door, the shining sun beaming on me as I walked to my car.

***

It was a rare day that I had off from work, but I decided to go home instead of finding me something to do. I was mentally and emotionally exhausted, and I just wanted to sleep and decompress. I had an exam I could study for and then graduation was literally next week. The crazy thing about life is that even when your world is crumbling, it still goes on. Pulling up to my complex, I almost turned back around once I saw that Dre's car was in his parking spot.

A mix of anger and relief washed over me. Angry, because his stupid ass stayed away and had me blocked for three days. Relieved, because his stupid ass was alive and well. If he would've stayed gone any longer, I was going to go to the police station and file a missing person's report.

Dragging my feet, I walked up the stairs to our second floor apartment and let myself in. I should've braced myself, because there he was, sitting solemnly on the couch, no lights on since it was still mid-day, and no tv or music on either. I looked him up and down and walked past without saying a word to him.

Going to our bedroom, I stripped out of my outside clothes and changed into a pair of shorts and a tank, climbing in the bed to take a long overdue nap. Just as I was about to get into a good slumber, I heard Dre banging on the door. Flustered, I hopped out the bed and snatched the door open.

"Why the fuck you got the door locked, Desiraè?" he demanded, brows pinched as if I was bothering *him.*

"What is it that you want, DeAndre? I'm really not in the mood for your shit. And if you coming in here to start your shit, gon' back in the living room or back to wherever the fuck you been for the past three days!" I spat.

Dre recoiled back as if I'd slapped him.

"Man, watch out" he tried to move past me, but I wouldn't budge.

"Look, I'm trying to talk to you," he said.

"You can talk right here," I scoffed, not in the mood at all for his funky ass attitude.

He ran his hand over his waves and through his beard, a clear sign that he was getting frustrated. Crossing my arms across my chest, I shifted my weight from one foot to the other, waiting for him to talk so I could lay back down.

"Look, I wasn't out cheating on you if that's what you thinking. I just – I just needed some time to clear my mind...."

I scoffed and sucked my teeth.

"DeAndre, there are things worse than cheating. Like oh, I don't know, leaving home for three days, blocking me on everything, turning off your location. You broke our promise to each other. So no, I don't give a fuck if you were cheating or not because you broke the main rules in this partnership. Doing nice things for me just to convince me to do some shit that I already said I didn't want to do right now, is worse than cheating. Ignoring me is worse than cheating. Clearing your mind isn't the issue, it's how you went about it. Blocking me was petty. What if something happened to you, and I would have had to tell the police or whomever that I don't know where my boyfriend is because we had a bad argument and he left and blocked me for three days? Do you hear how crazy that sounds? I wouldn't do no shit like that to you!"

Earlier in our counseling sessions with Dr. Love, we created a list of promises to each other. One of them was to promise not to abandon one another in times of strife. That it's okay to need space and time to clear our heads when we get into it, but never without informing the other person first. No where in the promise did we agree to block each other or disappear for days on end. I wasn't worried about Dre cheating. Though I knew that all men were capable, I knew that Dre was devoted to me. I just thought he respected me enough to not break his end of the bargain.

Dre hung his head, looking defeated and I just stared at him, my right leg bouncing up and down.

"Desiraè baby.... I did what I felt was necessary at the time. It's just that you – I mean I – we both said some hurtful things to each other that night and I needed to leave before it got worse. Then you threw my shit over the balcony and I just – I didn't want to say something to you that I would later regret, because you know how you get when you're mad."

Now I recoiled back as if he slapped *me*.

"What did I say that was so horrible to you that night, DeAndre? Because I remember calmly stating for the umpteenth time that I wanted to focus on graduating culinary school and then start taking the necessary steps to build my business. I did not disrespect you. I did not belittle you. I didn't throw your past in your face at all, yet *every time* we have this conversation, you're convinced that I am comparing you to a nigga that I ain't seen since Obama's *first* term, or being insensitive to the fact that yes, I *have* experienced multiple miscarriages and instead of respectfully dropping the subject, you accuse me of depriving you of the family you want to create. As if *my hopes, my wishes,* and *my dreams* don't matter. It is not my fault nor yours that you grew up in foster care. The loneliness you must feel, I'm sorry, but it is not worth putting my body at risk, nor my dreams on pause just so you can feel whole for once in your life. And, while I know you make enough money to do all that you named as far as providing for me and any future children we'll have, there are certain things I want to do for myself. I thought you understood that about me, but considering how you're acting – as I looked him up and down, "I guess you don't."

A loud silence hung in the air, the tension thick enough to cut with a knife.

In the back of my mind, the questions that Dr. Love told me to ask myself popped into the forefront of my brain.

Was love enough? No, it wasn't.

Was I being heard? No, I wasn't.

Was I being treated with kindness, even when we don't see eye to eye? No.

Am I okay with being ignored? Fuck no.

Am I okay with being left uncertain? Absolutely the fuck not.

"Desiraè, I'm – look man, I'm sorry. Look, I'll go to Dr. Love and talk to her. Maybe we can go together again. I just – I just really love you and I want us to be together. I'll chill on the kid talk and support you in whatever decision you make. I'm sorry baby. I do love you," he pleaded, stepping closer to me, trying to engulf me in a hug. I stepped back, not in the least bit moved by his admission.

I sighed, feeling my resolve slowly breaking.

"You still want to be with me right? I can fix this baby, just give me a chance. I love you and you love me, whatever you want me to do, I will do it. I won't ever bring up a baby again if you don't want me to. Just don't leave me – don't leave us."

More begging. Frustrated tears threatened to drop but one thing I knew for sure is that while I loved and cared for this man in front of me, I knew this wouldn't be an easy fix.

I gulped and heard my voice crack. "DeAndre, I need you to understand something: sometimes, love just isn't enough." With that, I shut the door, locked it, and dove into bed, hoping and praying for sleep to find me and a dream to distract me from my tumultuous reality.

Chapter Four

Desiraè

The next few weeks went by like a blur. Dre and I were still living in the same home, but not sleeping together and barely speaking. I was wrapping up my last few classes for school and pulling doubles at the restaurant, just to avoid coming home to see him. I worked non-stop, and barely talked to my mom and my friends. It felt like Dre and I were avoiding the inevitable, knowing that breaking up was probably the right thing to do, but neither of us wanted to initiate it.

On the rare occasion that we were home at the same time, the tension was so thick that it felt like I was being choked and backed into a corner. Never had I ever felt like or realized that love wasn't enough to sustain a relationship. Growing up, it was ingrained in me that love was all you needed, but maturing is realizing that love is low on the hierarchy of needs. Dre was a good man, but our differences were becoming clearer to me now. Not even with the whole kids thing, but also with him assuming that I wanted to be this kept woman. I was grateful for partnership – but I never wanted to be placed in a position where just because someone made more than me meant that they could treat me any type of way.

Plus, he broke our promise. Leaving for three days and not hearing from him during that time triggered something so deeply within me. We both put in the work to evolve our communication skills and one rash decision ruined it. I understand that emotions were high but now.... I just wasn't sure anymore. He said we could fix this, but I didn't see any effort from him nor did I put forth any on my own, because I truly didn't feel like my reaction to him was wrong. So if I felt this way, what was stopping me from just ending things as amicably as I could?

Sure, it would hurt but I wasn't happy.

The questions swirled around in my head as I pulled into my mother's driveway. I was popping up on her for an at-home brunch today, because I felt guilty for dodging her calls the last few weeks. We talked almost everyday, but this thing with Dre had me in such a slump that I couldn't stand to do anything except go to class and go to work. Before getting out of my car, I thought briefly about how my mother and I's relationship evolved over the years. God and therapy truly helped us come a long way because at one time, I thought I hated her, when I was really just hurt by her perceived abandonment. Although I would never get the answers I wanted from Gramz, I allowed my mama to start with a clean slate. While I believe that forgiveness doesn't always require reconnection, I am grateful that my mom and I reconnected. She understood me on a level that no one else did, and sometimes, that's all I wanted: to be seen, to be understood, to be heard, to be loved. Grabbing the bag of groceries out the car, I walked up to her red brick, two story home and rang the doorbell. Minutes later, she opened the door dressed in a cute two piece teal green workout set, though I know she wasn't doing any type of working out.

"You and that boy must be really going through it if I ain't heard from or seen you in weeks. Get in here, you look pitiful!" she exclaimed, engulfing me in a hug. I obliged, wrapping my arms around her tightly, trying to keep my tears at bay.

Mothers always know.

Walking to the kitchen, I unpacked the groceries of brioche bread, eggs, vanilla extract, honey, cinnamon seasoning, nutmeg, and turkey bacon. Nicole sat at the table and watched me for a while, gathering her thoughts while I started making the batter for the french toast.

"Alright, what's going on baby?"

"What makes you think it's something going on? I *have* been busy" I said, just to test the waters.

She scoffed. "Girl, tell that to somebody who doesn't know you. I know you've been busy but it's unlike you to go ghost like this, even when you're locked in. Even the group chat ain't heard from you, and y'all pop your shit in there everyday. Now, if you ain't ready to talk about it, I'll respect it for now. But if you change your mind, I'm here to listen too."

Slumping my shoulders, I turned from the stove and stared into my mother's eyes. In her early forties now, Nicole looked pretty youthful, but her eyes were just like mine: they held stories of immense pain, struggle, and triumph. She'd seen and experienced things she shouldn't have had to, yet developed wisdom because of it. For years, she felt like her light was dimmed, but she also held this spark that was determined to bring warmth and joy not just for herself, but all she encountered.

So, I told her everything. How the evening started, what happened in between, and how it ended, leading up to how things were now. One thing Nicole couldn't control were her facial expressions, so when I got to the part of what he said before leaving and blocking me, I knew she was about two seconds from getting into her car, driving to our apartment, and knocking him upside his big ass head.

Nicole didn't play about me, or any of her kids. She always gave people a warning but if you had to find out another way then you had to find out.

Once I finished, she leaned back into her chair and shook her head.

"Awww baby. I'm so sorry you've been dealing with that", a touch of sadness in her voice. "If things get to be too much, know that you are always welcome to come here."

I managed to offer her a half smile. My mama and her husband Jamaal were big on letting us know that no matter how grown we got, if we ran into any type of hardship or trouble, we could always come to their home, free of charge. In times like these, that was a blessing to hear because so many parents acted very weird to their children once they got to a certain age and needed help. Either they would kick them out early at 18, or charge them an arm and a leg for rent, or just make them feel shitty for facing any type of hardship. I was grateful to my parents for creating an environment where my brothers and I never experienced that.

"So, do you want me to offer some advice or did you just need to vent?"

I shrugged. "I don't know. I know you gon' offer some input sooner than later, so might as well say it now" I giggled, setting our plates down on the table.

Stuffing a forkful of French toast in her mouth, Nicole closed her eyes, savoring the taste. "Girllll.... You gets *down* in that kitchen, I can't wait until you open your restaurant!"

This time, I smiled for real. Mama was always so encouraging of my dreams. Once she took a few more bites and washed it down with a peach mimosa, she leaned forward and looked me directly in the eyes.

"Alright, here's what I think: if you know in your heart that you all aren't meant to be anymore, make peace with that in your mind and allow your feet to follow. Lack Mindset will tell us that just because we've experienced good treatment from one person and it ends, that we will never get that type of treatment again. That's simply not true Rae-Rae. You still haven't met all the people in this lifetime who will love you, be on the same page with you, respect you, and make you feel seen and heard. Compatibility is more important than chemistry and history. And remember, history can be rewritten at any time. You don't want to look up one day and realize that you've settled. So while I don't doubt that he loves you and that you love him, understand that love isn't always enough to sustain each season and perhaps his season in your life is up."

I sipped on my mimosa silently, the prosecco in it suddenly tasting bitter as the truth hit me like a ton of bricks. At one point in time, I thought that though me and Dre were different, our chemistry and history made up for that. The nigga literally took me in his home, saved me from destruction, and provided for me. But my mom was absolutely right – history could be rewritten at any time, and I was ready for a new chapter. Not to be with someone else – but to really lock in on what I wanted to do, to be free, and not feel guilty about it.

But yet, I still felt guilty. Guilty for wanting to leave after Dre did so much for me. I didn't have to pay bills at the apartment we shared. I worked because I wanted the restaurant experience. He footed the bill for culinary school. He supported me wanting to open my own restaurant, he just wanted a baby first. I felt so conflicted. On paper, he was everything the girls wanted. But behind closed doors, our differences were magnified and often created conflict. He wasn't secure in the fact that I chose him. Whenever we bumped heads on the baby thing, he called everything I experienced as a teen irrelevant, which got under my skin because while yes, the past doesn't matter, the lessons I've learned since then do. He was only romantic if he felt like he could get something out of it, and he never understood that sometimes, I was too tired for sex and that I sought to connect in ways that weren't always physical.

Momz and I finished brunch and she told me to go to my room in her house and take a nap. That nap turned into me waking up the next morning confused, realizing that I slept the entire day and night away and never made it home. I woke up to a dead phone and hella missed calls and text messages from Dre.

***

So, you just don't come home anymore? That's what we do now?

Man, turn yo location back on.

DeAndre: You a spiteful MF.

Desiraè, I'm really trying with you.

> So, you let yo phone die too? Hope whatever nigga you with can fight.

> My bad. I called yo mama looking for you and she said you was sleep.

> I'm fucked up about us Bae.

I rolled my eyes so hard that I was surprised they didn't get stuck. Dre was really crashing out and I wasn't in the mood to deal with it. Mind you, ever since coming back home, this was the first time he texted my phone in weeks. Conversation was non-existent and we essentially avoided each other.

So for him to crash out like he was doing? If I wasn't so irritated, I'd be laughing. Walking out my bedroom, I went to find my mother snuggled on the couch with her husband. Over the years, Jamaal became an integral part of our family. He was no-nonsense, very kind, could grill his ass off and was a great listener. He loved and respected my mother deeply, and she never had to worry about anyone coming to her as a woman or secret side babies popping up. He didn't have any biological kids of his own but you couldn't tell him nothing about me and my brothers. I loved him like he *was* my father, since my first one turned out to be such a disappointment.

I didn't let my mind wander on Daddy too long, but certain things you never forget. No matter how much me and Nicole bumped heads in the past, it would forever be smoke behind my mother and everyone knew that. Just like she didn't play about me and my brothers, we in turn also had a few screws loose when it came to our mother. His side children tried to reach out over the years but, my siblings and I truly weren't interested in having a relationship with them. Especially since their mamas were *still* ratchet and raggedy. They loved to pop shit on social media but Nicole and I were the types to drive up to Chicago, walk into their homes (since they loved dropping addresses) and smack fire from them for all to see. So naturally, my siblings and I kept our distance. The only thing we had in common was a man who was no longer breathing.

"That raggedy boy called looking for you last night," my mama announced. Jamaal looked surprised that she called him that, cuz Nicole *loved* her some DeAndre and vice versa. But now that me and him were beefing, he was her opp.

"Now why is he raggedy? He do something to you?" Jamaal asked, leaning up and sitting his drink down. One thing about it, my mama asked for permission – most of the time – to tell our business. Her and Jamaal talked about everything, but some things we had to tell him ourselves if we wanted him to know about it.

So, I filled Jamaal in. The whole time, he stroked his salt and peppered beard, brows furrowed as he listened intently. Once I finished, he asked me if I wanted feedback or if I just wanted to vent. I gave him permission to give feedback, not because I necessarily wanted or needed the advice, but because I just needed a male's perspective to see if I was tweaking or not.

"Well, Imma give it to you straight Baby Girl. It sounds like that lil nigga is jealous. While he isn't wrong for desiring a family, he *is* wrong for projecting on you, as if you haven't made yourself clear on what you desire for yourself. Sounds like he needs to go find a woman who can give him what he wants and leave you alone. He's a good dude on paper but problems like this ain't no easy fix and even if you compromise, one of y'all won't get what you want. So that's not compromising."

"What makes you think he's jealous of me?" I asked, remembering what me and Dr. Love talked about. She mentioned the same thing, and I still struggled with grasping the concept.

"Easy. He's a man that's used to doing and taking care of his woman because he thinks he can save her. Woman turns around, goes to school, gets knowledge, and has her own dreams that don't revolve around him... he's jealous. Jealousy is often motivated by fear of losing something. He's afraid that when you become this successful restaurant owner, you'll forget about him and all he's done to help you. See, this is where most of these young cats fuck up at. Instead of being honest about their fears and doing the internal work to fix it, they project on the woman where they fall short. When instead, they could be supporting and uplifting their woman...Making sure that she is staying on track with her dreams. Keeping her as stress free as possible. And I'm not even talking about financially. Yeah, these niggas be broke these days, but anyone can pay some rent or buy you material things. But how many niggas will listen to you, pour into you, and be empathetic to what you have going on? How many are willing to put their selfish desires aside, to heal their insecurities, and realize that they should never get too comfortable with a woman like you? So, I won't tell you if you should break up with him or not, but let no one make you feel guilty for doing what's best for you. And don't let *that nigga* make you feel guilty, period" Jamaal said.

"God forbid it and I would do everything in my power to not let it happen, but if me and ya mama were to ever part ways, I would let her have everything. I don't throw nothing I do for her or you kids in her face and I respect her no matter what. I respect her boundaries and if it's a no to something, then that's just what it is" he shrugged. "She doesn't like to repeat herself and I don't either. When we get mad at each other and need some space, I carry my ass down to the man cave and that's just that. Only bitch-made niggas try to match the energy of women or offer the silent treatment. But everybody can't be a real nigga like me, Baby Girl" he smirked, sipping his drink.

Mama patted his knee, nodding every so often to what he was saying while I just listened. My heart was heavy. It seemed like I was in a battle between my head, my heart, and my comfort zone. I had a lot on my plate, both literally and figuratively, and though I knew what I *should* do, I was scared. Scared of what life would be like without him. In comparison, Dre was *way* better than LaShawn. What or who was better than Dre? I hated to think this way, but it was my truth. And maybe, that was that lack mindset that my mama mentioned, rearing its ugly head and setting up shop in my mind. I looked down at my phone and saw that DeAndre was texting me again. He even started sharing his location again.

You still at yo mama crib?

Yes, DeAndre.

You see I shared my location again?

Yes… did you need something?

Yeah… you.

Come home baby.

Please. I'm sorry. I been fucked up about us.

I hate to sound ridiculous, but there was a small part of me that wanted to see him fight for us, minus the unnecessary crashing out. I missed how we used to be. There was a delusional part of me that believed that despite our major differences and me being unhappy, we could figure it out. Maybe start consistent couple's counseling with Dr. Love, maybe start back intentionally dating each other. Maybe I could get this birth control removed and give him the baby he wanted and postpone opening up my restaurant for a couple years. I could continue working at the restaurant. Maybe I could just *try* to see things his way. DeAndre was a good man. A good person. And, I know he loved me. He was imperfect, but aren't we all? Happiness is fleeting anyway, right?

I sighed. I was doing it again. Willing to compromise and put the happiness of others above my own. Operating in that lack mindset, and settling. I was... disgusted with myself. All this work in therapy that I've done over the years and here I was reverting back to old coping mechanisms.

Sucking my teeth, I pulled my phone back and tried to think of something to respond.

I'll be there.

When?

When I get there.

Silencing my phone, I sat back on the couch with my parents and spent the rest of the afternoon with them. My graduation was in the upcoming week and they were throwing me a graduation party at their house right after. My family loved to celebrate anything and everything so I was gonna let them do them.

***

After a few hours, I declined staying for dinner and walked to my car. Driving to our apartment, my heart began to feel heavier and heavier. Opting to take the stairs instead of the elevator, I inserted my key into the door and found Dre on the couch, engrossed in his video game.

When he heard me come in, he paused the game, stood and walked over to me, giving me a hug. Shutting the door behind me, Dre caressed me, and I just felt numb and confused. We stood there for a couple of minutes, before Dre started kissing me. A peck to my forehead, then my nose, then he lightly kissed my lips. I dropped my purse by the door and wrapped my arms and legs around him as he hoisted me up, never breaking our kiss.

My mind and body were now at war, because even though I was annoyed by him, I missed being touched by him. It's like my body craved connection while my mind wanted to disconnect. Leading me into our bedroom, Dre laid me gently on the bed, taking off my clothing items one by one, peppering light kisses and sucks everywhere. The familiar thump in between my legs made itself known, and my nipples hardened as he took one, then the other one in my mouth. My pussy was slick with desire, wanting to be handled in the best way. Dre trailed his kisses from my breasts to my stomach, to the top of my clit. Spreading my legs wide, I gave Dre full access to me, watching him lap me with hunger. Gripping the back of his head, I pushed him deeper, where it felt like his tongue was touching my heart.

"Dre, I'm finna cum....." I moaned, caressing his waves as his tongue worked in and out of me.

"Hold that cum for me baby, I'm not finished" he smirked deviously, putting his head back down and gripping my hips and ass to hold me in place. I bucked against him, fucking his tongue back from beneath him, winding my hips slightly as I felt my orgasm rise to the tip of my toes and shoot its way to my clit.

No, head was *not* an apology but the way Dre was eating it, I was ready to apologize to *him*. I wanted to say sorry for shit I didn't even do yet, that's how good his tongue lashing was. He reached up and rubbed my clit while he was tongue deep in me, making me feel a foreign sensation in the pit of my stomach. I was soaking, and if I didn't know any better, I'd swear that I peed on myself.

I gripped the back of his head again, while the urge to pee got stronger and stronger.

DeAndre was insatiable, and if I died today, my autopsy would show that I didn't have any pussy left, because the nigga ate it all. Abruptly removing his tongue from inside me and his finger off my clit, a stream of liquid and cum shot out of me, landing on his beard and lips, where he licked every drop.

Did I just squirt? Oh my God. This nigga made me squirt.

Taking a second to gather my bearings, from low lids I watched Dre take off his clothes, and suddenly I got a second wind. This nigga just ate me out like he had something to prove, so now I did too. Ever the competitor, I leaned up and pulled him on top of me. We started nastily tongue kissing again, and I tasted myself all over his lips. He then flipped on his back and pulled me on top of him, squeezing my titties while I positioned myself to ride. Balancing on my ankles, I hovered over his rock hard dick and teased his tip with my wetness.

Up.

Down.

Up.

Down.

Up again.

Down slowly.

Rotating my hips, I squeezed my pussy muscles and lightly bounced, taking all my frustration from the past few weeks out on that dick. Dre started fucking me back from underneath me, smacking my ass and digging his nails in my cheeks. I spun around with the dick still inside and rode him reverse cowgirl, leaning forward just a little so he could see how sticky and wet he made me. Throwing it back, Dre continued to palm my ass, moaning loudly which turned me up even more.

"Shit baby, I'm finna cum. Keep goin!" he moaned, and I was in a trance until he said that. Lifting off him, I turned to face him again, taking his hard dick in my hands and jacked it for a bit, while licking the tip with fervor. He tasted so good, that when he announced he was about to cum again, I inhaled him in my mouth, tapping the back of my larynx. He erupted, spilling all the kids he wanted to put in me down my throat and I kept sucking even after he was done nutting.

Mutually spent, I laid on top of him trying to regulate my breathing, our bodies heaving up and down after the session we had. He rubbed circles into my back with one hand and rubbed my booty with the other. I didn't expect us to have sex but I would be lying if I said that release wasn't needed.

But we still had important things to talk about. Things that couldn't be patched with mind blowing sex, or sucking the soul out of each other with bomb ass head.

***

"Dre." I nudged his shoulder, still on top of him as he slightly dozed off.

"Hmmm?"

"We still need to talk." He sighed sleepily and looked at me through lowered lids.

"We did enough talking baby," he said, pulling me closer to him but I shifted off him and laid beside him instead.

"Fucking is not talking, DeAndre. And if that's what you think it is, then..." my voice trailed off.

Dre sat up, rubbing a hand through his waves and beard.

"I ain't say that fucking is talking, Desiraè. What I'm saying is, I think we had a good time a while ago after not talking or touching each other for weeks, and maybe we should bask in that instead of getting all serious."

I scoffed. Giving him a *ok-nigga-you-got-it* nod, I got out the bed, grabbed my robe, and headed to the shower.

Knowing Dre, and knowing him well, he wouldn't initiate the conversation anymore. He'd think that just because we rolled around in the sheets, things would go back to normal. If he was really serious, he might even suggest going to sessions with Dr. Love again, just to pacify me.

Letting the water cascade over my face, I laughed to keep from crying. I wasn't sad exactly, but I *was* frustrated.

Coming out of the bathroom, Dre was no longer in our bed. Instead, he was back on the couch playing stupid-ass 2K. I shot daggers at his back and walked into the kitchen to pour myself a glass of wine.

Sipping slowly, I began to think of ways I could nicely approach this situation and came up with nothing. I wondered if it was even my responsibility to initiate it. It takes two to tango, right? So why did I feel like I was trying harder than he was?

Draining my glass, I filled it again and sauntered into the living room, easing onto the couch right next to him. Silently, I watched him hit three-pointers on the game and curse loudly whenever his teammates missed a shot.

Eventually, he got tired of losing, so he switched his game off and turned to look at me.

"Stop staring."

"I can look at what's mine," he grinned.

"Am I really yours though?" I asked.

It hurt to push those words out but I needed the reassurance. Dre's eyes flashed with a look of – well, I can't quite put my finger on it – but they flashed with something. Looking me directly in the eyes, I saw many things in his: A grown man in age, but lots of growing up to do. I saw that he loved me, I just wasn't sure if it was a choice or out of obligation. I could see that he didn't wanna lose me, but wasn't sure if it was because I meant that much to him or if he too, was afraid of what life would be like without me.

"Of course you're mine baby. I'm sorry that I haven't been showing you that over the last few weeks, but understand that I never meant to hurt you. I was just... just dealing with my own shit. You know I hate when we get into it. But, I love you. I always will. I want us to take the next step in our life but I can understand that you wanna wait. So even though I don't agree with it, I also understand that it's your body and your decision to make. We been in this too long to give up on each other this easy....I ain't never gave up on you, even when a nigga wanted to" he said, rubbing his hand through his beard. His rebuttal sounded convincing enough... if I was still young and dumb.

"Where did you go those nights when you first left?" I cut off, not in the least caring about the bullshit that came out his mouth.

His eyes flashed that same look from earlier, and I peeped it more clearly this time.

"I wasn't cheating on you baby," he frowned.

"I didn't ask that. And I know that. Stop deflecting."

"I'm not."

"You are."

"I'm not."

"You *are.*"

Dre sighed and pushed up from the couch. I stood up to follow him.

"How hard is it to just say where you were, DeAndre? You say you wasn't out cheating, so what were you doing? Why did you need three days? What made you turn your location off? Block me on social media? Block me from your phone?" I said at his back.

Dre sighed deeply. Froze before entering the bedroom and reached out to move me closer. I stepped out of his reach and crossed my arms over my chest. We stared at each other, not saying a word, though there were so many between us to say.

"I'm trying to talk to you and you are deflecting. If that's what this relationship is coming to, then maybe we don't need to be in it anymore. Maybe space from one another is what we need, if we can't have a simple conversation without you throwing a temper tantrum."

Dre's eyebrows raised and I saw a mix of anguish, heartbreak, and surprise cross his face. He got closer to me, pinning me between the wall and our bedroom door.

"You'd leave me baby? After everything?" he asked, in a voice that sounded far away. He was so close, I could still smell my pussy on his breath. I remained silent, anxious about what he was going to do. Dre had never put his hands on me, but this erratic behavior had me frozen in place. I couldn't begin to wonder if it was me who pushed him to act this way, or did I ignore signs that were already there?

"DeAndre, please get the hell out of my face!"

"Nah. Wassup? Give *me* an answer since you wanna fuckin' talk so bad," he sneered.

I closed my eyes and quickly counted to ten in my head. I didn't want this to happen.

To be quite frank, I regret even uttering those words to him and wished I could take them back. I always had to say the first thing that came to mind, not always thinking about the impact it would have on the person who received them and now look at me: Hemmed up by a man that's losing his sanity with every passing minute.

"DeAndre. *Please.*" I pressed my palms firmly on his chest and pushed him gently out of my face. He staggered back a bit, as if he snapped out of his trance and a look of dread replaced the far away look in his eyes. I stared at him cautiously, contemplating my own next move.

"Baby, I'm –"

I held up my hand and cut him off.

"Just... don't. You are absolutely right. We ain't gotta talk about it."

I turned to go into the bedroom. I wasn't staying here tonight. Couldn't stay here. Didn't *want* to stay here.

I pulled out my small duffle bag and packed three days' worth of clothes in it. I didn't even want him to chase me at this point.

Things were getting unhealthy between us, and I was fearful that if I just up and left him, he'd do something to me—or to himself.

That was no way to live.

I came back to the living room and Dre was nowhere to be found. I walked out the door and to my car, my destination set to my mother's house. It was around 11PM but I knew showing up at this time wouldn't matter to her or Jamaal, as long as I was safe with not a hair on my head touched. The fifteen minute drive passed quickly and my mother met me at her front door.

With no words exchanged, she embraced me and I broke down, releasing a deeply buried sob. They say it gets worse before it gets better, and I was afraid of how much worse it would actually get.

***

Three Days Later....

It was graduation day, and I should have been happy. Instead, it felt like I was on autopilot. I hadn't heard from Dre and he certainly didn't hear from me. Despite my final practicum going well, I was still feeling... heavy. The weight of what was next for me, both personal and professional, loomed over me.

Knock!

Knock!

Knock!

Someone on the other side of the door banged. I sighed and glanced at my phone. Graduation was at 10AM and I still had to get my hair curled and makeup done. The ceremony would be about two hours, and then the graduation party would start at 5PM. In between, I wanted to hide and decompress, but my friends had other plans. Swinging my legs over the bed, I got up to find my three best friends outside the door.

"I know you ain't think we was missing this day!" Bri yelled, holding up a makeup bag and roses in one hand. Angie and Robin followed behind her, with bottles of champagne and a bouquet of roses in their hands.

I burst into tears. Usually, I was not this outwardly emotional. But sessions with Doc over the years reminded me that it was okay to cry. So, I let my tears fall. I missed my girls and one of my unhealthy coping mechanisms was to isolate myself whenever I was going through something.

"Awww Dee, it's okay. You ain't gotta hide that you're going through something. You ain't pregnant are you?" Bri asked, patting me on the back.

"Fuck no!" I laughed through my tears. "I'm just... it's just... it's been so much going on. I'm sorry for ghosting."

"Ohhhh, don't mention it. It's your day. You worked really hard for this day, so whatever is the issue, will not take up space in your mind today. You are an official chef after today, D. Next up will be your restaurant and seeing you win is what matters most," Angie said.

I smiled warmly at my girls, sniffling a bit but taking in everything Angie had said. She was right. Today was *my day* and I worked my ass off to get to this moment. Nodding and dabbing my eyes with the tissue, I sat in the chair and let Robin beat my face, while Bri curled my hair. For the next two hours, we laughed, talked shit, and got a little buzzed off the champagne. My outfit for graduation was a simple white chef's coat, white pants and black pumps. I would change into a custom Chef's coat that my mom surprised me with later. It had red and white embroidery that outlined it, with Chef D. Rae on the front pocket while on the back it had an airbrushed design of our old house on Sangamon and the words "Mz. Earline's Kitchen" above it in the sky. I cried when she presented it to me, because everyone knew that I carried my Gramz with me everywhere. She ignited my love for cooking and I often flashbacked to us being in her kitchen, working in the candy store, and helping her with the soul food dinners. To see where I had come from, to where I was now, made me smile from ear to ear.

Robin put the final touches on my face and I swooned at what I saw in the mirror. I had long, natural looking cat-eye lashes, a smoky eye with a pop of red in my eye corners and my foundation made my skin look like glass. My hair was in a middle part quick weave, that was bra strap length with layers and curls. My chef uniform was pressed to perfection and my black Kendall Miles pumps set the entire look off. I walked into the living room and my entire family started hooting and hollering. Mama had hired event decorators to come to the house and do a red, black, and white balloon arch that was in the shape of a chef hat. In the corner of the deck, there was a 360 camera booth set up with all types of chef props. I saw the warmers out for food and got excited to taste the menu later of curry chicken, greens, garlic butter lamb chops, cubed garlic roasted potatoes, jerk chicken, thai chilli curried salmon, and roasted broccoli. There was also a taco bar for appetizers and the bar was open. Mama and Jamaal went all out for me and I was truly grateful.

After taking what felt like a thousand pictures, we headed to my school and my family went to take their seats while I went backstage with my classmates. We all hugged and greeted each other as we took our seats, waiting to be called. The ceremony was pretty straightforward. Chef Le-Breaux was our mistress of ceremonies, and a bunch of other professors came forward and gave remarks. Then, it was time for our names to get called and for us to receive our toques. Our white chef hats had pleats in them that represented the number of techniques we learned over the years and were tall. I scanned the crowd and saw my family, but then my eyes landed on DeAndre and immediately, my stomach knotted up. In his hands was a huge red and white bouquet of roses. Turning my eyes toward Chef LeBreaux, I mustered the fakest smile and tried to focus on not falling as I walked across the stage.

What the fuck is he doing here?

Aren't we broken up?

But I didn't have time to focus on that. I shook Chef LaBreaux's hand firmly and she pulled me into a brief embrace as the pictures flashed. "It's an honor to have you as a fellow chef, you will do great!" she whispered quickly in my ear. My heart swelled. I heard my family being loud as hell in the stands and didn't even care. They were all so proud of me and I was excited to eat, drink, and kick it with them and my girls later. My restaurant family was also stopping by.

Once everyone's names had been called, my classmates and I stood and waited on the command for us to throw our hats in the air. Pandemonium erupted in the auditorium and all you heard were screams and cheers of joy. We fuckin' did that. And now, the world was literally ours. I would finish out my summer working at Ruthie's, and then figure out what was next.

Leaving the auditorium, my family stood on both sides of the hallway and clapped and cheered as if I was a guest on *The Jennifer Hudson Show*. I Soul Train line-danced my way down, and Dre was at the end.

I quickly stepped back, startled by his presence. He pulled me into a hug and kissed my forehead, shoving a bouquet of roses into my hand.

Cutting my eyes at him, I silently warned him not to do anything stupid. Jamaal and my brothers would not hesitate to beat his ass, and I wasn't in the mood for no bullshit today.

I didn't technically uninvite him from my graduation—I was just surprised he was here, since we hadn't seen or spoken to each other in three days.

He wrapped his arm around me, and everybody snapped pictures of us—except my mama and Jamaal. I caught my mother's eyes and silently pleaded with her to come save me. She quickly moved closer to where we were.

Right before she could say anything to him, Dre loudly cleared his throat, and everyone's eyes snapped toward him.

He smiled sheepishly and looked down at me.

"I wanna thank everybody for coming out to my baby's graduation today. Though I paid for it, it was her who put that work in," he started. I rolled my eyes. It was something so smug in his tone when he mentioned putting me through culinary school and I wanted to knock him over the head with these damn roses.

"I'm proud of you shorty," he continued, pressing a kiss to my forehead. "As she embarks on this new journey in life, know that Imma be there every step of the way. To see Desiraè grow from this lost teenager to a woman that is so sure of herself, her future, and what she wants out of life, makes me want to keep her in mine forever. We've had so many ups and downs throughout our relationship, and I'm man enough to admit that I didn't always deserve her. Still, she persevered and did her big one when it comes to this culinary shit. So Rae baby, I just have one question for you...."

All the color drained my face as I watched Dre's goofy ass pull out a ring box, velvet press play on his phone to a song, and lowered himself on knee.

"I'on think you wanna do that bruh...." Jamaal bellowed, taking a step towards us. My friends and my brothers looked confused, since they had no idea that me and Dre were at odds.

Dre ignored all of them and it felt like my feet were in quicksand.

This couldn't be happening.

This couldn't be happening.

*This **couldn't** be happening.*

I kept chanting this in my mind, and to make matters worse, we were attracting a crowd.

"Desiraè Janelle Thomas: I've loved you since I was a young nigga who's locker was right next to yours. Over the years we've been through so much, especially as of late, but we've always made our way back to each other. If you rockin', I'm rolling. Would you do me the honor of rocking my last name until our caskets drop?"

I looked back and Jamaal was fuming, my mama was trying to hold him back, and the girls and my brothers just looked shocked. My mouth felt like sandpaper and if I had a genie, I'd wish to just disappear.

The question lingered in the air and I heard nothing but claps and cheers from the outside crowd.

Leaning forward, I whispered in his ear, "No! And get your dumb ass up! We are *done!*" and pushed his roses in hands.

Bewilderment crossed his face and I motioned for my girls to come on. Dre took a step forward like he wanted to grab me, and Jamaal was on him like white on rice. He hemmed Dre up so fast and spoke in a low but even tone, "Leave her the fuck alone bruh. You fucked up, so be a man and let her go. And what type of fool proposes at her graduation day anyway?! Getcha dumb ass on boy before we all go to jail out here."

I quickly sprinted away from them, heading to the car, wiping tears away. I felt so many things at once, mostly a combination of sadness, embarrassment, and relief. The girls joined me and we sat in silence for the ride back to my mother's house.

"Sooo... I guess we got a few more things to celebrate today," Bri spoke up, breaking the silence. I cut my eyes at her and she held her hand up. "Let me finish. "Our best fucking friend graduated culinary school, and you're a single woman. Sounds like a turn up to me!"

I shook my head. This day felt like the longest week of my life, but she was absolutely right. I was a certified chef, and a newly single woman. Sounds like a celebration to me, too.

Chapter Five

Desiraè

Three Months Later

"So, how have things been since you turned down the proposal Desiraè?"

It was a Saturday afternoon and I sat across from Doc, contemplating how I would answer her question.

The crazy thing about chaotic shit happening is that life has a tendency to go on. You are rarely given time to pause and reflect. Some days I felt like I was on autopilot and other days, I felt every emotion you could feel with a breakup.

Three months after turning down DeAndre's proposal, life was returning to normal. The day after the graduation, proposal, and my party, I moved out because according to my mama and Jamaal, wasn't no nigga putting me out... again. My entire family and friends ended up having to block him, because every day for three weeks straight, he kept finding ways to contact me. The straw that broke the camel's back was when this nigga showed up unannounced one random Thursday afternoon at my mom's house, and it took three police officers, a firefighter, and a couple neighbors to pull Jamaal and my brother Dayvon off him. After that, it seemed like DeAndre went ghost.

I shuddered at the memory. It's not that they were *trying* to jump him, but him coming over uninvited had Jamaal on go. And Dayvon couldn't stand niggas who failed to understand that no means no. It probably didn't help that Dre tried to "kidnap" me and I use that term loosely because even though he snatched me up and tossed me over his shoulder, he never got the chance to put me in his car because Jamaal tackled his ass, sending both of us flying across the front yard. After they made sure I was okay, Dayvon beat the boy so badly, I was sure that he was going to be walking with an overly black eye and limp for the remainder of his life.

How one could go from so in love one second to blocked on everything with a restraining order in place the next second was beyond me.

But stranger things in my life have happened.

"I'd say... trying to create a new normal for myself, I guess," thinking of my routine that consisted of still working at Ruthie's, doing small catering orders, and attending bi-weekly sessions with Doc. Life felt mundane at times, but that was okay, right?

"You know it's okay for life to feel mundane at times, right?" Doc queried, seemingly reading my mind.

I nodded in agreement.

"And it's also okay to have some challenges adapting to such monotony after experiencing abrupt change." I nodded again, mentally recalling the many sessions Doc and I have had over the years about my nervous system trying to reset itself after experiencing trauma. The thing is, I was *exhausted* with the constant reset. It was like no matter how much work I put in to cultivate peace in my life, some bullshit was always around the corner.

"You know better than anyone what you've gone through and what you've overcome. And even if life feels a bit uneventful or unsure *now*, know that it won't always be like this. You're deserving of the peace you seek Desiraè. Don't forget it" Doc continued, signaling an end to our session.

I am worthy of the peace I seek, I chanted silently to myself while pulling out the parking lot of Doc's office. I wanted to believe it, but at the same time it seemed so far-fetched.

At least, that's what I often told myself.

***

Driving to start my closing shift at Ruthie's, my phone dinged with a familiar sound from Instagram letting me know that I had yet another DM. Ever since I started posting recaps of my catering and restaurant kitchen creations, my DM's were filled with inquiries and praises. My following grew from a few hundred to what seemed like fifteen thousand overnight. I wasn't a fan of social media, but I appreciated the recognition a person could get just from sharing their passions. Going viral always surprised me but as long as the outcome resulted in happy clients and income, I welcomed it.

Parking in my spot, I looked and saw that I still had about ten minutes before I needed to clock in, so I took out my phone and scrolled through Instagram. Going over to my DMs, I responded to a few inquiries and then saw a message from a familiar bane of my existence.

KingShawn.071:

> You gone keep ignoring me Lady Rae?

I rolled my eyes. Refusing to follow him back on Instagram, I tried to go lurk on his page but it was private. My fingers lingered over the message and right then and there, I mustered up some energy to reply.

ChefDRae:

> What is it that you want LaShawn?

KingShawn.071:

> Damnnnn. It took you this long? Lol Come fwm.

ChefDRae:

> I would rather scrape my coochie down Halsted street.

KingShawn.071:

> You wild asf shorty

ChefDRae:

> And I'm dead serious too.

KingShawn.071:

> Shidddd, I am too. Fr doe, come fwm next time you in the city.

ChefDRae:

> Sorry, I don't come fw with married men. Stay out my inbox LaShawn!

KingShawn.071:

> Hell nah and follow me back too lil big head ass girl

Shaking my head, I exited the app and gathered my bag to head inside to the restaurant. I found it astonishing that it had been years and LaShawn still seemed to act the same. I had no idea why he wanted me to come fuck with him but apart of me felt like this was all a scheme to see if he still *could* fuck with me. Single or not, I wasn't stupid enough to go backwards with that man.

But I'd be lying if I didn't feel a teensy bit of satisfaction that he was thirsty to reach out to me. I smirked, cuz one thing about them tables? They sure do turn.

***

Pushing the message out my mind and getting locked in for my shift, I walked into the employee entrance and spoke to the line cooks, dishwashers, and kitchen managers.

Ruthie's was a high-end restaurant that had a heavy rotation of customers on any given day. People liked eating here because not only was the food top-tier, but the ambiance was just right as well. Many customers came through for date nights, business meetings, and even proposals.

Wrapping my shoulder-length goddess locs in my hair net and putting on my apron, I washed my hands and got down to business.

Everybody in the back of the house referred to me as "Chef" and constantly looked to my guidance and expertise on dishes. Many times, I went to management and even our owners to suggest new dishes or ways to improve upon current ones. Some ideas they liked and some they didn't, but the point was, for some reason they trusted me.

I took pride in my skills but also treated everybody with respect, because though I just graduated from culinary school, there were still many things I didn't know—but was eager to learn.

"Hey Chef. Table 33 askin' for you" my General Manager Sapphire came in and announced. I looked up with a questioning look and then nodded, only looking back down to finish putting the garnish on a dish that was getting ready to be carried out. Snatching off my gloves and disposing of them, I followed Sapphire out of the kitchen and down the long hallway to Table 33. It wasn't uncommon for customers to request for the chef to come out, but Table 33 was in the executive suite, meaning people with real big money and titles were dining with us.

Sometimes, celebrities came in and dined with us but the staff would've already been notified if that was the case. Getting closer to the table, a small smile appeared on my face upon noticing Chef LaBreaux. With her at the table was a dark skinned bald man with a salt and pepper beard, and a white woman with shoulder length copper hair and jade green eyes. Chef LaBreaux looked pleasant as always, thanking Sapphire and then turned her attention to me.

"Frank, Emily, I want you all to meet the head chef here at Ruthie's. This was my star pupil and recent culinary school graduate, Desiraè Thomas. She goes by Chef D.Rae online though." I shook Frank and Emily's hand.

"We've heard such great things about you and the food here at Ruthie's is to die for!" Emily exclaimed in a British accent. Frank smiled and nodded, taking a bite of his miso butter salmon, spiced broccolini, and garlic mashed potatoes.

"You're young, but I can tell that you run that kitchen with efficiency," Frank said between chews.

I smiled bashfully. "Well, thank you both. I can't take all the credit though, my team back there makes it easy to lead them."

Chef LaBreaux smiled at me, her eyes sparkling at me with a sense of pride. Though I never came right out and asked her to be my mentor, she was definitely someone I looked up to. Hearing her praise me filled me with a sense of pride too, making me stand up straighter and puff my chest out a bit more.

"I forgot my manners. Frank here is a renowned chef who owns over twenty-five international restaurants, specializing in a fusion of Afro-Asian cuisines throughout countries in Africa, Europe, and Asia. Emily here works for the Food Network, and is responsible for the success of many shows getting greenlight over the past twenty years. They're here stopping through town before they go back to their respective parts of the world and they asked me to take them to the best restaurant in town, so I brought them here," Chef LaBreaux explained.

Wow. They're all so accomplished, I thought to myself.

"We know you have to get back to your team, but before you leave, please tell us what is next for you after Ruthie's ?" Emily asked expectantly. My face grew hot and a lump formed in my throat. Just as quickly as the self-doubt and nerves creeped in, one quick glance at Chef LaBreaux made me swallow that lump and give Frank and Emily direct eye contact as I spoke on my dreams.

"I plan to finish out the year working here since I am a new graduate, but in addition to this, I also run a small catering business where I take a few orders per month to build up clientele. My ultimate goal is to open a restaurant that honors my late grandmother, who is the sole reason I even got in the kitchen."

I practiced this answer so many times, imagining if I was a guest on the Oprah or Tamron Hall Show and I had fame and recognition for my restaurant. Frank and Emily sipped their glasses of Veuve Clicquot champagne and nodded their heads, glancing at Chef with small smiles.

"Such an ambitious young woman" Frank clapped quietly, and we all shared a laugh. Looking at my watch, I smiled at the table one last time and thanked them for coming by to meet me.

"Desiraè," Chef called out.

I turned and waited a beat before she handed me a business card.

"I am proud of you, and I do believe that you will accomplish all your dreams and then some," she said. "My phone number is on this card. On your next off day, I'd like you to call me so we can arrange to meet for lunch. I have a few opportunities that I think will align perfectly with some of your goals."

I nodded, promising her that I would call, and hustled my way back to the kitchen where things still seemed to be running smoothly.

***

A couple of days later, I was off and had absolutely nothing to do, not even a therapy session. Instead of sleeping in, I got up, showered, and dressed for the day in a cream colored Fancy Homebody two piece lounge set. Whipping a quick breakfast of French toast and turkey bacon with a side of green apples, I ate while I mentally planned my day. I looked at the business card that Chef LaBreaux gave me and ran my fingers over the gold and black detailing. Pushing the nerves that threatened to bubble up in my stomach aside, I dialed her number and waited until she picked up on the third ring.

"Desiraè. I was expecting you," she said instead of hello.

"Good morning Chef. Is now a good time to talk?"

"Absolutely. Before we get started, how are you?"

"I'm fine. Finally have an off day for the next couple of days so I am happy about that."

"Very good. Early in your career, you'll work nonstop if you are passionate about it. But don't forget to practice self-care when you can, even if it's in the smallest ways."

I nodded as if she could see me. Self-care was something that I had to remember to practice, because it did often feel like I was working non-stop. And with plans to open my own restaurant, I knew that my work load would increase if I didn't take the time out to build my own team. As much as it warmed my heart to open my business, I often felt overwhelmed, too. No matter how glamorous social media made it seem, taking an idea from your head and actually executing it was hard work.

But I was built for it.

"Anyway. The reason I wanted to talk to you is for a number of reasons. I am intrigued by your ambition and the sheer talent you have in the kitchen. I've been a chef for twenty years and teaching for the last ten, and I can't say I've seen many like you. Your tenacity and eagerness to learn and do more is admirable. There are a few jobs in Chicago I'd like you to consider and not only do they pay extremely well, but they will elevate you to new heights and new customers, which is pivotal when you have plans to open your own restaurant like you do."

At the mention of Chicago, my mind briefly went to LaShawn and I's last Instagram exchange and I quickly pushed the thought out of my head. Chicago was where I was born but aside from a few trips here and there, I stayed away from the city.

"Tell me more."

"Of course. So the first is to become interim head chef at my pop-up restaurant. It is a temporary position, since my current chef will be going on maternity leave soon and I need someone sharp, efficient, and as tenacious as you to fill in for her for the next six months. The hours will be long and the menu changes every week but I know you can handle this. We have a starting pay of two-hundred dollars per hour and can even help you secure housing for the time-being. I own an Airbnb not far from the restaurant."

My brows rose in surprise as I quickly churned the numbers in my head. Two hundred dollars per hour times a forty hour work week meant that I could be making close to eight thousand dollars *per week*. That's about $32,000 *per month*. I ain't never seen that type of money before, and   almost questioned if my fresh-outta-culinary-school ass was even worthy of it. I didn't know anyone making that type of money and never even imagined it for myself.

"Don't doubt yourself, Desiraè. I know you are fresh out of culinary school and while I do have a network of friends and colleagues I can ask to fill in, I think the industry needs someone fresh and new. How you elevate even the most basic dishes is commendable. And, I want to give you a chance" she continued.

"I'm–I'm... I am honored," I finally found my voice. I didn't know if Chef LaBreaux was psychic but with her being from New Orleans, I didn't put it past her.

I heard her clap her hands.

"Very well then. The next opportunity aligns with your catering goals. Every year, the Mayor of Chicago and some other big wigs host what's called the Black Excellence Ball. It showcases the movers and shakers of the city—both prominent and smaller Black-owned businesses. I want you to set up a grazing table with some of your best dishes. This event attracts over a hundred thousand people and will give you the chance to build your network in Chicago. It'll be helpful when you open your restaurant, because you'll already have an awaiting clientele.I know you've already built a buzz on social media, but longevity in this industry means you've got to get in the field. Strategically placing yourself in the right rooms puts you in front of the right people.

I want to see you *win*, Desiraè. The question is: are you ready to win?"

My mouth went dry as I processed all that she said. I had Proverbs 18:16 tatted on the inside of my wrist that reminded me that my gifts would make room for me. As much as I enjoyed working at Ruthie's , I knew that what I wanted out of life was much bigger than what I was currently doing. Were these opportunities that Chef LaBreaux presented proof that my gifts were making room for me?

Sipping my water, I replied that I was ready to win. Because, although I was scared, I wanted to win. I wanted to excel. I wanted to prove to myself that I was capable of doing this and that all my hard work would pay off in the end.

"Excellent. Your start date will be the day after Labor Day. I know that's three weeks away, but as you know, this industry moves fast. I'll send over the hiring documents and the AirBnB information. Please think it over and if you have any questions, don't hesitate to reach out." I agreed and with that, she ended the call.

I let out the biggest scream of joy sending my mama and Jamaal running into the kitchen. I quickly recapped my conversation with Chef LaBreaux and they both told me how proud they were of me.

"This is *big* Rae-Rae. Only the beginning. Whew! Only three weeks to pull together a going away party, but I can handle it. What do you want the theme to be? Maybe we can just have a kickback. You feel like catering your own party? Oh girl! I'm so proud of you." My mama was going off on a tangent, pulling out her phone to jot down notes.

"Give me a second mama... I'm not sure if I want a going away party yet, this is a lot to process. And I for sure don't wanna cater my own party... if I have one," I snickered as my mama cut her eyes at me.

"Oh we gone celebrate! This is really just the beginning and we are proud of you. You set your sights on a goal, graduated culinary school, and now you have an amazing job offer. This is putting you on track to make your dreams come true, baby."

Jamaal nodded. "She's right, Baby Girl. At least let me throw somethin' on the grill. We ain't gotta make it a big deal but we do need to celebrate you."

"I will let y'all know. Right now, I just wanna take a quick nap," and they snickered. On my off days, they knew I didn't want to do much but catch up on rest, especially if I had a big decision to make.

Retreating to my bedroom, I laid down and it felt like my mind had over three hundred tabs open at once. Overwhelmed yet filled with gratitude, I said a quick prayer to God to let His will be done and to order my steps and lulled myself to sleep.

***

"Is there anything else that has you nervous about this move to Chicago, Desiraè?" Doc asked, sipping on a cup of chai tea. A couple days after my conversation with Chef LaBreux, I gave her my answer and signed the offer letter. I also promised my mom that they could throw me a small kickback a couple days before I was to get on the road to Chicago. I only wanted my friends, my brothers, and her and Jamaal there. Saying goodbye to Ruthie's was bittersweet. The love they showed me before I even started culinary school and even after I graduated would be something that I always remembered. They threw me a "wishing well" party where the pastry chef made me a cupcake tower that replicated a wishing well and everyone gave me small notes and tokens of appreciation wishing me well on my next journey. I cried the happiest tears, totally not expecting it. I would miss my Ruthie's family deeply.

I also made sure that I was in Doc's office at least once a week before I left. Starting new chapters wasn't easy and sometimes my brain made me think that I was stepping into a lion's den with no protection. I went back and forth between anxiety, fear, and self-doubt. Doc assured me that this was normal, but I don't know... it felt unbearable at times. I know Chef LaBreaux believed in me, I had the support of my family and friends, and knew I was capable of putting the work in, I was just... nervous. I didn't want to fuck this opportunity up. I was a perfectionist with all I did and had a tendency to be hard on myself.

I sighed and shifted my eyes, looking down at my lap.

"Desiraè?"

I glanced up and sighed again. "What if I see him Doc? Chicago is a big but small city."

"Has he still been hitting you up via Instagram?"

I sighed and focused on the lavender and coconut scented candle burning at the coffee table separating us. Doc stared at me intently, not rushing me to respond.

"Yes." I finally said, cringing inwardly.

"And have you been responding?"

"Yes but...."

Doc raised her eyebrow, silently encouraging me to finish.

"Let me ask you something..."

"Go ahead, Desiraè."

"Am I wrong or stupid for entertaining him?"

"Do you think you're stupid or wrong for entertaining him?"

Chewing my bottom lip, I didn't want to answer. Truthfully, my ego was stroked whenever I would peep that he watched my story, double tapped on my pictures, and slid in my DM's. It was like the roles had reversed, because when I was younger, I was the one thirsty to hold his attention. Now, it was like he was thirsty for me. He constantly complimented me and he even cash app'ed me two bands one day and told me to get myself some nice cooking shit with it.

Doc leaned up and looked at me. "Alright Desiraè, let's lay out the facts," she said and I groaned. One thing about it, Doc was going to hold me accountable and make me answer my own questions. Her therapy style was so unique and matter-of-fact. She didn't sugar coat things and that's probably why she made the money and had the impact globally, that she did.

"So. LaShawn is someone from your past. The first man you ever loved and although the relationship was tumultuous at best, you cared for him and were deeply attached. You all part ways and you haven't seen or heard from him in years. He finds you on social media and starts reaching out to you. Likes, comments, and views all on your page. And truthfully, it *is* stroking your ego. Especially, as a newly single woman. But let me ask you this: Is your ego getting stroked more important than your peace of mind?"

My shoulders slumped. Doc had this way of asking things that made me feel like she ripped out all my edges. Bouncing my leg, my eyes hyper focused on the candle burning, her question lingering in the air like the scent the candle was leaving.

"I think you look at things too black and white Desiraè. Stupid and wrong are not adjectives I would use to describe you in regards to interacting with him but I would implore you to decide what's more important to you; your ego getting stroked or your peace of mind. You're about to move to Chicago and you feel tempted. You're worried that if you see him, you will revert back to that young girl who was easily manipulated by him. Except, you are grown now – not just in age but in wisdom too. While some people *can* change, why do you think a married man who clearly has no respect for his marriage *and* who deeply traumatized you would do so?" Doc finished.

Well damn. There goes the last bit of my edges.

But she was right. I *was* worried that I would run into LaShawn or want to meet up with him when I touched down. I *was* worried that all the healing I did over these last few years would revert me back to that young girl who simply wanted to be loved again. And even though the conversation between us was minimal, –mostly just me saying thank you to his compliments– it was still crossing the line. And even though I couldn't stand LaTrice's chipmunk looking ass, she *was* his wife *and* the one he chose in the end.

But Doc was right. As a newly single woman, it did stroke my ego for someone I was once connected with to be on my line. While I didn't plan to get into another relationship any time soon, I did sometimes yearn for attention. So while it didn't make me stupid or wrong, it did make me aware of just how human I am.

"You right, Doc. I just... I don't know. I don't want him back at all but it's not like I have a roster or anything either... I thought the ball was in my court since he came looking for me," I defended my choices.

"And the ball *is* still in your court. You just have to decide if you want to continue to play the game or not."

The timer dinged, signaling that our time for the week was up. We stood and embraced each other. This was my last in person session with her since I was moving and her Chicago location was full at the moment. But she assured me that she was only a phone call away. I pulled out of the parking lot feeling a mix of perplexed and... heavy. Like, should I just go ahead and block LaShawn?

Common sense was telling me yes, but pride and ego were asking what for? He wasn't really disturbing my peace, and if I was being honest, something inside me subconsciously posted things just to bait him into responding. It was childish, but at the moment... I didn't really care.

I scanned my phone, bypassing messages from someone wanting me to feed 50 people with a budget of $300, yet they wanted an all seafood menu, comments on my latest video, and funny memes and videos the girls sent in our group chat. Going to my story, I typed 'BIG ANNOUNCEMENT COMING SOON' and posted it. Less than thirty seconds after posting, that familiar username replied to my story.

KingShawn.071:

> fuck you gotta announce?

Me:

> You got notifications turnt on for me or sumn?

KingShawn.071:

> FOH. Idk how to do all that. You gone let me know or what?

Me:

> You real nosey.

KingShawn.071:

> About you? Hell yeah.

Me:

KingShawn.071:

Mannnn. You capping.

Me:

no cap in my rap big dawg. What do you want?

KingShawn.071:

I been told you to come fwm.

Me:

And I told you that I would rather drag my coochie up and down Halsted before I do that.

KingShawn.071:

You always been wild asl shorty.

Me:

I always been dead ass serious too.

KingShawn.071:

Stop acting lame man

Me:

If I'm a lame, why you wanna know my business so bad then?

KingShawn.071:

You always been my business Lady Rae… ain't shit changed.

Me:

damn, when you become a comedian G?

KingShawn.071:

Wym?

Me:

I ain't been yo business since Obama FIRST term. Them wife and kids is yo business. Not me.

KingShawn.071:

you do the most man

Me:

And yet, you stay yo bean head ass in my inbox daily.

KingShawn.071:

mannnn.

Me:

Exactly. Ain't got shit to say.

KingShawn.071:

if you would come fwm, you ah know exactly what I gotta say.

Me:

I would rather drink flamin hots with cheese for breakfast than do that.

KingShawn.071:

bro… what is wrong with you?

Me:

besides the fact that you nosey as hell? Nothing.

KingShawn.071:

Mannnn I'm gone.

Me:

I'll see you tomorrow

I exited out the app and pulled into my mom's driveway. Today, my ego and pride won. Tomorrow might be a different story. But for now, I was going to allow my ego to be stroked and pray to God that it didn't backfire on me in the end.

Chapter Six

Desiraè

Chef LaBreaux was being modest about the Airbnb she had me staying in. It was in the heart of downtown, on the 75th floor and the building had every amenity you could imagine. It was a three bedroom, two bathroom loft style apartment, with huge floor to ceiling windows, a state-of-the-art chef's kitchen, and a wrap-around balcony that went from the primary bedroom to the kitchen that had a gorgeous view of the Chicago skyline and the river. Where Bloomington was quieter and didn't have skyscrapers and thousands of people being out and about 24/7, Downtown Chicago was live all the time. This loft could fit my mother's entire house in it and still had leftover room.

And I felt out of place.

Noticing the nervousness on my face, my mother paused her unpacking of my clothes and looked over at me. "You belong here Rae-Rae, and pretty soon, you'll believe it. If you weren't capable, you wouldn't have been asked to take on the job. Now stop stressing baby." she called out, then turned around and started organizing my clothes by color in the huge walk in closet. Although I insisted on driving up here alone, I was glad that my mama paid me no mind and came up here with me. My nerves were all over the place and I was struggling with imposter syndrome. My first day at Le Reaux was the next day, and I felt my stomach knotting up every time I thought about it. I just hoped I wouldn't fuck up, and then my reputation would be ruined.

I just couldn't believe that a young girl from Englewood was now in the heart of downtown Chicago in a loft that cost more than what some people make in a year. Chef LaBreaux was a wealthy, extremely accomplished chef and for some reason, she believed in little ole me. I could only dream to obtain this level of success. Making a mental note, I reminded myself to write in my journal about just how grateful I am for these opportunities that kept falling in my lap.

Ambling out of the bedroom, I made my way to the kitchen and paused at its beauty. Taking a picture of it to save to my Pinterest board later, I surveyed the layout. It was an open concept with a huge island in the middle made up of black granite and wood. The floors were marble and the same color as a white chocolate Hershey bar, with specks of black in it. At the island were six barstools that were also black, with gold detailing on the arms and legs of the stools. Behind the island was a large farmer's sink, two ovens, two dishwashers, and plenty of counter space. On the counters were everything from an Air Fryer, a Bartesian, and a Ninja smoothie maker. The backsplash on the walls weren't your typical tiles that you saw in most kitchens, instead it was printed wall paper in hues of black, white, and a pop of burnt orange. To my left was a cozy breakfast nook, the same burnt orange on the wall paper decorated booth of the nook and the tables and chairs were black. Leading off the breakfast nook, were the sliding doors that led to the wrap around balcony.

I was in heaven. I could tell that Chef LaBreaux spent a pretty penny on the decor in this home and knew that the six-hundred-dollar per night price tag on this home made the investment on the decor worth it. Making my way to the island, it was minimally decorated with a matte black fruit bowl and fake fruits like green apples, oranges, and even pomegranates in it. Leaning against the fruit bowl, was a matte black envelope on it and my forehead crinkled in surprise seeing my name on it in gold vinyl lettering. Tearing it open, it read:

Welcome to The Chateaux. I trust that you and your mother arrived safely and found everything up to your expectations. If there are any issues, press the button on the control panel by the fridge that is labeled MAINTENANCE and they will take care of it within eight hours. I am excited to have you taking care of Le Reaux and though it will be challenging at times, I believe you are more than capable of handling yourself and this restaurant. If you have any questions, need to vent, or simply need some advice, please feel free to call me or leave a message with my assistant at any time.

Opportunities like this don't come too often, Desirae. But I knew that when you first stepped into my classroom a couple years ago that you would go far in this life. Don't let imposter syndrome tell you that you don't belong, because you do. Have an amazing first day tomorrow, and I look forward to hearing about it

~Chef LaBreaux

I felt a small smile warm my face, reading the note over and over again. As rich and accomplished as she was, Chef LaBreaux was so humble, welcoming, and didn't hesitate to lift anyone up. She was also real as fuck, and didn't sugarcoat anything that came to this industry. I was so grateful that our paths crossed.

Walking into the kitchen, my mama let out a low whistle and looked around. "Miss Chef Lady really set you up *nice*!" she exclaimed, looking out the windows, then opening up the fridge and spice drawers, before finally sitting at one of the bar stools. I giggled. My mama had a nickname for everybody, it didn't matter who you were. I nodded and walked to the fridge. In it were expensive bottles of wine I couldn't pronounce and no food. My stomach grumbled, realizing I hadn't eaten anything today.

"You know what I got a taste for? Some BaBa's or Harold's" my mama questioned and then answered herself. I smirked, because being downtown meant that we were nowhere near a BaBa's and everybody knew if the neighborhood didn't have any Black people in it, then you did not go to that Harold's. Except the one in Hyde Park, that one was just nasty forever.

"Ma, we are nowhere near a BaBa's. But I haven't had a pizza puff with mild sauce and lemon pepper on it in so long," I groaned. "Then again, a six piece with salt, pepper, and mild sauce with a Calypso sounds fye too."

I was being indecisive. I just knew I wasn't in the mood to cook a damn thing today since I had to be at the restaurant at five sharp tomorrow morning.

"Girl, you have a car. Change your clothes and let's go eat so I can get back on the road."

Returning to the room that was mine for the next six months, I picked out a simple white sundress that hugged my curves, green slides from Shein, and the small green Telfar to match. Grabbing a pair of Lorvae shades, I kept my goddess braids in a bun and glossed my lips with the Fenty lip oil that just came out.

"Ok girl, you cute!" my mama exclaimed, glancing up at me from the couch.

"What can I say? I look different outside my work clothes" and we cackled at my imitation of Alicia Keys from that one music video.

Heading down to the parking garage, Mama got in her car and I got in mine, since she was leaving after we finished dinner.

Heading to the Dan Ryan, I turned on my slow jams and looked at the scenery as we crawled through Labor Day weekend traffic. Chicago summers were unmatched, and though the weather would change soon, I was happy to be here to catch the tail end of it.

The beautiful water, the tall buildings, the hustle and bustle of the city made me nervous—but made me feel alive at the same time.

Looking to my right, I saw the familiar 71st Street exit and had half a mind to go visit my old block.

Pulling up to 87th, I was a little surprised at how different it looked. The original Harold's had been replaced with some random ass restaurant and moved across the street where the Wendy's used to be.

We couldn't even sit down, so after ordering our food, me and Mama sat in my car to eat once we got our orders.

I missed mild sauce so much. It didn't matter that I could cook anything, sometimes you just wanted the simple hood delicacies from your childhood.

Savoring the taste of the chicken, I looked out the corner of my eye at my mama, who had her head on a swivel.

"You ever miss the old block?" I blurted. She turned towards me and squinted her eyes.

"Sometimes.... Yeah.... I do," she admitted.

A loud silence lingered in the air between us, the radio playing the same six songs on Power 92.3 being the background noise.

"Do you wanna go visit?" I blurted again. Like me, my mama had a lot of memories growing up on 71st and Sangamon. It was the same block she met my father on, and the same block she lost a lot on too.

Shaking her head, she rolled her eyes. "Not today, Desiraè. It's getting late and with this traffic, I need to get home before ya step daddy sends out the search warrant for me," her voice was playful but the humor didn't quite reach her eyes.

Sometimes, I think her past life was a trigger for her. All the years she spent away, unable to talk to us, not speaking to Gramz, and then building a new life for herself in Bloomington made her unwilling to visit the old block. I think she carried a lot of guilt and even though Gramz was in the ground, the house was sold, and she had a better relationship with all her children, anytime any of us brought up going by the old block, she shut the idea down immediately.

I sighed, looked at the time and nodded my head. We finished our food in silence and then she took our garbage to the trash can and came to sit back in the car.

"I thought you had to go?" I asked.

"I do, but I wanted to leave you with some parting words and a small gift."

Curiously, I looked at her as she reached in her purse and pulled out a small black box with a red bow on top. Unwrapping it, it was a sterling silver necklace with a heart pendant, and on the back of the heart was a picture of me, her, Jamaal, and my brothers. It was taken at my going away kickback and everyone had the biggest smiles on their faces as they wrapped me in a hug.

On the front of the pendant were the words *Close To Your Heart*. She then handed me another small box from Pandora, and in that was a charm bracelet that had a tiny chef hat, a champagne glass, and a butcher knife charm on it. Tears welled up in my eyes and I embraced her, thanking her profusely for my gifts. My family was everything to me and were people that were fully in my corner. I never had to question or doubt them.

"I'll never get tired of telling you how proud we are of you Rae-Rae. You've overcome things most people would have thrown the towel in at and created a whole new life for yourself. It is amazing to witness. You're not a little girl anymore, but you will always be *my* baby. Remember that you were built for this. Lean on God and remember that you can always lean on us too. I love you. We love you. Your first day will be amazing, don't stay up all night stressing."

Giving me a tight squeeze and a kiss on the cheek, I watched my mom get in her car and pull off in the opposite direction, heading home. I followed suit, heading back to the Air BNB to get prepared for the next day, but as I passed that familiar exit on 69th, I felt a pull, like a little voice in my head and quickly found my way on Sangamon.

***

The block was like a ghost town. When I was younger, you always saw kids playing on the sidewalks and in the streets. Labor Day weekend meant that the smell of barbeque would be in the air and loud music would be playing from someone's car speakers. People would be out on their porches, drinking liquor or lemonade and conversing with their friends while keeping a watchful eye on the children milling around.

It wasn't like that anymore and a part of me felt... shocked. Like the wind had been knocked out of me. I slowly creeped down the street and saw so many abandoned and boarded up homes. I knew shortly after Gramz died, many other elders in the neighborhood passed on year after year too. I just didn't expect the neighborhood to die right along with it. I stopped in front of Gramz's old house and just looked at it.

What once was a house full of life now looked destitute. I didn't know anyone who lived there now, but when I was little, I remembered her having her screen door open while she sat in her chair in the living room watching TV, while I sat on the porch. I remember she used to holler at us about running in and out of the house, complaining about us letting her air out, even though half the time, the window air conditioner didn't work. I remember –

My reminiscing was cut short when I saw a black on black Range Rover truck pull up directly behind me. I gripped the steering wheel so hard that my knuckles turned white. Looking through my rearview mirror, I watched the driver hop out, looking eerily familiar. Instead of shoulder length braids, this man had a fade with deep waves and a goatee beard combination. Unlike the tall white tees and Girbaud jeans of the past, this man had on some blue and black basketball shorts that said Rhude across the front and a fitted plain white t-shirt.

I peeped a shiny watch, an earring in his left ear, and a pair of Jordan's that matched the shorts perfectly. This familiar stranger walked up to the house that used to be our next door neighbor's home and knocked twice before being let in by a dark-skinned man. Minutes later, he came back on the porch with the same man, shook up GD, and chopped it up with him, looking at my car. My windows were tinted so he couldn't see me, but I knew exactly who he was.

Time had done LaShawn Davis well. I couldn't even cap.

His brows furrowed as he looked at my car and back at the man who was on the porch with him. The man on the porch was also fine, skin the color of dark roasted almonds and a tattoo of a crown on his throat. He reminded me of that rapper Skepta, who looked menacing at first glance but I could tell that if he smiled, it would be the most beautiful thing in the world.

LaShawn eventually came off the porch and right up to my window, knocking fast three times with the butt of a gun.

Shit.

I didn't expect him to do that.

But it was obvious that he would because of course I looked strange as hell since we were the only two cars on the block and he obviously didn't recognize mine.

I contemplated not rolling down my window until he said, "Open this window or I'm shooting this shit out."

So I did. And the look on his face was like he had seen a ghost and then his signature smirk came out.

"Ahhhhh! I knew yo shit talkin' ass was gone come fuck with me! Get out the car Lady Rae," he said, unlocking my door and swooping me in his arms. I stiffened. He buried his face in my neck and swung me around as if I was a soldier returning from war. Then he sat me back on my feet and we just stared at each other.

"Damn, man. I ain't think I was ever gon' see you again," he said, breaking the silence.

"You wasn't."

"Yet you came and fucked with me though," he retorted.

"Consider it luck and nothing more," I rolled my eyes. He laughed and rubbed his hand through his beard.

"Still talking shit but that's okay. What you doing in the hood man?"

"Minding my business," I retorted. LaShawn smirked and shook his head and I watched his eyes glaze over me, taking me in from head to toe.

"You ain't lil Rae-Rae no mo'. You always been fine but now you finer and a lil thick," he said, licking his lips. I rolled my eyes and begged my facial expression to remain neutral.

Even though he was saying nothing spectacular, his words were still stroking my stupid ego and I didn't wanna give him the satisfaction of seeing me smile at his words. Just then, his phone rang back to back three times and he ignored each call.

"What you doing out here though? You just visiting or you staying for a while?" he asked, his phone interrupting us for the fourth time. He looked down at it, eyes crinkling in annoyance before picking up.

"Trice, what the fuck is yo problem?!" he roared. He walked back towards the porch, pacing the sidewalk as they talked.

And just like that, I snapped out of whatever nostalgic spell I was under. This nigga was my ex, a very toxic one might I add, and married to the bitch who jumped me and made me lose my first baby.

Yeah... let me get the fuck off Sangamon.

But for some reason, my feet wouldn't move. I watched and listened to him argue with her, something about how he's been dodging her and hasn't been home in a couple days because he was too busy running the streets and in some hoes face.

Clearly, nothing had changed but the year because I remember when I was on the other end of his phone, sounding just like her. Chuckling, I opened my car door and slid in the driver seat, ready to take off to leave those two to their argument. Noticing me put the car in drive, LaShawn hung up and jogged over to me again.

"Aye yo Rae! I'm sorry about that. Her ass be tweaking man," he stressed. I just looked at him and then smirked.

"As I was saying though, you should let me get yo number. We can take a drive down Lake Shore, go get sumn to eat – whatever you wanna do."

I frowned and shook my head. "Absolutely *not*. You are *married*. And I'm just not interested."

LaShawn always had very long lashes so when he rolled them, they touched the top of his eyebrows as he scoffed. "Yo ass just hear what you want to," he began spinning his web.

I held my hand up. "Honestly G, I've heard enough. You can't rewrite history, LaShawn. Go home to your wife, y'all kids, and stop trying to link with me. You saw me today. Consider this the last time that you will."

He nodded. "Yeah, aight. Imma see you again Lady Rae," and he tapped the hood of my car. I rolled my window up and pulled off, adrenaline pumping. The ride back to the Air BNB took only thirty minutes with some slight traffic and since I had a parking garage, I didn't have to waste my time parking.

I couldn't cap: LaShawn looked good on the outside.

Sometimes when we leave situations we expect them to crumble without us. We want their hair to fall out, teeth to rotten, and for their barber to forever push their linings back. I remember being so bitter in the beginning of my healing journey.

I wanted him to get beat up, robbed, and go broke. I wanted him done worse than the Power Puff Girls used to do MoJo JoJo, but life has been kind to him. He was obviously still getting money, he was married, and he had children. But, I wasn't doing bad for myself either.

I was about to start getting money, I wasn't ugly, and more importantly, I was at peace. I didn't have to worry about somebody's raggedy ass son stressing me out. I didn't have to worry if they were lying, or cheating, or would switch up on me just because I didn't want to do what *they* wanted me to do. I didn't have to worry about constant embarrassment.

Honestly, I began to feel bad for LaTrice. We both fought over that nigga hard in high school and for whatever reason, they got married but it was clear it wasn't a happy or healthy one. And, while it stroked my ego a bit that he still found me attractive, let's be so for real: if I was the old Desiraè, LaShawn wouldn't be paying me any mind unless he wanted to.

Who wants to continue to live life feeling unappreciated and over-looked?

Not me.

I walked to the fridge and pulled about the bottle of wine I couldn't pronounce and googled the name of it. Google led me to an article on none other than Chef LaBreaux, who created her own wine brand imported straight from France and I chuckled. What doesn't this lady do?

Pouring a healthy amount in her mocha colored wine glasses, I went out to the balcony and overlooked the skyline as the sun was setting. The day was eventful, but I had to shift my focus to more important matters at hand. After running a bath in the beautiful clawfoot tub and making sure my uniform was ironed for tomorrow, I climbed into the cozy California King bed and drifted to sleep.

***

Waking up at 4AM was no hoe. Even though I slept like a baby, I was groggy as fuck. I quickly dressed and then checked the address to the restaurant. It was only a two minute drive and a fifteen minute walk.

Deciding that I would walk, I headed out the door a bundle of nerves. Chef LaBreaux gave me a set of keys to open the door to the employee entrance and after walking in the cooler morning air, I was fully awake now.

Slipping in the back entrance, it was about 4:45AM and I noticed that I was the first person in the kitchen. The lights automatically came on as I moved and my breath caught in my throat as I observed the state-of-the-art commercial kitchen. There were stainless steel appliances everywhere and it was so clean that you could eat off the floor. There were two prep stations, two clean up stations and my favorite part were the stoves. I counted six of them, and they all had multi-unit ranges and combos of gas burners, a griddle, and a fryer-steamer station.

Le Reaux's kitchen was a culinary heaven. The restaurant itself was equally beautiful. High ceilings, plush seating, bathrooms with huge floor to ceiling mirrors, and lots of natural sunlight set in a zebra print, red, black, and gold color scheme made this place aesthetically pleasing.

What made Le Reaux unique was that its menu rotated weekly. Each week was themed after an international place or local cuisine. If the kitchen produced too much food, they partnered with local shelters and soup kitchens to give the food away for free. The bar also followed suit, with its bartenders crafting specialty cocktails from each country, complete with decor and special garnishes to go along with it. It was a social media sensation, and because they only popped up two times a year for six months straight, the reservations were booked up until March. The restaurant employed hundreds of people and Chef LaBreaux ran a tight ship.

Which meant that I needed to get into formation.

Checking the time, it was now 5:30 AM and that meant that by now, staff should've been arriving. Heading quickly to the back, I saw about twenty-five people milling around, doing everything from washing their hands to starting the prep for today's menu. Pushing down the nerves bubbling in my stomach, I stepped in the middle of the kitchen and cleared my throat.

A few people glanced my way but everyone else ignored me. Music was blaring loudly so I found where it was coming from and unplugged the bluetooth speaker which cut the sound.

A hush fell over the kitchen, and now everyone was looking at me with the stank eye. I forced myself to smile and not let my intimidation show on my face or in my body language. Taking a deep breath, I started my address to the crew.

"Good morning everyone! My name is Desiraè Thomas but you can call me Chef Rae or D. As you all know, I'm the Interim Head Chef while Catherine is out on maternity leave. I'm excited to learn, work with, and lead you all in her absence."

"You look kinda young. You fresh outta culinary school or something?" a heavy-set Italian woman with stringy black hair interrupted. I heard a few chuckles and felt all eyes on me.

I swallowed the lump on my throat and squinted at her.

"I'm sorry, I didn't open the floor for questions and commentary, and we haven't done introductions yet. What's your name, I didn't catch it?" I said in a clipped tone.

It got so silent that you could hear a mouse piss on a cotton ball as me and this lady stared at each other. Finally, she sighed and rolled her eyes.

"Shelly. Shelly Bianchi."

I nodded. "Thank you Shelly. It's nice to meet you. I'm not sure what you do yet, but I do plan to get to know you all over time. As for my age, it doesn't matter. I *am* fresh out of culinary school, but I was *hand picked* by Chef LaBreaux to come here. So even if you don't think I should be here, understand that the person who signs our checks thinks differently. Now, if you all have questions for me, I'm happy to answer them when we get some time. For now, I ask that you all listen to these morning announcements without rude interruptions." I looked Shelly's pasty ass right in the face and her eyes showed a mix of embarrassment and awe.

Internally, I could have told her to mind her fucking business but a part of being a leader was learning how to talk to people even when they pissed you off. I never heard Chef LaBreaux raise her voice or cuss at anyone she worked with so I would work just as hard to control that side of me as well.

But this was Chicago, so sometimes you had to tell a goofy where they had you fucked up at.

Professionally, of course.

I breezed through the morning announcements and then went to the office to check on morning delivery updates. As I powered on the computer, I heard a knock on the door and Shelly popped her head in.

"What's up Shelly?" I asked, half-focused on her and half-focused on the fact that we were supposed to open in two hours for the morning rush, yet we were missing two hundred cases of heavy whipping cream, strawberries, and butter.

"I just wanted to apologize for my outburst earlier. I ain't mean nothin' by it," her Italian Chicago accent thick. "I've been working in this industry for a while and I can tell you already got what it takes. So... sorry."

I nodded. "I appreciate Shelly. Once I said my piece, it was already water under the bridge. These six months are gonna fly, but while I'm here, I just wanna make sure things are as seamless as they should be. Now, if you'll excuse me, I need to figure out why the hell we're missing a delivery that should've been here yesterday," as I pushed out my seat and looked for the delivery company's number. Shelly nodded and yelled over her shoulder that she would be around if I needed.

The rest of the day flew by and by the time I made it back to the loft, I was tired as hell. I washed off the day, ate my leftovers from the food we made today, and collapsed on the couch.

Remembering Chef's words in her note, the day was indeed challenging but I knew that in due time, I was built for this.

***

One week turned into two weeks and that turned into a month and while the hours were long and I was exhausted, I felt...content. The money wasn't bad either. I had more money than I knew what to do with and since I didn't have to pay rent at the loft and only worry about my phone bill and car insurance, I stacked a lot of my money in preparation of finding a space for my restaurant. The name was already trademarked, I had the LLC already, and I had money saved for a billboard and other marketing materials I might need. There were other things that people didn't think about when opening a restaurant and some days it overwhelmed me. The thought of having to spend money on equipment, then think about who I wanted to hire because I knew it was impossible to do alone, had me *stressed.*

My favorite way to relieve stress was to take a drive on Lake Shore Drive and vibe out to the music. After locking the doors to Le Reaux, I hopped in my car and drove the familiar streets to the busy expressway. No matter the day or time, LSD was always bussin'.

Some nights I would take it all the way north to its beginning at Hollywood Ave, and other nights I would take it far south, stopping at the intersection of 67th and Jeffery before heading home. Deciding to drive south, I weaved in and out of traffic, mentally going over my to-do list the next day.

Tomorrow's menu was Asian cuisine, and we had a couple celebrities and food influencers coming through to create content and review the food. Getting a reservation these days was harder than getting a pair of limited edition Jordan's, but we stayed full. I knew Chef LaBreaux was happy that business was booming.

Somehow, I looked up and found myself back in Englewood. I drove past the BaBa's that used to be on 72nd and Morgan, then went around Kennedy King College, looking at the blank space that the Whole Foods once occupied. When I was coming up, we ain't have no Whole Foods in the neighborhood. We went to Food 4 Less on Ashland, Aldi's, Jewels, or Pete's on 83rd. Now it was a Chipotle, a Starbucks and other businesses.

Aside from the sit down restaurant that was funded by the college, I realized that my hood didn't have many sit down restaurants, and that bothered me. It was already a food dessert, but in comparison to other neighborhoods in Chicago, I wondered why many didn't invest over here.

Turning from Halsted, I drove past my old high school and chuckled at memories of me acting a damn fool in there over LaShawn. It was amazing that I graduated, in the top ten of my class at that, but I'd always been smart.

Just didn't make the smartest decisions in choosing men.

While other girls were enjoying things like school dances, going to sporting games, innocent crushes, and hanging out with their friends, I was caught up in a boy who was older than me, trying to prove my dedication and loyalty to a nigga who didn't give a damn about me forreal. I wonder what life would have been like if I had just walked past that nigga the day at the barbershop.

Sighing deeply, for some reason I drove past the old barbershop, and that's when I saw it. A vacant restaurant space that was in between a beauty salon named Reigning Beauty and a barbershop named Krowned. Across the street, I saw another business called Vibes and Lines and it said it was a bookstore and a wine bar.

I made a mental note to come back and check that out, because my mama was an avid reader and loved her some wine. Getting out of the car, I walked closer to the commercial building and saw that it had a For Lease sign. I couldn't see much but it was medium sized and had an open concept layout with double doors to the entrance.

Putting the phone number on the door in my phone, I made a mental note to call them tomorrow when I got a break. Though many people thought I was crazy, opening a restaurant in the neighborhood I grew up in was a dream of mine. People talked hella shit about Englewood and its violence but there was a lot of community here when I was coming up. I wasn't a superhero, but I figured why couldn't I be someone who contributed something positive to this community, just like Gramz did when she was alive?

Her dinners were the glue to the community and she didn't always do it for the money either. It didn't matter if you were short on funds, homeless, a crackhead – Gramz fed everybody. And the people loved her for it. I wanted to embody that same heart, that same spirit of giving, that same –

"What the fuck is you doing out here shorty?" a gruff voice said from behind me, interrupting my thoughts. My body stilled for a moment and I slowly turned to a tall, dark figure behind me. He had a medium build with an all black Nike Tech sweatsuit on and all black Air Force Ones. His energy seemed oddly familiar but it was dark as hell, and I couldn't really make out his facial features.

Finding my voice, I said, "Minding my fuckin' business." I wish I didn't leave my purse with my mace in it, in the car. Dude snickered, and I furrowed my eyebrows in confusion.

If he was about to rob me, I wasn't going to stick around for it. Walking around him, I hit the locks on my door as he called after me. "You need to be more careful, especially at this time of night. I can tell yo ass ain't from around here."

Pausing to open my door, I looked at him over the hood of my car and realized where I knew him from. "There you go minding my business again. I grew up right on 71st and Sangamon," having no idea why I even volunteered that information. He stared at me for a second, then nodded.

"Well, yo ass don't live on that block no more, so just... be more careful shorty. It can get spooky this time of night."

Instead of a response, I opened my door and started my car, driving off on his ass.

Then it hit me.

Dude was the same one that LaShawn pulled up on when I stopped on Sangamon the other day, and I didn't know what to make of him. Despite coming off rude, he did sound a bit caring, and for that I could appreciate it.

Pushing thoughts of Mr. Mystery Man outside my head, I thought back on the space I had found. I called my mom on the drive home and told her all about it. Though supportive, she was skeptical about the location, but I assured her that I would do my research before making any hasty decisions. But deep down inside? Something was telling me that what I discovered today would be the beginnings of something big.

Chapter Seven

Desiraè

Five months later....

"Alright, people! Tonight is a huge night for us. We're expected to serve over a thousand people in five hours. That means things will move fast, and we gotta be on point. By now, you all should have gotten your stations and duties for the night. If there are any questions, please find Shelly or Nicole. I believe we have a surplus of food, but if there are extras, *please* take some home...just remember to leave some for the houseless. Dayvon will transport whatever we don't eat. If you know you ain't much of a people person, keep your ass in the back and refill the items. We don't ever want folks accusing us of bad customer service or food running out. More importantly, have fun tonight!Clean-up crew, the best way to stay organized is to pick up as you go, so you won't have much to do at the end of the night. Jamaal here is your go-to person for that." I took a breath and looked around at my team of twenty people for tonight's event.

The Black Excellence Ball was tonight, and true to her word, Chef LaBreaux got me in as one of the vending caterers. There were hundreds of Black-owned businesses present, and guests had the opportunity to sample countless cuisines from around the city.

Over the past few months, Shelly and I had built a bond based on mutual respect. She had my back and I had her front when it came to that kitchen at Le Reaux. My mama, Jamaal, and Dayvon came down to help with this event and I enlisted help from some other employees at Le Reaux to help out for tonight.

Bri had created and ordered me a custom table cloth that had my logo and business name on it. She also created the cutest business cards for me to hand out, that were in the shape of little menus. While all the food we were giving out tonight was free, she also created a cute digital tip jar. I required my team to wear all black and Bri made them custom name tags to wear on their uniform shirts.

Though I was making good money now, I wasn't one to spend it on frivolous shit – but I *loved* spending my money on cookware and catering items and getting my hair done. I had state-of-the-art chafing dishes that matched the gold and emerald color scheme of the event, a serving tray set up with a swing, and three tables in an L-shape. I was putting an elevated soul food twist on a grazing table.

For the menu, I had short rib of beef sliders, honey garlic lamb chop skewers, collard greens with smoked turkey tips in gold appetizer cups, jerked marry me salmon pasta bowls, baked macaroni and cheese, fried party wings, seafood gumbo, chicken sausage gumbo, and even a couple vegan versions of the dishes.

For dessert, I had banana pudding cheesecake in martini glasses, cookies 'n creme cupcakes, and pound cake cupcakes with a strawberry glaze icing. For drinks, we had this classic punch that Gramz taught me how to make which consisted of red Hawaian punch, sherbert ice cream, pineapple juice, and ginger ale.

With the amount of people I had, setting up took only an hour and a half, and staff for the ball were already trying to sneak and get a sample or two since the food smelled so good. The event was held in the historical Old Post Office building and it was beautifully decorated, though I thought it was stunning without all the decorations.

The high ceilings and historic charm made me feel like I was transported back to the Prohibition era or something. People could say whatever they wanted to about Chicago, but my city had some of the best history, food, attractions, and architecture, period. I wrapped my speech up and saw Angie and Robin capturing footage for my social media recap. I had started doing these mini vlogs called *A Day In The Life of A Future Restaurant Owner* and although I didn't care for social media and the posting, I really did them to remind myself to keep going. The girls convinced me to hire a camera man because Bri was convinced that I should start a Youtube channel and felt that this event would be the perfect introduction video.

Since she was my unofficial marketing executive and brand manager, I just listened and approved without too much pushback. I had a love-hate relationship with social media. Business owners not only had to worry about running their business, we also had to create social media content and be a constant presence online. It was nerve wracking at times.

So many people relied on their social media personas but weren't shit in real life. I know it sounds harsh, but the difference between me and them was that I was who I was both on and off the net. Too many times, I've seen videos of chefs getting bashed on social media because their social media personas didn't meet the expectations for professionalism and quality of food.

I didn't play that. Not only would the food be good but my professionalism would be on point too. And, I was selective about what type of clients I would take on. I didn't care if you were a celebrity, social media famous or how much money you were offering, if it didn't align with my personal values, I wasn't doing it. Even at Le Reaux, Chef had a policy that she didn't care who you were – you were to treat the staff and others at the restaurant with respect, or security would escort you out. I couldn't count how many times well known people were refused service after being rude to servers or bartenders or other patrons.

After wrapping my speech, I ran to the bathroom to use it and make sure I looked presentable.

Though I had been up cooking since 4AM, my mama convinced me to make time to get my hair and makeup done tonight. My uniform consisted of black slacks, some comfy black Crocs, and my custom chef coat from graduation.

My hair was in a ginger colored, shoulder length half up, half down quick weave with two buns and two bangs. Robin did my makeup, which only consisted of lashes, brows, a skin tint, and the Fenty glow powder on my cheekbones. On my fingers, I had custom press on nails which was a basic french tip but had a small, 3D chef hat and knife set on my ring and middle fingers.

Taking a picture and posting it to my Instagram story, I pocketed my phone and headed back to my tables. During my walk, I was in awe of all the vendors that were spread out in the lobby area of the venue. I ran into one of my favorite chefs I met out here, <u>Chef Kita of Kita'z Kitchen.</u>

Her food was so bomb and people stayed flying her out all over the world to get her experience. She was also very sweet and down to earth too, and she didn't play about her professionalism either.

She had been in the business for almost a decade and she was definitely someone I looked up to. After chatting with her, I finally made my way back to my table and the event was now in full swing. Since I had more than enough staff, the line was flowing smoothly. I was right in the mix, chatting with guests and introducing myself to them as the chef.

Angie made sure every guest left with a business card and some wanted to book me on the spot for some of their upcoming events. I explained to them that I would be opening up a restaurant soon, and they would be able to dine in with me soon.

In the middle of a conversation with the owner of a media company called <u>The Triibe</u>, I heard a voice that sounded like nails on a chalkboard. Turning my attention to the far end of the table, I squinted and peeped LaShawn in an all black custom suit with a pair of those ugly Prada gym shoes, minimal diamond jewelry on his neck, wrist, and ears with a fresh haircut.

With him was LaTrice, dressed in a mermaid style gold dress with a corset that had her titties sitting nicely. Her jet black hair was styled in a buss down middle part with the trendy Kash Doll curls that framed her face. Her matching gold heels had her a bit taller than usual and even though I didn't want to admit it, she looked nice. In fact, she was never an ugly girl, just acted ugly. Hell, we both did over that stupid ass man she ended up marrying. Pushing those thoughts out my head, I made my way towards them to see what the issue was.

LaShawn peeped me in front of them, and his expression was a mix between surprise, proudness, and like he had seen a ghost again. Then it switched to a poker face, as he tried to pull his wife away from the table.

"Excuse me, what seems to be the problem?" I asked in what I hoped was my most professional voice. My employee explained that LaTrice was arguing with them whether or not there was pork in the collard green cups because her dumb ass couldn't tell the difference between pork and turkey. Not to mention, there were place cards that had all the ingredients listed on them. So not only was she dumb, the bitch couldn't read either.

LaShawn sure knew how to pick 'em.

LaTrice squinted at me as she took in my appearance, recognizing me immediately.

"Wait a minute, don't I know you? Ain't yo name Desiraè or some shit?"

LaShawn pulled on her hand. "Naw you don't know her. Let's go man, the program is about to start and we can't miss cuz receive his award."

LaTrice shook away from him, put one hand on her hip and cocked her head to the side, eyes boring into mine as she mentally put the pieces together.

"Nah, Shawn. This yo old bitch from high school! The one who we jumped and she lost her baby. This why the fuck you wanted to come over here and taste this nasty ass food?" she accused, getting louder and holding up my line.

I counted to ten in my head, neither myself or LaShawn saying anything to her. Sometimes, no matter how healed and mature you got, there were still some people whose asses you wanted to beat every time you saw them.

LaTrice was that person for me and I was pissed if I had to make an ass of myself and drag her in front of all these people. I excused my employee, and looked dead at LaShawn and LaTrice.

"My name is Chef Desiraè Thomas, and I own this business. I can assure you that there is no pork in this dish. Not only can you taste the difference between pork and turkey, but there are also place cards that list every ingredient in every dish you see on this table. I pride myself on letting patrons make decisions on what they are putting into their bodies, in case of allergies or dietary restrictions. Please, listen to your husband."

Leaning over the table getting close enough to smell her breath, I concluded, "Not only are you holding up my line, but I can promise you that I am not someone you *want* to know, no matter how much you *think* you do."

LaShawn kept trying to pull her away but it's like her feet had cinder blocks on them. She angrily narrowed her eyes and they flashed with embarrassment. Here we were at this fancy ass event with the who's who of Chicago, and this bitch wanted to act like it was fourth period at Harplan High School.

I wanted to dog walk her so bad, but my reputation and integrity was on the line. I worked too damn hard to be out here acting like a ghetto bird. Even though Michelle Obama said when they go low, we go high, I wanted to take it to the pits of hell.

I remembered that fight after school like it was yesterday. I remembered how they snuck me, the feeling of the bricks being slammed into my stomach, and waking up in the hospital after passing out. I remember the blood loss and the depression that followed afterwards. That was too much for a child to bear, yet I thought I was doing something noble by taking it on the chin.

Enough time had passed where I wasn't a crying mess every time I remembered the children I lost, but who ever really gets over child loss anyway? Grief ebbs and flows. In a strange way, I do feel like the child loss protected me from being attached to Shawn forever, but it still hurt. And for that bitch to gloat about jumping me and *murdering* my child, I wish I would've pressed charges on her when I had the chance.

"Girl please. Stay away from my fucking husband!" she snapped, turning on her heel and letting LaShawn pull her away.

***

My chest rose and fell and I felt my entire body get hot. I headed the opposite way towards the bathroom, walking fast as hell, refusing to let these stupid tears fall in front of everybody. Finding an empty stall, I practiced the breathing techniques that Doc taught me, then pulled out my phone to send her a request for an emergency virtual session the next day.

Somebody had to talk me off the ledge because what I wanted to do them both would surely land me life in prison. Walking out of the stall, I noticed my mama standing by the sinks, waiting on me. She held her arms out and I rushed into them, sobbing. She said nothing, just gave me space to cry and rubbed circles on my back.

I cried for a good ten minutes, frustrated that I couldn't go and whoop that girl's ass. When I stopped crying, my mom fixed my lashes and gave me eye drops to decrease the redness and puffiness.

Once I was calm, we wordlessly walked back to my table, where the crowd was still thick. I networked with so many business owners and even stopped to take a few pictures with people who recognized me from Instagram. In the last hour of the event, the curator called the vendors on stage to give them a shout out and token of appreciation.

As I scanned the crowd, my stomach dropped to my toes. Seated on the front row, was *DeAndre* of all people, and with a date. He was looking real cozy with a pretty light skinned girl in a royal blue ball gown, and he was rubbing on her *very* pregnant stomach.

Could this night get any worse? It was absolutely mortifying to see not one but *two* exes. If these were the tough battles that people said God gave his strongest soldiers, I was ready to go AWOL. Put me on the weakest soldier list, immediately!

I quickly said thank you, accepted my gift bag, and scurried off the stage. There was nothing I wanted to do more than go home, run a hot bath, and pour the biggest glass of wine. To say that this evening was a *lot* was an understatement. As I scurried back to my table, I bumped into the woman that was with DeAndre.

"Sorry!" I shrieked, walking even faster because clearly, God had jokes.

"Oh no, it's okay! I should've been watching where I was going" she said. "Do you know where the bathroom is? This baby is on my bladder," she chuckled and palmed her stomach. I paused and glanced over her, noting that she favored Keri Hilson with the light eyes, but was taller and more on the thick side. Pointing to the nearest one, I turned on my heel again but she kept following me.

"Wait, I follow you on Instagram. You're the girl that's gonna open a restaurant soon, right? I love your videos!" she gushed, seeming to forget that she had to pee two minutes ago. I forced a smile and nodded my head, glancing over at my table to see that my team was starting to break down.

"Wow, you're so pretty. And I tasted some of your samples earlier. Everything was good, and me and my baby really enjoyed the short rib sliders. When is your restaurant opening? My fiancè and I live in Bloomington, but plan to move up here before the baby is born," she yapped.

Fiancé?

I couldn't believe this was happening. I mentally started doing the math in my head and wondered how in the hell DeAndre had time to find a girl, get her pregnant, and then propose to her in less than a year.

And why the hell did I feel some type of way about it?!

I know me and Dre ending was for the best but aside from the restaurant and pouring into my own business, I didn't have anyone. I didn't have a roster and though dudes sometimes shot their shots in my DMs, I wasn't going out on dates either.

Was something wrong with me? Why didn't I have anyone?

Peeping my face, my mom immediately came up to me and asked what's wrong, but I told her that I would tell her later.

Dre's fiancèe came up to the table and I instructed my mom to make her a to-go box with whatever was left. She was so grateful, she started crying a bit... pregnancy hormones, I guess. I excused myself and went to the bathroom that was tucked away from the crowd on the second floor.

I needed a second.

Really, I needed *more* than a second but that was all the time I had to spare at the moment. Once we finished cleaning and packing up, my family and friends were coming back to the AirBnB with me and then leaving the next day. I just wanted to be alone but knew their presence would distract me from my thoughts. I checked my phone and saw that Doc could squeeze me in at 2PM tomorrow and I was grateful. I had so much tea for her, I couldn't believe it.

Coming out of the bathroom, I bumped right into LaShawn who was standing in front of the door. I threw my hands up in exasperation, because at this point, you have got to be kidding me!

"Yo, Rae... chill...." he started, blocking me from moving around him. I jerked my head back and glared at him. Angrily chuckling, I tried to get around him once more before letting him have it.

"Chill? Chill? G, be so for real! You and yo bitch came over to my table and like the raggedy hoe she has *ALWAYS* been, she decided to start some shit with me. I *am* chill. I *been* chill. Because when I coulda dragged her up and down this venue for what the fuck she said, I decided to be a fuckin' professional."

"Rae...look man...I'm sorry –"

I cut him off. "Yes, you are fuckin' sorry. It's been years and you are *still* a sorry excuse for a fuckin' man. While she's proud to have "won" you as if you're some type of prize, I realize that you are not a prize...you really ain't shit. Ain't never gone be shit neither... a sorry fuckin' excuse of a man is what you are and I regret meeting yo bitch ass. I regret ever thinking I was in love with you, and even though it sucks that the babies I carried never made it earthside, I'm glad as fuck that I don't have no attachments to yo bitch ass. You and that pie face bitch make me sick! The fact she thinks you're a prize is comedy to me G. The fact that you proudly married and procreated with a bitch like that is funny to me too, but hey. Everybody settles for something in life right? Except me. Ain't no way I woulda continued to settle for yo bitch ass, so I'm glad I got away while I could. LaShawn, don't say nothing else to me for the rest of your life. In fact, I hope you and that stupid bitch die tonight just so I can make sure you don't say shit to me and you better not contact me from the afterlife either. The next time you or that bitch says something to me, I swear to God the devil himself is gonna have to pull me off of her and that's on *my* kids!" I snapped, then pushed him out of my way.

He grabbed my wrist and I hauled off and slapped the shit out of him, the loud **WHAP** echoing in the empty hallway.

"LET FUCKIN' GO OF ME!" I shrieked, and felt my voice cracking.

Shaking him off, I continued my way downstairs, seeing that everything was packed up and ready to go. I rented a Uhaul for the bigger items and everything else was going in Dayvon's car so he could drop it off to a shelter. I hopped in my car without saying bye to anybody, and pulled out of the parking garage like a bat out of hell. Less than ten minutes later, I headed up to the apartment and ran to my room and locked the door. Sliding down the wall like I was Summer Walker, my head fell in my hands as I let out the most gut wrenching sob I had ever heard from myself. □

***

How could an amazing night go to shit so fast? Why did I have to see both of those bozos tonight? Why did —

KNOCK!
KNOCK!
KNOCK!

"Desiraè, open this damn door!" I heard my mama yell. I pulled myself from the floor and opened it, looking at her with a red face and puffy eyes, leaving her at the doorway. I walked to the bed and got in, burying myself under the covers. Mama came in, closed the door and then followed me to the bed, getting on the other side. We laid in silence for a while, while I tried to regulate my breathing.

"So... tonight was a lot. But, before we get into the bad, can we celebrate the good? You did your first big event, premiering yourself to the city. That's something to be proud of baby. You had such good reviews, and I checked your Instagram. You're at 30K followers now. And all your business cards are gone, I know someone is gonna call you. I peeped that some people were trying to book you on the spot," she started.

I just blinked at her, slightly spacing out. She was right, I did have things to be proud of but I couldn't even focus on all that because of the drama that followed shortly after. Why was it that drama always followed me? I was so sick of it.

"Want to tell me what else happened?"

I sighed, and began filling her in on the night. From the argument with LaTrice to meeting DeAndre's fiancèe, to cursing out LaShawn and slapping the shit out of him, I told it all.

"Shit."

"Yeah....."

"I don't know what to say to make you feel better baby... I really don't know. How would you like to be supported?"

I shrugged. "Honestly, I wanted to be alone tonight but I think I need the distraction with everyone here. I'm gonna take a bath and when I get out, we can all eat some leftovers and polish off those bottles of wine."

Mama nodded then kissed me on my forehead before I got out of bed and headed to the bathroom to run my water. Soaking in the tub, I replayed the evening's events in my head and dove deeper into the water until it was up to my ears. Then I sunk lower, letting the water fill my nose and mouth, and then lower until...

Wait a minute. I can't go out like this.

Bucking my eyes open, I quickly sat up and drained the tub, deciding on showering instead. I read somewhere once that the brain was the strongest yet weakest organ in the body. I hadn't had any suicidal ideations or attempts since my first and last time many years ago, so I had no idea why I would go underneath that water like that. Intrusive thoughts were a muthafucka.

Changing into a black satin pajama set, I went to the kitchen feeling sad but I still put on a brave face to make everyone else besides my mom think I was okay. Pouring up a tall glass of wine, I gulped it down and then refilled it until we finished the food, cleaned the kitchen, watched a movie, and then fell asleep. Being wine drunk helped me fall asleep instantly, and luckily, nothing crazy happened in my dreams.

***

"I wanted to take a chafing dish and bash her over the head with it, Doc!" I yelled at my iPad screen, pacing back and forth in the living room.

"Desiraè....." she sighed.

I shrugged. "You asked me how I felt and I'm telling you, if I didn't care about my reputation, I would've mopped the floor with her bean head ass."

"I understand. But I asked you how you *felt*... not what you wanted to *do*. Get your emotions wheel out, let's talk through this," Doc replied, and I groaned.

I had a love-hate relationship with the emotions wheel that Doc made me use over the years. The default for humans is that we are often angry but we refuse to acknowledge the underlying feelings associated with that anger.

"Feelings are nuanced," is something that Doc often said. I hated pulling it out because some days, I truly didn't feel like doing the work. But my therapy sessions didn't work like that. There was never a session that passed, where I wasn't gonna do the work.

Ugh.

Pulling the wheel up on my phone, I waited on Doc's instructions for what to do next.

"Based on what you said you wanted to do, what emotion on the wheel matches that action?" she asked.

"Anger... It made me feel angry."

"Okay. Can we explore that further? Look at the wheel. What is that anger powered by? Do you think it is powered by something else?"

I stared at it for a beat and sighed. "Provoked. I felt provoked."

"By what she said to you? About causing you harm back in high school and you suffering a loss?"

I felt a lump in my throat and nodded.

"Okay. Look at the wheel again. Is there any other emotion here that resonates with anger and feeling provoked?"

"Betrayed," I whispered. Doc remained silent, allowing me to elaborate as she peered at me over her glasses.

"By whom?"

In a shaky breath, I whispered LaShawn's name. Feeling my face get hot, buried emotions rose to the top and spilled out of my eyes like a rainfall. I *hated* crying over this nigga and I hated myself even more for allowing all that I did when I was younger. Like, if I had a time machine, I would yank myself by my kinky twists and keep me locked in the house until I was eighteen. I would have walked past that nigga when I went by the barbershop or pretended I was deaf or something. Any option was better than dealing with him all those years.

But I couldn't. Though I physically got away from him, the remnants of our toxicity engulfed me like a cloak. And seeing him and his bean head ass wife did nothing but trigger me.

Ugh! Why couldn't I be like other people, who brag about how detached they are and how they're able to move forward easily? Is something wrong with me, or is everybody lying?

"How did LaShawn betray you?"

I closed my eyes to try and stop the rainfall of tears. Reflecting on the loneliness, the confusion, and abandonment from back then made me feel lower than low. Though I would never *now,* you couldn't convince me back then that his behavior should've been expected. Though he was older, we were both so young, and because he was a man, it should have been expected that he wouldn't stay faithful to me, right?

"Desiraè... you're rationalizing again. Let's refocus. How did LaShawn betray you?"

I sighed. "He betrayed me by not being there. He wasn't around for the fight. He wasn't at the hospital. And, if I recall correctly, he ghosted me for weeks at a time. When I finally did see him again, I saw him and that bitch riding in his truck, without a care in the world... like I didn't matter."

Doc nodded. "Now that we've identified the feeling, what do you think you need to process and move through it?"

I shrugged. "I don't know. I just know I want him and that bitch to stay away from me. I can't promise that I'm not going to whoop her ass the next time I see her."

Doc smirked, used to my antics by now but I was dead serious. Her and LaShawn deserved something very bad to happen to them and I couldn't promise that the next time I saw that clown-faced bitch, she wouldn't have an imprint of my foot on her forehead.

Bugging out on me over a nigga that ain't worth the edge control I put on my baby hairs was beyond me. Maturity made me realize that LaShawn was definitely the problem back in the day.

Going back and forth between me and her was a sure fire way to cause conflict. But LaTrice just *HAD* to take it a step further and choose to disrespect me too. She just couldn't play her role or accept that the nigga had moved on. Nooooo, she tried to bully me from day one and realized that she couldn't. She allowed her jealousy to control her actions.

On the surface, most people might think she won. She had the jewels, the kids, his last name, and whatever other perks came with being his wife. But at what cost?

Years of lies? I could bet all my money in the bank that he hadn't stopped cheating. Not to mention, I'm sure they couldn't keep their hands off each other, and not in a good way. Me and Shawn used to fight so much. The shit was toxic. Ain't no way she thought I couldn't stay away from him.

Besides, I wasn't the one who looked him up on Instagram. I wasn't the one finding any little way to talk to him. I wasn't the one sending him random cash apps just to get a conversation.

Why is it that the female gets all the smoke behind these raggedy ass niggas?

As women, we have a tendency to give all the anger to the woman and after all the crying, cursing the nigga out, and maybe destroying his property, we stay right with his ass. How is that anything to be proud of? Knowing that I used to be like the girls I just described, I was disgusted by my past actions.

Thank God for growth though.

"It's okay not to know. We can shift gears a bit though. You said you saw DeAndre in the crowd with a girl that you later met as his pregnant fiance. How did *that* make you feel?"

I paused for a moment. I had forgotten all about him and ole girl because I spent the majority of my session ranting and raving about Dumb and Dumber.

"Confused. Like, I don't want him back or anything like that but it was just...weird to see how his life moved on without me. And, the girl seems nice or whatever. Like, she came up and told me how she was a fan of my work and all. So, I don't feel the same way about her like I do LaTrice. But, I wanted nothing more than to disappear."

"I imagine it can be quite jarring to see someone you shared so much time with as a complete stranger now. Especially when it seems as if they have moved on quicker than you. How are you coping with the breakup?"

"Honestly.... I've just been working. I haven't really thought about him in months. He's blocked on everything and I haven't gone lurking. I don't allow myself to receive updates on him from my family and friends...not that they would anyway, but yeah. But seeing him in that crowd made me realize that life is short. He really wanted to have a baby and get married. I guess he succeeded," I sighed somberly.

While DeAndre was a good partner for me in the beginning, as we grew, our incompatibilities did too. I realized I was operating in a scarcity mindset when I was with him and that ain't no way to live either. I wasn't a perfect partner by any means but my imperfections aren't the reason to stay in a relationship where my desires aren't even being heard or respected.

But you live and you learn.

"It's completely normal to grieve a relationship, Desiraè."

"Is it really grief though?" I opened my mouth to object but Doc held her hand up to stop me.

"You've been with the same person for over five years of your life. It is perfectly normal to have feelings of hurt, confusion, regret, anger, and everything in between when making the right decision. I'd be concerned if you felt no type of way about him moving on to someone else so quickly.

You're human. It's okay. I hope you are making time to take care of yourself instead of drowning yourself in work. If you don't confront your feelings, they'll eventually confront you."

I remained silent, processing what she said. We wrapped our session shortly after and I began to get ready for the day.

Therapy sessions usually left me depleted but per usual… I had things to do. Today's adventure consisted of me going back to Englewood to meet with the property owner for the space I saw in September and then my lawyer to go over the leasing agreement. My time at Le Reaux was coming to an end in just three short weeks. The prior head cook was finishing up maternity leave and while I had grown to love Le Reaux, I was ready to get the ball rolling on my restaurant.

Nervous, but ready.

***

Pulling up to the street, the neighborhood looked much different in the daytime. Englewood was once a bustling hub of Black owned businesses according to history books. Disenfranchisement, crime, poverty, and food desserts began to plague the community but research let me know that there were organizations and individuals trying to make my old hood safer and vibrant again with resources and businesses. I wanted to add to that. Getting out of the car, the weather was what we called fake Spring in Chicago. The weather was warm enough to only have to wear a light jacket or hoodie, but we all knew that we would be back in the forties and snow by the end of the week.

Walking into the building, I greeted the property owner and two hours later, we had an agreement. The keys would be in my hand on April 17th. From there, I would start the small cosmetic upgrades, make sure all my licenses were up to par, and then start interviewing people. I wanted to have a soft launch for Memorial Day weekend and then be open for business fully by August 8th. August 8th was Gramz's birthday and that is how I wanted to remember her. I was able to negotiate the rent for a reasonable price at $2,500 a month. I still had to price the cosmetic upgrades, but Jamaal said he'd do them for free as long as I purchased the materials. I knew I wanted new bathrooms and new floors so far. Then I needed to pay an inspector to come through and make sure all the pipes, electrical wiring, and other related things were up to par. My plan was to lease for two years and then eventually either expand locations or buy land to build a larger restaurant on.

I felt a mix of overwhelm and joy. Pulling out my phone, I started recording myself on Instagram.

"Hey Youtube, welcome back to my channel!" I joked. "Nah, on some serious shit, I'm feeling happy but slightly overwhelmed. I got big things coming and I can't wait to show y'all the journey," I panned the camera to the empty space. After watching it a few times, I posted it to my story, made a reel out of it, and then sent it to my family and friends group chat.

"What big shit you got coming?" I heard that same gravelly voice from a few months ago asking out of nowhere. I jumped, then shoved my phone in my bag before answering. Quickly glancing at his appearance, he was dressed in all black again, this time in a black jogging suit that had <u>The Chi Is Elite</u> on the front of the hoodie. He still looked mean as hell, but his eyes held something that I couldn't read right away. His throat was covered in an intricate crown tattoo and though I couldn't see the rest of his body, I just knew that was tatted as well.

"Damn. You scared me," I joked. If I had to guess his height, he stood at about six foot two, and his shoulders were kinda broad. He really reminded me of that British rapper Skepta. Low cut caesar haircut with some deep waves, and a well manicured low cut beard and mustache/goatee situation complimented his smoldering chocolate brown eyes.

"I'm... I'm opening up a restaurant soon," I gushed, for some reason being excited to share with this complete stranger. His eyes slightly lit up, and then returned to his normal unreadable expression.

"That's wassup. What kind?"

"Elevated soul food."

"What the fuck is that?"

I smirked, because most people had that response when they asked me what type of food I'd be selling.

"Like...normal soul food... just elevated. Cleaner ingredients but not lacking on the flavor at all. New ways to present classic dishes."

His brows furrowed. Then he very curtly blurted out, "Man, what the fuck make you think people around here gone wanna buy that shit? Can yo ass even cook?"

I jerked my head back like he slapped me and in a sense he did, because his delivery was harsh.

I sucked my teeth and glared at him. "First of all nigga, yes I can cook. My Gramz taught me everything she knew when I was coming up and I worked in a restaurant for five years, graduated from culinary school last year, and was the temporary head chef at Le Reaux downtown. Do yo research on me before you get to assuming!"

He smirked. "Ion gotta do my research on you. I know exactly who you are. But not on no hating shit, let me tell you this: most mufuckas around here ain't gone give a damn that you worked at a fancy ass restaurant downtown. Most niggas around here ain't never even been downtown. These the same mufuckas who still go to BaBa's for a pizza puff with extra mild sauce and lemon pepper on it with a Mistic on the side. I know you social media famous and shit but if you really want longevity, you gotta get off the internet and get in the field. Don't come around here, acting like you doing the hood a favor cuz you not. I know you used to live over here but you ain't *been* here. Get to know your new community cuz if you don't, ain't a soul gone take you serious."

To say I was taken aback was an understatement. "How is it that you know a little bit about me and I don't even know your name?" I blurted. This nigga had me fucked up.

He smirked again. "Reign. Reign King. I own this barbershop and my twin sister owns the beauty salon right there. Her name is LaReina but she just goes by Reina."

I glanced at the shop behind me and made a mental note to check it out soon.

Reign.

Though I considered him a bit of an asshole, his name definitely fit his aura.

"Well... It was definitely not a pleasure to meet you," I smirked. "But thanks for the advice, I guess. I'll keep some things in mind but the rest you can keep to yourself." And with that, I walked off on him and headed to my car.

Driving off, I reflected on what he said. He was right about one thing, okay maybe a few things but one thing I could agree on was getting off the internet and in the field. And I had just the perfect idea to do that.

Chapter Eight

Desiraè

Reign had me fucked up.

However, what he said played on a loop in my mind as I packed dinners in my car and drove to my destination. Since it was important to get off social media and get in the field, I was going to sell dinners to business owners and their customers, starting with Reign's barbershop.

Did I know him well enough to do some shit like that?

No.

Was I scared that he would treat my goofy ass?

A little bit.

But was I confident that my food was good and that people would love it?

Yes. Hell yes. I got *busy* in the kitchen, and couldn't a soul tell me different.

Popping the trunk, I pulled out my black wagon and packed the fifty dinners I had neatly inside. I cut through the parking lot and looked up at the sign. My stomach began turning but I held my head high, squared my shoulders, and pushed open the door. The color scheme of the shop was a unique shade of periwinkle blue and gold. They had a waiting area with gold leather couches with a gigantic flat screen tv mounted on the walls that played sports highlights on mute. In the middle, was a receptionist desk that had *Krowned* on the front written in gold script. On both the left and right sides of the shop, were gold barber chairs filled with customers. I counted about ten chairs on each side. In the back, they had pool tables. Shaking off my nerves, I walked right up to the receptionist desk where a pretty brown skinned girl with bright golden brown hair was scrolling on her phone. Upon seeing me, she eyed me curiously before I spoke.

"Hey. My name is Desiraè. I'm about to open up a restaurant soon and was wondering if it was cool for me to sell some plates to y'all?"

Shorty looked me over and I suddenly felt a little self conscious. I had on my black and red *Mz. Earline's* staff tee, some flared black jeans and some black and white panda Dunks. I was in between hairstyles, so I put my hair in a top knot with two bangs in the front that were slightly curled.

"Shit... what you got? How much?" Shorty asked. Pulling out a hot styrofoam container from the wagon, I popped it open, showing her the contents.

The menu today was lemon herb garlic salmon, garlic mashed potatoes, and broccolini. For dessert, I made some banana pudding cheesecake. I even made the special punch that I had at the ball that I kept in small mason jars with the restaurant's logo on it. If you didn't eat fish, you could substitute it for lemon herb garlic chicken thighs with the same sides.

Shorty inhaled the scent of the food and looked over it. "You take Cash App?" she asked, ready to eat. I confirmed that I did and she paid me instantly, grabbing her dinner and devoured it immediately. She took one bite and closed her eyes, moaning and rocking side to side.

"Damn! This shit good as fuck! Aye y'all! Make sure yall ass get a plate from the chef lady, yall baby mamas is *not* cooking like this!" she turned around and yelled.

All the barbers looked up and I made my way over to them. I introduced myself to each one, and they all had similar reactions to shorty at the front. I sold out since I only brought about twenty five in with me, but I had more in the car. Going back to the receptionist desk, I peered around looking for Reign.

"If you're looking for Reign, he's in the back in his office" shorty, who I learned went by Goldyn said, reading my mind. "But aye, promise me you'll come back. I wanna buy another one for later. That shit was fye!" she exclaimed. I promised her I would and she promised she would tag me on Instagram. Making my way to the back, I carried one last dinner and knocked on his door.

He yelled for me to come in and I took in his office. It wasn't the largest, but it was big enough for a couch, a mini fridge, a desk and two chairs. On his walls were all types of black and white photos of Black historical figures like Muhammad Ali, Malcolm X, and Ida B. Wells. He was sitting behind his desk, typing away on his iMac, with a pair of reading glasses on. He was dressed in all black again, this time in a hoodie that had Fake Decent on it.

"Oh wassup?" he peered up at me. "Fuck you doing here?"

I rolled my eyes. "You are rude! Anyway, I came to bring you a plate... I'm selling dinners and your shop sold me out but I saved one for you."

He smirked and motioned for me to sit it on his desk. Opening it up, he nodded at what he saw and then closed it, setting it aside.

"Good looking. Did you need something else?" he asked.

My face grew hot. "You not gone say thank you?" This nigga was rude for real!

"Did I ask you to come bring this me?"

"N-no... but, the courteous thing to do would be to say thank you. Yo bean head ass probably ain't ate all day or nothing." I shot back, folding my arms.

"I saw you when you walked in looking all shy. My staff already hit the groupchat saying yo shit was fye. Good looking Desiraè, I appreciate it." He offered a small smile and put his eyes back on his computer. I stared at him for five seconds, feeling slightly dismissed.

I stood up, tucking my tail between my legs and headed towards the door.

"I see you took my advice. Make sure you hit my sister shop and the bookstore across the street. Joyy and Cherrice are good people."

"Yeah... that's the plan" I replied.

"And Desiraè? You can come sell plates whenever you feel like it," he said.

I offered him a small smile and then exited. On my way out, I passed a few of the barbers my business card and told them to follow me. They asked me when was the next time I was coming back and I promised them soon.

***

After bringing Goldyn another container of food for her to buy, I made my way two doors down to the beauty shop, Reigning Beauty. The vibe in here was immaculate. The color scheme was a periwinkle blue with a splash of cranberry, and one wall was completely made up of Essence, Jet, Ebony, and Hype Hair magazine covers.

All the stylists were dressed in all black and had periwinkle and black smocks on with the shop's logo on the back. Similar to the barbershop, a receptionist desk was the first thing I saw, and there were about ten chairs on each side as well. At the receptionist desk was a tall, caramel macchiato colored woman with thick, perfect eyebrows, a long, sleek, high ponytail, and the same smoldering brown eyes as Reign. She was dressed in all black sans the smock, and her shape was modelesque with a small waist and heart-shaped booty.

"Welcome to Reigning Beauty. Who are you here to be serviced by?" she asked, scrolling on the iPad to check me in.

I smiled and shook my head. "Actually… I'm not here to get serviced yet," and my hand brushed over my top knot. "My name is Desiraè, and I'll be opening up a restaurant soon. I was selling plates and wanted to know if your shop was interested in buying some."

"My brother didn't tell me you were pretty," she smiled.

My brows crinkled. She looked like Reign a little bit, but I asked anyway to be sure.

"Your brother?"

"Reign King. He owns the barbershop you just walked out of. I'm LaReina, but most people just call me Reina. I own this shop" she smiled.

"Wow! Your shop is pretty. But yes, I'm selling food. You're the receptionist at your own shop?" I questioned.

Reina tittered. "Usually, I'm behind the chair but my receptionist called in sick and the boss has gotta do, what the boss gotta do," she shrugged.

I liked her energy already. I tended to gravitate towards people who were bosses in their own right but also not afraid to get their hands dirty. I handed her a container and told her it was on the house, but she insisted on paying me for it, and then she allowed me to go around and peddle to the hairstylists and their clients. The ladies sold me out quicker than the men at the shop did and sung my praises, inquiring when and where the restaurant was opening and if I did catering gigs.

As nervous as I was about doing this, my heart was full. Going back towards the receptionist desk, Reina was checking out another customer and smiled at me. "So I know you'll be back and in my chair soon, yes?"

We exchanged Instagrams and I had to say, I was impressed with her work. She specialized in natural hair, quick weaves, ponytails, and wigs. She also had a braider on site and a girl who specialized in faux locs. Her prices were reasonable and unlike some of these hairstylists out here, she didn't require her clients to come washed and blow dried already.

There was even a small beauty supply store that supplied all the hair, products, and tools one would need. Reigning Beauty was truly a one-stop shop and I was definitely booking an appointment soon. Walking to my car, I noticed that the same blacked out Range Rover truck from the other day was waiting behind me to take my spot. I quickly put my head down but it was too late.

"Desiraè! Aye! Let me chop it up with you," LaShawn called out.

I let out a long sigh.

I wasn't sure if God was testing me, but I'm pretty sure I asked him to take me off the strongest soldier list.

Instead of responding to him, I got in my car as calmly as possible, only for him to be knocking on my window. Biting on my bottom lip until I drew blood, I rolled it down slowly, cracking it half an inch.

"What. The. Fuck. Do. You. Want. Nigga?" I gritted out slowly.

"I just wanted to apologize again man. We left off on bad terms and regardless of what you think Desiraè, I don't like for us to be at odds. You know how Trice is man... mad cuz she always wanted to be you and mad because she can *never* be you. Her behavior was uncalled for and I'm just... I'm just sorry man. I ain't mean to cause all this shit in yo life" he said, nervously running his hand over his waves.

His whiskey colored eyes looked sincere, but the ice around my heart wouldn't melt at his apology. It was too much anger, too much resentment, too much hurt. This accountability and apology would have meant something when we were younger and still together, but now that we were older, I didn't feel a use for the words that were falling on deaf ears. I just wanted to be left alone. I stared at him, chest heaving up and down while contemplating my words. He stared back, searching my eyes for something, *anything* that would indicate that I accepted his apology.

"Okay." I finally said.

His head shot back, and his brows furrowed. I'd never been this calm before and I could tell my response shocked him.

"What you mean okay? That's all you got to say after all that?"

I sighed, then looked at him. "LaShawn, I really have got better shit to do. I don't have time –"

"Nah, G. You gotta give me something more than that. I just poured my fuckin' heart out to you and all yo ass gotta say is some fucking "okay" like

I'm a lame or something? I'm lame to you now Rae?!" his voice was getting louder and louder as he cut me off and I just stared at him.

"SAY SOMETHING!" he yelled, yanking on my car door handle.

"I know you can stop yelling at me! The fuck!" I snapped, exasperation bubbling up and threatening for the most vile shit to spill out of my mouth. One would think that after me cursing him out last week, he would just leave me alone but this was LaShawn Tramell Davis I was talking about. This nigga lived for this toxic shit and I was tired.

Putting my car in drive, I pressed hard on the gas and sped forward, leaving his goofy ass standing there. Getting caught at the red light, I looked in my rearview mirror to see an all black Navigator zoom down the block then reverse, hitting LaShawn at full force, smashing his body in between the back of the Navigator and the front of his Range Rover. The truck bumped him a few times like this was smash truck or something. Then, the Navigator reversed down the block, hitting a left. I quickly turned my car around and put my hazards on, hopping out and running towards him while everyone else inside the shops came rushing out.

"AYE! EVERYBODY BACK THE FUCK UP! SOMEBODY CALL 9-1-1!" I heard Reign yell. I pushed my way through the crowd and the sight of Shawn's body almost made my knees buckle. His white Amiri shirt was soaked with blood and his eyes were squeezed shut, soft groans coming out his mouth as he cried out in agony.

Locking eyes with Reign, I pulled my phone out and dialed 9-1-1. Seven minutes later, paramedics and police pulled up and they loaded him onto the stretcher, with Reign and Reina hopping in the back. My feet felt like they were made of cinderblocks yet somehow I made it back to my car, trailing the ambulance to the hospital.

Chapter Nine

Desiraè

I hated hospitals. The smells. The uncomfortable ass chairs. The waiting around. The inevitable death behind the doors. It all creeped me out, yet, here I was.

Well, it felt like I was watching myself be here because my body automatically went numb. LaShawn was no saint, but why would someone purposely run him over like that? I didn't know if he was still selling drugs, but I didn't put it past him. Hustling was all he knew, passed down from generation to generation. It wasn't the most morally sound thing to do, but he did it because as the oldest son, his family depended on him. Business must've been lucrative because even when we were younger, he paid his mama's bills, his own, and even gave me money. Material wise, I didn't want for anything when I was with Shawn. He was known to lace me in diamonds, buy me cars, designer jeans, and whatever else I wanted.

None of it mattered though. People often made jokes about whether or not you wanted to cry in a Honda or a Rolls Royce, but... I didn't want to cry at all. No amount of money or gifts could make up for not being treated right. I didn't care what these bitches on the internet said. Until they had the experience of having everything they wanted yet getting disrespected at every turn, I wasn't paying any of these girls any mind. Hoes would sell their souls for some money and a bag.

Broke bitches.

Walking down the hallway, I spotted Reina and Reign in the waiting room. I felt awkward as fuck, but I pressed forward anyway. Tears were streaming down Reina's face and Reign had this stoic, far-away look in his eyes. Every so often, he would reject calls and mutter something inaudible to himself, looking pissed. I stood there silently, not really knowing what to do but chose to sit down next to Reina and rub her shoulders.

She cried harder, laying her head on my shoulder, wetting my sleeve with her tears. Moments passed, and I see Reign looking more and more tense as the minutes go by. Leaning forward with his elbows resting on his knees, he dropped his head in his hands and sighed. Reina stopped leaning on me and laid on her brother's back, rubbing circles in it. Murmuring so lowly, that only he could hear it. The waiting room was amuck with activity, and I felt my stomach churning more and more. I was starting to feel bad about what I said to him at the ball. I told him that I wished him and his bitch would drop dead, and now here he was laid up in the hospital.

I laid my head against the wall and closed my eyes, hoping this was just another bad dream. My mom was blowing my phone up, probably after peeping my location but I sent her a text letting her know I was fine and that I would call her later.

***

"WHERE THE FUCK IS MY HUSBAND?! WHAT HAPPENED TO HIM?!" LaTrice's voice cut through the chaos of the waiting room like nails on a chalkboard. My eyes popped open, and Reign and Reina just stared at her until she peeped us sitting together. Despite the distraught look on her face, she was well put together. She had on some pink wide legged pants, a cropped white silk blouse, a denim trench coat and some white pointed toe heels. Her signature jet black lace front adorned her head and she had minimal jewelry on. Rushing over to us, she stopped short when she saw me and narrowed her eyes.

"Twins, what the fuck is this bitch doing here?" she spat out.

"Trice, chill on her," Reign started. Reina turned to me. "You know her?" she asked, clearly confused by the interaction.

"Watch your fuckin' mouth when you speak on me, LaTrice" I replied. I wasn't in the mood to deal with her theatrics today, and I would hate for her to be the next one put into the hospital.

"Nah, bitch, I told you to stay away from my fuckin' husband and here you are in this fuckin' hospital. Bitch, he don't want you and I done told you that plenty of times. You shouldn't be here, this is for *family* only, you barren pussy ass bitch!"

My flip had switched and before she or I knew it, I leaned up, closed the distance between us and socked her in her face a couple times.

WAP!

WAP!

WAP!

"And I told you to watch your fuckin' mouth when you speak on me bitch! You so worried about me and mad that you can't be me, that you need to be wondering if it's your husband that wants me!" and I popped her ass again. Reign stood up and the hospital security rushed over to separate us, while Trice tried to climb over the security's shoulder to get to me while Reign had a firm hold on me, calming me down.

"Aight, that's enough! I know she disrespected you, but this really ain't the time and place for all that, D."

"I'm sorry y'all, I'm just sick of that bean head ass bitch! Maybe I should leave...." I turned to grab my purse.

Reina put her hand out to stop me. "Girl, you ain't gotta go nowhere. She's pulling that wife card like my cousin ain't been trying to get her to sign those divorce papers for a year now," Reina chimed in, rolling her eyes.

Wait, so that's how they all knew each other. They're cousins.

Though me and Shawn dated for a while, I didn't meet all his family, only his immediate ones. We never went to any family reunions or summertime cookouts because Shawn was busy hugging the block and in and out of jail more than anything.

"Reina, shut the fuck up telling they business! I know you don't like LaTrice, but that's still Cuzzo's wife and the mother of his children." Reign sternly chimed in and Reina hushed, but gave Trice the stank eye, who was still being rowdy with the security guard until he threatened to put her out.

"So, how do you know our cousin?" Reina asked again.

"We dated a while ago... he was my first love. First everything, really." I muttered.

"And y'all still keep in contact?"

I shook my head. "No. I haven't seen him since I was about 18/19. He found me on Instagram and he would comment and message me but I wasn't giving him no play."

"But you pulled up on the block a few months ago" Reign pointed out. I looked around Reina and straight at him.

"I used to live on that block with my Gramz. I didn't know he would be there," I felt the need to defend. Reign looked at me like he didn't believe me, and Reina just stared off into space. Eventually, things fell silent between us and Reign got up to get some snacks out the vending machine.

"He likes you, you know that right?" Reina blurted out of nowhere.

"Who? Me?" I felt my face contorting at the thought. Reign was fine as hell for sure, but he was also my ex-boyfriend's cousin.

"Reign. Usually, he's hella rude to females and honestly would have sent you on your way the moment you walked in here, but he didn't. I know my twin… he likes you. The moment you walked into his shop today, hell even before, he was putting everybody on notice about you. Told us you were opening a restaurant soon and that we should support you. Reign doesn't do that for everybody, only women he likes," and she gave me a weak smile.

I couldn't even process that. So I responded with nothing, until I had questions of my own.

"Y'all blood cousins?"

Reina nodded. "Yeah. Through our daddies. We grew up in the hunneds though, and then our OG sent us off to the suburbs because Reign was starting to get into trouble. When we got older, we didn't see much of each other but Reign and Shawn used to run the streets together before he got out the game and opened up his barbershop. Him and Shawn are co-owners."

Well, at least he was doing something with his drug money, I thought to myself.

"What kind of trouble?" I asked.

Reina tittered. "Girl, Reign used to be bad as *fuck*. Stealing cars, robbing stores, fighting at school, you name it – he was doing it. Our dad passed away when we were young and it's like he got worse after it. So, my OG felt it was best that we go to school in this bougie ass suburb and go live with our grandma for a while. Reign was giving those white boys a run for they money! And wherever my twin went, I was going. Shawn still dabbled in the streets but my twin completely turned his life around. After he opened up his shop, he helped me open mine and we've been in business for the past four years." Reina spoke fondly of her brother, wrapping up the pieces of how everyone was connected to each other.

Reign came back, an unreadable expression on his face and sat down next to his sister. She leaned back on his shoulder while he scrolled through his phone, declining more calls. LaTrice sat across from us on the other side of the room, staring daggers at me while she nursed her lip with an ice pack.

***

It felt like hours passed before a dark-skinned Indian man with a white coat came out with an unreadable expression on his face.

"Family of LaShawn Davis?" he called out, and Reign, Reina, and La-Trice rushed over to him while I stayed planted in those uncomfortable chairs. I couldn't hear what the doctor was saying but from reading their body language, it wasn't good. LaTrice wailed out, Reina shrieked and ran out the waiting room, while Reign's face contorted like he was in pain.

"NOT MY HUSBANDDDDDDD!" LaTrice screeched, falling all into Reign like a weeping willow. My chest and throat got tight while I watched Reign console her. The doctor looked apologetic and I heard him say, "I'm sorry ma'am. We did all that we could do," and dropped his head while slowly backing away. LaTrice continued to act a fool and security came over again. Whatever Reign said to him had him tucking his tail and I was feeling the contents of my stomach come up. My body went numb and I felt myself run out of the waiting room to my car. Unlocking the doors, I slid in the driver seat and the levees broke. I realized that those dreams I was having last year were no longer a figment of my subconscious.

I was now living in a reality where the first boy I ever loved was no longer here and I had no idea how I should feel about it.

Chapter Ten

Desiraè

Collasped lungs.

Aortic dissection.

Seizure during surgery.

Dead.

LaShawn was dead and I felt like it was all my fault. After all, I was the one who wished death on him.

I didn't know how to feel, but I knew I felt like I was trapped in a never ending bad dream. To know that someone would so callously take his life like that...I wondered if that would've happened if I hadn't walked out of the hair shop when I did. If I just would've heard him out, or even offered to take us on a drive away from that block. Would Shawn's life have been spared then? Tears wanted to come out, but they were buried under thick, suffocating silence. I felt distant and detached from my body, like I was watching myself go through the motions.

"Rae baby... you gotta get up and eat something," my mom's voice cut through the loud silence. When I left the hospital, I found her outside my apartment door, pacing the floor. In a rush, I told her what happened and then next thing I knew, everything went black. I had fainted. I woke up in my bed and thought I dreamed everything but a quick scroll on Instagram showed that being awake was more painful than dreaming. All up and down my Instagram timeline, were R.I.P. posts, dedicated to LaShawn. It was even worse on Facebook. Every other post was a picture of him and if that wasn't annoying enough, all the posts in between those were news articles articulating the incident.

I deleted the apps off my phone.

That was three days ago, and I hadn't done anything with myself besides roll from one side of the bed to the other.

"I'm not hungry Ma," I muttered.

"But you haven't ate in three days, baby. I understand how you're feeling, but come on. It's just a jerk salmon wrap from <u>Ain't She Sweet.</u> Take three bites for me."

"Ma, you don't understand how I feel. I said I'm not hungry!" I snapped.

I felt her sit on my bed towards the edge and pull my covers back. The room was otherwise dark, because I hadn't opened the black out curtains or turned on any lights.

"So you forget that your father was my first love, my first everything too? Imma let you slide with the tone because I know you're grieving, but please believe that you aren't the first or the last person to navigate the death of someone they once loved." And with that, she walked out of my room.

Immediately, I began to feel bad for what I said. Our situations were definitely parallel to each other in a lot of ways. Begrudgingly, I dragged myself out of bed and went to use the bathroom, almost scaring myself when I walked past the mirror. My hair was disheveled, breath smelled like an old pot of greens, and my coochie was begging for some soap and water to hit it.

I don't think I've ever let myself get this bad before. After showering and changing into an oversized shirt and some cotton shorts, I shuffled to the kitchen to find my mom and Dr. Love sitting at the counter.

"Doc, what are you doing here?" I asked, announcing myself.

"I called her over here because you're grieving, Desiraè. I don't want you to sink into a depression" my mom replied.

I shrugged, walking to the microwave to warm up my food. "I'm not depressed," I replied flatly.

"Maybe not now, but it is possible you can slip into it because of...of what happened."

I sighed.

"Ma, I am not you. We wasn't even together. I'm not the one who had children by him or got married to him. We dated a long ass time ago. Just because daddy's death sent you into a spiral, doesn't mean that I'm gonna do the same. Please, just leave me alone!"

"Desiraè..." Doc started, while my mom and I locked eyes with each other. Her eyes mirrored mine, except hers had a bit of hurt behind them.

"Nah, Doc...let her ass talk. I'm up here trying to help her and she wants to act.. I don't even know how to describe how she's acting right now, but

I know I don't have to put up with it," and she stood up to grab her keys and her purse.

"Nicole, sit down," Doc finally spoke up.

"But Doc–"

"AHT. I said *sit down*," she bellowed.

Nicole sat down, pouting and avoiding eye contact with me.

"Desiraè, you find a seat too." I sat across from Doc.

"Now, it's been a while since I've had a session with you two. Don't worry, we won't be having one today. Because neither of you are in a place to receive what I have to say. And that's fine... therapy is available when you're ready, nobody is forcing you. But what I notice is a mother that is powered by her own trauma trying to help a daughter who won't even acknowledge her own grief and trauma. Nicole, just give her time. Desiraè, in time you will learn that you can't push everyone away. Do with that what you will," Doc said, pushing away from the counter and grabbing her large painter's tape colored Telfar bag.

"Call me when you're ready to do some work. And Desiraè, even if you won't acknowledge it, I am sorry for your loss. Take care now." And with that, Doc sauntered down the hallway disappearing. Nicole and I sat there, too stunned to speak. After a while, my mama grabbed up her purse and keys. I wanted to stop her, to ask her to stay because I was scared to be alone, wanted to say sorry for blowing up on her, but it was like a weight was in my throat, so the words wouldn't come out. So I watched her leave, the deafening silence getting louder.

***

I erased the message. Whenever someone died and people asked you how you were feeling, they didn't really want the truth. They didn't want to hear about the despair, or the depression, or the never ending darkness of grief. People didn't want to hear about how you couldn't stop crying one minute, feeling angry the next, or how becoming hyper aware of the fact that we all gotta die someday was tweaking you out. Instead, people wanted to hear about how you were this pillar of strength and how you were making it. Or how you were "fine."

Except, everything wasn't fine.

So, I erased that message. Because Reina and Reign had just lost their cousin. Of course they wouldn't be on the up and up. I felt stupid for even asking. I didn't have either of their numbers, but me and Reina exchanged Instagrams. So, after a full week of wallowing in my own pity, I decided to reach out. I downloaded the app back on my phone and searched for her name. Surprisingly, she hadn't posted. But Reina didn't take me as a girl who would post intimate details of her life on her hair page. And Reign didn't have an Instagram account at all, aside from the Krowned page.

Clicking on the message icon again, I thought a bit before I said what I wanted to say.

I set my phone down and handled my hygiene, then decided to order groceries for what I wanted to make. My appetite wasn't 100% back, but I figured that cooking for others would get me back in the swing of things. I decided to order three cornish hens, string beans, and make some baked mac and cheese for them.

Simple.

I checked my phone and saw that Reina responded.

Reigning.Beauty.Reina:

> Hey girl… thank you for checking on us. Things have been crazy, but that is so sweet of you… what you cooking? ☒ lol

Me:

> Do y'all like cornish hens? And string beans? And baked mac and cheese?

Reigning.Beauty.Reina:

> OMG ☒ hell yeah! My last client is at three. Idk where my brother is but you can stop by the shop and leave his plate with me… I promise I won't eat it lol

I told her I would see her soon and then got up to start seasoning the birds. My cornish hens and mac and cheese were a hit every thanksgiving, and I added in three cheeses for them along with a savory cheese sauce. Everybody had their special way of making it, but I knew my baked mac was one of the best, because Gramz taught me. A little over two hours later, I packed everything in carry out plates and packaged them in the insulated custom bags I got made with my logo on them so the food could stay warm.

***

Pulling up to Reina's shop felt eerie. A week ago Shawn was crashing out on the street. Now he was gone. Swallowing the lump in my throat, I got out the car, walked in the shop and found Reina putting the finishing touches on a client's heavily layered middle part sew-in. It was a cherry red color and looked bomb against the woman's cinnamon colored skin.

"Hey girl!" Reina chirped, sounding in better spirits than I expected. She spun the client around, and snipped the last couple of layers, with focused precision on each strand. I asked her where she wanted me to sit the food, and she motioned for her counter.

"Have a seat Rae, I wanna chop it up with you."

Ten minutes later, Reina was done, paid by her client, and we headed to the back in her office which was just as nice as Reign's, if not nicer. She had grey hardwood floors, cranberry colored couches, and large floor to ceiling mirrors. Placing the bag on her desk, Reina wasted no time tearing into the food. I made enough to last her and Reign for a couple days.

"Rae, this food is *so good*!" She exclaimed between bites, her hand covering her mouth. I smiled, loving that she was able to find some joy in her pain. "Reign is gonna love this. We loveeeee cornish hens and he lovessss baked mac and cheese. Who taught you how to cook like this? How is it not a nigga snatching you up and married right now?"

I tittered. "Girlllll.... My Gramz and culinary school. She used to have me right with her selling dinners every weekend when I was younger," smiling at the memory. I decided not to comment on the marriage part. I was so mentally exhausted, my brain couldn't even fathom that Dre was somewhere engaged with a baby on the way. I rather pretend that that tidbit of information didn't matter and didn't exist.

"Well God bless yo Gramz and culinary school cuz gahdamn! When you say your restaurant is opening? I can't believe its gone be right next door. You finna have us all fat but yo pockets gone be fatter! I know that's right!" she clapped, then sat back in her chair, rubbing her stomach.

We shared a laugh. "Thank you so much for this Rae. Can you believe this is one of the first full meals I've eaten all week?" she shook her head and looked away briefly, then back at me with a somber expression. I nodded. I could believe it. This situation was hard, especially for her and her family.

"I'm really sorry for your loss Reina... so very sorry," I admitted, for more reasons than one.

"I appreciate it. But, I should be asking how you're doing," she replied.

I shrugged. "Rae, I know I don't know you that well yet, but... you lost somebody too. I'm not sure what kinda terms yall was on but, he was your first love. It's okay to feel whatever you feel. Don't let nobody bully you out that shit, not even LaTrice's irritating ass" she rolled her eyes.

I took her words in. A part of me felt like that even if I hadn't said those vile words towards him, I still didn't have the right to mourn him since we were broken up. I had moved on with my life and he had moved on with his. We weren't friends but we weren't enemies either. Aside from the dreams I would have and then us talking on Instagram, there was no connection.

So why was I so sad? Why did it feel like a piece of my heart was missing? Why did it feel like the weight of the world was on my shoulders?

"Are you going to the funeral?" Reina asked, breaking through my internal thoughts.

My mouth went dry and my pupils started to dilate. I didn't know how to answer her. I wanted to be honest, but I also wasn't keen on sharing my feelings with strangers.

"I don't know…" I trailed off. Reina's brows furrowed and she leaned up in her chair.

"Girl, fuck LaTrice's ass. Yes, she's his wife but on the lowest of keys, Shawn had been trying to get her to sign papers for the last year or so. She just refused and would use his kids as pawns as if he wasn't funding her whole lifestyle. Those two were toxic as hell for the longest, and before I met you, I always thought Shawn was settling for her ass. Not like he was faithful to her anyway. Bitch used to come in the shop raising hell trying to fight clients cuz of Shawn until I banned her ass. Ion give a fuck what's going on with yo nigga, don't bring no bullshit to my place of business."

My brows raised. Not at the mention of Shawn and LaTrice's drama, but how open Reina was being right now.

"Girl… I hear you. But I think it's just best if I stay away. When I say me and that girl can't be in the same room for long, I mean it."

"What is the beef between y'all? I remember in the hospital, she was screaming about staying away from her husband… yall was fucking around still?"

I shook my head and sighed. "No.. not at all. Our beef goes back to high school." I sighed again, choosing my words carefully. "Reina, what I'm about to tell you may change whatever perception you have of me, but it's my truth and I've grown from it."

Reina leaned up in her chair, nodding for me to continue.

"Me and Trice's beef goes back to high school. I met Shawn when I was like fourteen, he was eighteen. We started dating, being in a relationship, and a lot of girls didn't like that. She used to try and start shit with me in school all the time. At first, I didn't know that she and Shawn had a fling before me. But he was a fine ass nigga, so in my mind it was expected. What I didn't expect was for her to try and bully me. I ignored her mostly. Here she was two grades ahead of me, trying to start shit. We had one fight and I dragged her up and down King Drive. Shawn used to tell me that she was jealous all the time, but he failed to mention that he was dealing with both of us at the same time.... Because I didn't know any better, I put up with a *lot* from your cousin. He was my first *everything*. I was even pregnant by him. We planned to keep the baby, and everything was fine at first. Then one day, Trice and her gaggle of bitches jumped me after school, and I lost the baby."

Reina was on the edge of her seat, then reached out and grabbed my hand, which I reluctantly gave her. "Damn... I am *so* sorry. What the fuck? Wow. As if I ain't have a reason to dislike that bitch before..." she shook her head.

"What made it worse is that Shawn was nowhere near the hospital. He used to pick me up after school, but he wasn't answering that day. I went weeks without seeing him, hearing from him. When I finally did see him... he had Trice all in his truck, skinning and grinning without a care in the world."

"Oh my God, I wanna go dig that nigga up and he ain't even in the ground yet! What the fuck? On behalf of my entire family, I am SO SOR-RY you went through that... Trice should be ashamed of herself. What the fuck..." Reina shook her head in disbelief. I decided to keep the rest of my story to myself, and spare her the details of the toxic dance me and Shawn did before I started dating Dre. It was cringey talking about it out loud because even though my age could be attributed to it, I was really down bad. I didn't have the first clue about how to assert boundaries, to stay away from him, or even what it meant to date casually.

"So yeah... I catered The Black Excellence Ball last month. Me and her exchanged some words, well, mostly her getting slick at the mouth because I had to maintain my composure and keep working. But me popping her in the mouth at the hospital –"

"Was well deserved! Listen, I hear you! But I think you should still be there. The whole hood is coming. And you gone be the baddest bitch in there. The fuck Trice thought?" Reina hopped up, and walked around her desk.

I shook my head. Reina pulled my hand, making me stand and looked me squarely in the eyes.

"Just... think about it. It's on Saturday, at Glory and Honor Missionary Baptist Church. The colors are GD blue and black. I don't know how you're feeling but whatever it is, it may help by seeing him be laid to rest. Here, put your number in my phone," and she pushed the device in my hand. I saved my name and number and stared at her, shifting my weight on each foot.

"Now, follow me. I have this style I wanna try on you. When's the last time you had a silk press?" she called over her shoulder, walking out of her office. My feet followed her, and the whole time I was at the shampoo bowl, I felt conflicted.

This funeral was going to be a shit show, wasn't it?

Chapter Eleven

Desiraè

I'd only been to two funerals in my entire life.

The first one was my father's when I was twelve-years-old. I'm not sure if I missed my daddy much, because finding out he cheated on my mother, got other women pregnant, and left my mama to carry the weight of his unpaid child support put a bad taste in my mouth whenever I thought about him. So, I didn't allow my thoughts to honor his memory too often.

The second funeral was Gramz's when I was eighteen. I loved Gramz with everything in me. She took in four kids who weren't her own and did the best she could in raising us. I know I used to stress her out with my shenanigans but she never made me feel alone. She was always in my corner... I just wish we had more time together, especially once she got sick. I remember how at her funeral, there were so many people paying their respects and saying such nice things about her. She was a pillar in the community and damn near a neighborhood hero. Everyone from the alderman to the drug dealers and addicts respected her.

LaShawn's funeral would be my third, and I wanted to stay buried underneath my covers. I wanted to pretend that this was all a bad dream, and that he was still alive, well, and talking shit. Him and the word 'dead' being in the same sentence didn't even sound right. I kept going back to my Instagram messages and I even found the login for my old Myspace page, where my entire page was dedicated to him. He was the only person in my Top 8 and I had *Mrz. Davis 43ver* falling from the page. We had so many pictures together that it was ridiculous. My Instagram messages were filled with catering inquiries, tags from people's reviews on the dinners I sold, but nothing from LaShawn. He wasn't swiping up and commenting on my story and he would never heart my stories again.

A lump formed in my throat but the tears wouldn't fall. I felt broken for this very reason. Before I could dwell on what was wrong with my tear ducts, I hopped in the shower to get dressed for the services. I went through the ritual of moisturizing my skin from head to toe and then dressed in a pair of black and blue pin-stripped high-waisted dress pants that flared at the bottom and a blue dress shirt. Reina silk pressed my hair but cut it into layers that went slightly past my shoulders and convinced me to let her add a royal blue track in the bang. I looked like a GD version of Aaliyah, but I couldn't lie – it was cute. I didn't bother to put on any foundation or eye shadow, just covered my eyes with a pair of dark, oversized Lorvae sunglasses. I sprayed my Venus Vs. Mars perfume I made a month back and headed to the living room, where Nicole was sitting on the couch to my surprise. We stared at each other silently, trying to read each other's expressions.

"Ma, I–"

"It's fine, Desiraè," she held up her hand to stop me. "We can talk about it later. My job as your mother is to be there for you, not judge how you are grieving, nor place my experiences on you, even if they are similar." She stood up to wipe imaginary wrinkles out of her pants. She was dressed in all black with a blue blazer on top of her black dress shirt. "I ain't gone always get it right, but Imma always try."

I nodded. I felt like shit for blowing up on her but I'd apologize later. I was just appreciative that she showed up to come with me, because this shit was hard. I never thought I'd have to experience something like this, and even though my worst enemy was experiencing it too, I wouldn't wish it on her either. Nicole closed the distance between us and held her arms out for a hug. I obliged, and for a split second, everything felt alright in my world. Willing myself not to cry, she squeezed me a little tighter, and then we separated. Grabbing our purses, we piled into my car and made our way to the church. The wake was at 10:30 and the services started at eleven. I wasn't going to the repast or afterparty, no matter how much Reina begged. I had to draw a line somewhere. My heart fell to my toes as soon as we reached the parking lot of the church. Judging by the amount of cars and the sea of people donned in blue and black walking to get in the church, LaShawn's death brought the whole city out.

***

"I'm ready when you are," my mama turned and looked at me. "We don't have to go in, if you're not ready." I nodded, practicing some breathing exercises while some gospel song played quietly on the radio. It was actually a beautiful spring day for April, where the sun was shining and the weather was warm enough to only have to wear a light jacket if you wanted to. Taking one last deep breath, I grabbed my door handle and stretched my legs out, standing over the car. Nicole rounded the car and grabbed my hand, and together, we walked towards the church. Each step felt heavier than the last and my heart dropped further and further. I looked around for Reina and peeped her and Reign off to the side with some other people. I detoured and went to speak. Reina looked up from her phone, dressed in all blue with an airbrushed picture of her and Shawn on the back of her blue bomber jacket. She wore dark shades too and her hair was in a half up, half down style with two bantu knots and a blue and black swoop bang.

"Rae!" she shrieked, and almost knocked me over giving me a hug. Reign popped his head up and caught my eyes, giving me a slight nod before turning to talk to a guy next to him. I introduced her to my mom and then we turned to walk into the church. The ushers inside were handing out obituaries, a singular blue rose, and buttons that had a picture of Shawn throwing up GD. I smirked and shook my head. This shit was ghetto as hell, but so fitting for this homegoing service. Walking into the sanctuary, I saw that it was filling up already, so we took a seat in one of the last three rows. The cobalt blue casket was ominous, and I still couldn't believe that this was actually happening. Death is weird, man. Because while it's understood that we all gotta go one day, you always imagine that it happens when you're old as hell. Not in your twenties or younger with so much life to live. And despite how I felt about Shawn, I felt like he still had so much life to live – without me though. Before I knew it, I felt my mom grab my hand and enter the line to go view the body and I wanted to bolt up outta that church. But I allowed my mama to guide me through, pulling me behind her as we waited our turn. There were tears everywhere, from who I assumed was his family.

"LAWDDDDDD. NOT MY NEPHEW!" A woman who reeked of vodka hollered in front of us. She was on the skinny side, the color of coffee

beans, and had a lopsided wig on, dressed in jeans and a blue dress shirt. She hollered a couple more times, leaning all over the casket, tears pouring down her face. The man next to her was rubbing her back and said, "I don't even know why you making all that damn noise Geraldine! Hush up, you holding the line up!" Geraldine lurched backward as if she'd been slapped. "Wait a minute Jerry, who is this? This ain't my nephew!" Jerry peered into the casket and then looked back, embarrassment painting his light caramel colored face.

"Geraldine, this ain't the right church is it? *GAL!* Yo drunk ass doing all this crying and carrying on and we at the wrong damn church!" Jerry grumbled and snatched her arm so they could get out of line.

See what I mean? Ghetto.

After that commotion, it was now my turn to view the body and unlike Geraldine, I couldn't mistake the identity of the person inside. Unfortunately, I was in the right place, in my right mind, and felt like I would pass out any second now. The casket was beautiful, but the person inside didn't belong there. Adorned with blue and white roses, I stared down at Shawn laying lifeless with an artificial smile on his face. His facial hair was lined nicely and he was dressed nicely with a white button up shirt, a diamond chain, and a blue New Era baseball cap. I couldn't say that it looked like he was sleeping, because Shawn always used to sleep with a scowl on his face. He wasn't no smiling ass nigga for real.

I hope you haunt the niggas who did this to you, because this is stupid Shawn...why would someone do this to you? You got kids who need you, nigga.... I'm sorry for what I said to you. Maybe you should hop up and tell everybody that you're faking... it is April Fools Day after all. Shawn... wake up G. This isn't funny anymore.

Next thing I know, I feel loads of tears streaming down my face, and my mother pulls a Kleenex from her purse, pats my cheeks with them, and whispers that we need to take our seats because other people are waiting and service needs to start. We walked past the front row and I passed by Miss LaShawnda, Shawn's mother. I didn't see much of her when Shawn and I were dating, because she was heavy in the streets, getting taken care of by her drug dealing son. Shawn took care of his whole immediate family and not once did I hear him complain. She appeared to still be well taken care of, dressed in a short, A-line skirt with the same bomber jacket that Reina and Reign wore. Further down the row, I spotted LaTrice, two young girls that looked like carbon copies of Shawn, and a little boy who looked no older than one. They were all dressed in black and blue, with smaller airbrushed jackets on. My heart immediately broke into millions of pieces and I empathized with them. Those kids, those little girls especially, had to grow up in a world without their father's love and guidance. That little boy would never remember who his dad is, because he was little when he was taken from him. Those girls would never see their father again, unless he came and visited them in dreams like Gramz did me sometimes. That sucked. After offering condolences to Shawn's mother, I hugged Reina, and nodded wassup to Reign. Trice loudly sucked her teeth, but she was smart for once and kept her smart comments at bay. I leered at her, rolling my eyes even though she couldn't see them through my shades. She wanted to join her husband so damn bad.

But, I was a changed woman. Not today, or any day moving forward, would I argue or fight over a man...especially one that's in a casket. At some point, the stupid shit had to end and Trice could go to hell for all I cared.

I would be moving with love and light from this day forward. After this, I was sure I didn't have to run into her bean head ass again.

The service started, the pastor preached, and I zoned out until some woman got up and started screeching on the mic as she sung a song. I was sure Shawn would sit up in his casket and tell her to shut the fuck up then. It should be a crime to be a horrible singer at a funeral, like God you can't strike people down for that? Because if not, you should! Once she got off the mic, there were a few more people that got to come up and speak, saying nice things about Shawn. There was one woman who came up, holding a newborn.

"Hi. Many of you all don't know me, but I'm Paris, and this little boy that I'm holding here is LaShawn Junior..." and the church gasped. Chaos ensued and it took about ten minutes for it to calm back down so that the pastor could finish his benediction and the processional could start. Me and Nicole turned to each other and burst into quiet laughter, reminiscing on my father's funeral and how ghetto *that* was.

Shawn was something else, boy. I almost felt bad for LaTrice, but hell... she knew the type of nigga she was dealing with. Then I began to feel bad, because regardless of knowing who you're dealing with, nobody *deserves* to get cheated on and a child being born outside of you. Then I thought about it some more and thought that maybe this was her karma. Then I realized that none of this shit was my business, so let me turn these thoughts off.

I snapped out of my trance and watched as six men including Reign close the casket, removed the flowers and stood three on each side as they carried the casket down the aisle. Reign's face was stoic, his smoldering brown eyes unreadable but his energy gave off a mix of anger and sadness. I felt so bad for him. Reina explained that he and Shawn were very close, and that even though he wouldn't show it, he was taking it very hard.

The tears started coming down again, and I didn't bother wiping them this time. This was heartbreaking. This was maddening. This was fuckin' stupid.

After the first few rows filed out behind the pallbearers and family, we walked outside to watch the casket get loaded into the blue hearse. LaTrice was hollering and screaming while walking to the limo and Reina and Reign headed in our direction. Reina's shades were still on but the puffiness and redness of her nose and cheeks gave way to the tears she shed.

"Rae! You coming to the burial right?" she rasped.

Reign frowned. "Leave that damn girl alone, Reina." He looked at me. "Aye, thank you for the food and shit. You ain't gotta come, don't listen to my messy ass sister."

"Shut up Reign! I'm not being messy, she lost somebody too!"

I watched them go back and forth, Reina obviously a little tipsy and Reign too high to care for real.

"Hey... It's really okay. I don't need to come to the burial. I paid my respects," I interrupted their arguing. I gave Reina a hug as she sulked and then I turned to give Reign one too. My body fit into his perfectly and it felt like electricity was shocking through my body. It dawned on me that this was the first time I'd hugged a man that wasn't related to me in months. Before long, the hug was over and I felt two pairs of eyes on me and Reign. Awkwardly, I grabbed Nicole's hand and power walked to my car. My mother walked over to the driver's side and looked at me curiously after she started the car.

"That's a good look, Rae-Rae."

"What is, Ma?"

"That young man."

I shook my head. "Girl, no. That is Shawn's cousin and apparently they were very close growing up. I'm not on that..." I denied. I thought Reign was cute but how raggedy would I be for liking my dead ex-boyfriend's cousin? That nigga Shawn wasn't about to be haunting me in my dreams. With his jealous ass.

"Mmmhmm. Mark my words. That's gone be your little boo" Nicole smirked, pulling out of the funeral procession and heading to the expressway. My stomach was grumbling and while in a perfect world, I woulda been at the repast but ain't nobody want funeral chicken seasoned with tears. Plus, I felt awkward and out of place. Ma pulled up to <u>St. Rest on 87th</u> and we found a table immediately. After the waitress took our drink orders, my mama took off her shades and just looked at me, her facial expression unreadable for once. I squirmed in my seat, my mind going back to the last time I was around her and the words I said. I felt bad again and reached across the table to grab her hands.

"Ma... I'm sorry for what I said when you were just trying to help," I apologized. "I don't have an excuse for it, just that Imma shake back from this grief shit."

"I accept your apology Rae. Grief is odd like that, and you won't always navigate it correctly, if there is even such a thing as grieving correctly. I wanted to knock you out, but realized that I was projecting my feelings onto you. So... I apologize too," She smirked.

Nicole Thomas was one hell of a woman and our relationship came a long way. Truth is, I loved her deeply, and knowing that she had been through hell and back and still carried a light about her made me want to be a better person. She wasn't perfect but her intentions were pure. I would never know or maybe even understand all her choices, but I could respect the fact that she owned every single one of them. A comfortable silence fell between us and then our food came. After smashing the food, we left with our bellies full and our hearts even fuller.

"Promise me something Rae," she requested. I turned to look at her. "Promise me that you won't let yourself drown like I did. Use your resources before it's too late."

With that, she gave me a hug and kiss on the cheek and then left my apartment, leaving me with things to think about.

Chapter Twelve

Desiraè

"*R*ae... Rae... I'm-I'm-I'm sorry man. I wish I woulda got my shit together when we was shorties. I'm so sorry Rae.*"*

I lifted my head from my pillow and peered at Shawn sitting on the edge of my bed. I always wondered if angels had to wear the same clothes they wore in the casket, and here Shawn was dressed in his blue, white, and black with a golden aura around his fitted cap.

"What...what are you doing here, Shawn?" I asked, sitting up.

"Trying to right my wrongs. I really want you to know that I'm sorry, okay? And if it's okay if I come see you sometime?"

A lump formed in my throat. Shawn scooted closer to me, grabbed my hand, and cradled me in his arms.

"I finally get what you were trying to say to me. I had no right to expect forgiveness from you. Apart of me could blame it on me being a young, dumb, reckless, nigga but all that shit was a choice. I'm sorry I didn't choose better."

"Shawn.... I'm mad at you."

"I know, baby and I'm sorry about it."

I shook my head. "No, not because of what you did when we were younger...well, that's a lie. I don't fuck with you because of that, but because you left-left me!" I cried. All the tears I kept in since I saw the accident, to going to the hospital, to attending the funeral poured out of me. No amount of consoling could stop the tears and the anguish on Shawn's face.

"What-what are they supposed to do without you?" I asked, referring to his family. He didn't respond, just reached out and wiped the tears cascading down my face. My feelings towards him felt polarizing. I resented him for the way he treated me and marrying La Trice, yet I grieved his death and my feelings hurt for his family. Now I was reduced to memories.

I hated it here.

"Rae baby... I'm sorry," he expressed, tears streaming down his own face.

"I... I forgive you Shawn. It's-It's...–"

"It's not okay. I'm sorry. But you will be okay one day. Someone is going to come in and love you the right way, the correct way. If anybody deserves that, it's you. It's gone be somebody you least expect too, but he a thorough nigga. Take care of yourself, Lady Rae"

Just as I was about to say something else, I blinked and then everything faded to black.

Chapter Thirteen

Desiraè

I bolted from my sleep, my heart beating a million miles a minute, and my face damp from my tears. That dream last night tweaked me out. I couldn't understand why my feelings were in haywire like this but I didn't like it. But my mother's words when she left me played in a loop, and I couldn't let myself drown. I wanted to be proactive. Immediately, I got online and booked an emergency appointment with Doc. She accepted immediately and I laid there for a while, then got up to get dressed. A fuchsia-colored <u>Fake Decent</u> sweat suit adorned my body with a pair of fresh white Air Force Ones. I snatched the blue tracks out of my head and brushed my hair into a messy bun, making a mental note to call Reina for an appointment or get some braids from one of the other stylists at her shop.

Ambling to the kitchen, I mustered up enough energy to make a quick sausage and egg breakfast sandwich and a strawberry banana smoothie. While chomping on my food, I scrolled through my social media and emails, and realized that I needed to go check on the space. I also needed to check on the girls, my brothers, and call my mama back. The last few weeks had gone by like a blur and I needed to recalibrate. I scrolled through

Reina's Instagram and saw that this was her first time posting in a few weeks. It was a beautiful compilation of videos and pictures from her, Reign's and Shawn's childhood, all smiling, laughing, and looking happy. The song was a Rich Homie Quan one, and before I knew it, I was wiping tears from my eyes again. *"Til We Meet Again, Save A Seat in Heaven For Me.. #KingShawn4Lyfe"* was the caption. I dropped blue hearts in the comments, and three minutes later, my phone started ringing.

"Rae, girl! I called to check on you!" Reina's loud voice announced once I picked up. I smirked.

"I'm okay. You good? You been hella quiet," I asked, while I started washing my dishes.

"Even when I ain't, Imma always be good G. What you doing today?"

"I got therapy in a few and then Imma stop by the restaurant and check on the progress. I got a weird ass email about some plumbing issues and I need to see if this is going to delay the soft opening," I sighed.

There was a pregnant pause and I looked at my phone to make sure the line was still connected.

"Hello?"

"Yeah girl... I'm still here. I'm just shocked that you in therapy. Not that there's anything wrong with it, I just thought that therapy was for crazy people, and you seem pretty normal to me."

I understood where she was coming from, because that was a common misconception in the Black community. Whole time, being in Doc's care all these years helped me learn that therapy isn't just for "crazy people" and that all of us could benefit from going at least once, *especially* Black people.

"My normalcy depends on who you ask," I chuckled. "But yeah, I've been going for a while, off and on for the last few years. My therapist is amazing."

"That's wassup, Rae! I admire you. Well, I hope you have a good therapy session girl. Oh, before I forget, is it okay if I give my brother your number? He runs a spring break barber camp for high school students, and he wants to know if you can cater it. Just some lil shit, like sandwiches, wraps, wings, and that punch you be making."

I beamed. Reign was dope to me, and really cared about giving back to the community.

"Yeah, that's cool."

"Good, because I already gave it to him anyway –"

"Reina!"

"What? My brother likes you, but he tries to play the shy act like he don't be having these hoes down bad out here. But, I can tell he wants to do more than just fuck you –"

"REINA!" I cut her off. "*STOP.* I was in a relationship with y'all cousin for crying out loud. That's messy, and I'm not like that."

"Yes, when y'all were kids. You ain't got no babies by him. And that nigga is no longer with us. Reign ain't had a girlfriend since God knows when and I just think –"

I hung up on her. She texted me two minutes later.

Messy Ass Reina

> You ain't have to hang up on me hoe! ⬚ It's strict around here.

Block me back LaReina ⬛ I see exactly why he calls you messy!

Yeah, whatever sister in law! Stop by the shop when you done doing what you do.

I liked the message, then chuckled and shook my head. Reina was crazy, a bit messy, but I liked her energy. I finished getting ready and then headed out the door to my appointment.

***

Dr. Love's Chicago location for Love Rehab was beautiful. It was grand in stature, and the inpatient facilities looked like a college campus. I was greeted by her pleasant staff and marveled at how far she had come. She had dedicated rooms for art therapy, a rage room, a group therapy room, and more rooms that allowed clients to express themselves freely. I walked to her office and was greeted by the smell of lavender and cashmere scented candles and soft sounds of Cleo Sol playing. Doc was seated Indian style on her plush sea foam green couch, dressed down in a pair of wide-legged jeans and a turquoise flowy top. Her zebra print glasses and knotless braids styled in a bun pulled the entire look together.

"Desiraè," she smiled and motioned for me to have a seat in the seafoam green chaise lounge chair. I settled in and stared at her for a minute, knowing that she was giving me time to start.

"What's something small that brought you joy this week?" she asked, breaking the ice. I didn't have any other experiences with therapists to compare with, but I knew that Dr. LaKeisha Love was unorthodox compared to many of her peers. She's done this exercise with me before, and every time, I get stuck on big moments instead of small ones. It's supposed to be an exercise that helps me practice gratitude and stay present. But my mind constantly feels like it's a thousand tabs open at once, so I am rarely ever present.

"Ummmm...." I shifted uncomfortably on the plush lounge chair. "I... made a breakfast sandwich this morning. I showered, put on clothes, and made a smoothie. I had a conversation with a friend that made me laugh a little bit." I started naming the most random things off.

Doc nodded, and gave me a reassuring smile. "Okay... what happened at the funeral? Anything funny happen?"

I smirked. Doc knows she loved some tea.

"Actually... a couple things. It was this drunk lady there who thought Shawn was her nephew, and her boyfriend or husband realized they were in the wrong church and drug her out." I started laughing, so hard that I started bawling. Like heart wrenching sobs, that shook my whole body.

Doc remained silent and passed me some tissues so that I could wipe my face. It took me a good little minute to calm down.

"I'm sorry. I don't... I don't know why I started crying like that," I sniffed. Doc cocked her head slightly to the right, studying me.

"You know it's okay to cry right? You are likely feeling a mix of emotions. And it's okay to sort them out."

"But that's the *thing*. I don't understand why this is hitting me so hard when we weren't even together."

"Since when do you have to be in a relationship with someone to grieve them? Are there rules to grieving?"

My face flushed. Was I being too technical, too hard on myself? Were there rules to grieving?

"No...but... Doc. It's confusing. Like I'm so confused on how to feel, and it changes every second it seems like. Like, I said some fucked up shit to him and I *saw* the accident happen. I saw his blood staining the street and his clothes. Right before the accident, he was crashing out because I wasn't really responding to him and I just – I feel like if I would have never told him to drop dead, he would still be alive. This is just –"

"Desiraè," Doc crossed the threshold and sat next to me, grabbing my hands. "Let's try and unpack this. It is normal to feel anger, hurt, resentment. But I can assure you that *you* aren't responsible for what happened to LaShawn. It is unfortunate, but I can't allow you to carry that burden. That's much too heavy to carry and don't you think that after all this time, you deserve to lay some things down?"

I bawled. The tears cascaded down my face in endless waterfalls, soaking my neck and shirt. The pain could no longer be contained and I was afraid that my heart would give out on me if I tried to hold on to anything any longer. This shit sucked. Hands down. LaShawn broke my heart countless times over the years, but this right here took the cake. This wasn't something that he could apologize his way out of, buy his way out of, or even fuck his way out of. How could a man who irked me so much break my heart like this? Doc rubbed small circles in my back, letting me cry as long as I needed to. It felt like I was drowning, and something was weighing me down, preventing me from coming up for air.

"Grief is funny like that. It's non-linear, just like healing is. I'm not sure when you'll feel okay, and maybe, for now, that isn't the goal. Maybe the goal is to welcome those uncomfortable feelings. Sit with them. Cry with them, scream about it, throw things. Yeah... I think that's your goal here. To just be. You don't have to be strong. You don't have to hold it in or convince yourself that you are unworthy to grieve someone you once loved. Grief doesn't work like that. It has no qualifiers. There's no trophies for it. There's a saying that grief is just love with no place to go. So cry it out, Desiraè. Mourn him. It is okay. No judgement here," Doc spoke softly, but firmly at the same time.

My shoulders shook, as I nodded my head, hearing her clearly. The most I could do was try. One day at a time, right?

***

After crying my entire face off, I walked out of Doc's office feeling.... Well, I don't know how to articulate it. Not lighter, not freer, but a bit more optimistic that I would eventually be okay. It would take a while for me to grasp that there were no qualifiers for grief. Because, as shitty as LaShawn was towards me, I would be a liar if I said all the times between us were horrible. And I guess that is why I shed some tears over his death. Love never had any rhyme or reason to it. Love didn't care if your relationship was healthy or not. Love didn't care about if he ghosted you at your darkest moments or if you harmed each other physically.... Love was just... it was just there. Making the worst people appear loveable, letting people redeem themselves over and over again. As much as I liked to pretend that LaShawn didn't impact me, he did. In both life and in death.

Ugh. I couldn't stand that nigga.

Pulling up to the restaurant, I looked around and was astonished at how normal things seemed. If I hadn't seen it with my own eyes, you would never know that there was a gruesome car accident/murder that took place only a few weeks ago. I glanced across the street at Vibes and Lines Book Bar and made a mental note to stop in there to introduce myself and check it out. Climbing out of my car, I walked past Reina's shop and waved to the receptionist before I made my way to my space. With everything going on, I hadn't been as present as I would have liked, but now that the funeral was over and done with, I had to focus back on my goals. All I cared about was opening my restaurant. So when the contractor sent me an email about a plumbing issue that could potentially set me back three months, I was pissed. I paid good money for an inspector to look at everything, so how did they fail to inform me that the plumbing was piss poor? It was too late for me to find a new spot to open this restaurant because I was already locked into a two year lease and it would cost way too much to break the lease and eat the costs. Sulking, I made my way into Reina's shop and plopped down in her chair exasperated. Her brother was there too, looking at me curiously but not saying anything aside from his usual "wassup" when I walked through the door.

"These fools are talking about they're gonna have to rip everything out and start from scratch because of this plumbing issue and it's pissing me off because I wanted to have a soft opening next month during Memorial Day Weekend!" I huffed, typing a nasty email to my realtor and lawyer because the whole situation had me fucked up.

"Awww man D. Don't be mad. Delays don't mean that you're denied and if you have to push your open date back, is it really the end of the world?" Reina tried to reason with me, but I wasn't in the mood to hear it.

"Yes, it is the end of the world because I had a plan and this shit is throwing a monkey wrench in everything!" I rubbed my temples and pouted a little because I was so pissed. I had already given them so much money and still had even more to invest in this restaurant before I could even open it to the public. The cost of food, supplies, and equipment was steadily rising and I was afraid that I wouldn't be able to keep up. I slumped further in my chair, trying to figure out what I would do.

"Aye. My twin is right, there's a solution to everything," Reign cut in. I snapped my neck towards him, furrowing my brows in confusion.

"Oh yeah? What is it?"

"I can take care of your plumbing issue for you," he stated nonchalantly.

I looked over at Reina, and she just smirked. There was obviously an inside joke between the two of them that I wasn't let in on.

"Yeah... whatever," I waved him off and pulled my phone back out to see if my emails had a response yet.

"No for real, D. Reign has a construction company and he built both our shops. He definitely knows his way around plumbing too," Reina spoke up. I looked between the both of them, shocked. Reign was so mysterious. He didn't say much but he was always observant, listening, watching. I would've never pegged him to be someone who owned a construction company. I guess this is why they say you shouldn't judge a book by its cover.

"Really?"

He nodded.

"Okay... how much is that going to run me? I already wasted ten thousand dollars," I huffed, rolling my eyes.

Reign stared at me and I don't know – his eyes made me want to get lost in them, as corny as it sounded. I had to stop looking at him because he was my dead ex-boyfriend's cousin. I couldn't even play like that.

"You catering the food for my barber camp right?" he responded. I forgot that Reina asked for my number to pass to him but he never reached out and I had been so busy that I never thought to follow up.

"Yeah... I can."

He nodded. "Aight, consider it even then."

"Reign! I can't let you do that. It's not an equal exchange. Your menu would've run you a few hundred at most and I give discounts to small businesses and nonprofits anyway," I protested.

It was his turn to wave me off. "Look, I got you. And Imma still hit you with some bread when the camp is over."

Just as I was about to open my mouth to object, he stood up when his phone started ringing.

"Aye. Imma get up with you, I gotta take this," he said and exited out the shop. I turned and looked at his twin in bewilderment and she was holding back the most childish smile.

"What, Reina?" I snapped. She burst out laughing.

"Y'all got it bad for each other" she cheesed. I waved her off and stood up myself, to leave.

"I'm serious D. He doesn't usually do shit like this. My brother only tries to solve the problems of people he loves... or in your case, really likes. Mark my words," she giggled.

I rolled my eyes. Reign was fine as fuck – no lie. But I didn't think he looked at me like that, especially knowing about me and Shawn's history. Reign seemed like a man of principles. Loyal to soil. So unless shown otherwise, I was going to keep it professional with him. I left Reina's shop shortly after, worry plaguing my mind, but decided to release control and just nap for the rest of the day.

Hell. I'm just a girl.

***

773-326-1967:

> This the chef lady?

Me:

> Depends on who's asking ⬚

773-326-1967:

> Yeah, this yo ass. Wassup? This Reign.

Reign.

Unintentionally, I felt the corners of my mouth turn up as I saved his number with a crown emoji next to it.

> Hey Reign! How can I help you?

Reign ⬚:

> So about the Spring Break camp. My bad for hitting you so last min. The shit starts tomorrow. Imma throw you some bread for it. I just need something to feed these lil niggas. Wings, sandwiches, whatever kids eat, idk. Is 3K straight?

I paused. Though it was last minute, I felt that Reign was doing me a solid by doing my plumbing stuff that I needed. Plus, with everything going on,

I kind of wanted to give him a break. Though we were all still getting to know each other, I had good feelings about him and Reina. Ignoring his question about the price, I typed back.

Me:

> What time do you need me to drop the food off tomorrow?

Reign ⬛:

> Like 12, I guess that's when them lil niggas could get a break.

Me:

> And you want lunch for them every day or just for tomorrow?

Reign ⬛:

> Everyday if you can… I fuck around and order some Shark's or Italian Fiesta for the last day.

We continued to text back and forth about details and then I decided to get up and go to the grocery store. I decided to do hot wings and garlic fries for the first day, jerk chicken and jerk salmon wraps for the second day, a taco bar for the third day, and fried catfish and spaghetti for the fourth day. On the last day, Reign insisted that he order some Sharks or Italian Fiesta for them, even though I told him I could make mini pizzas for them but he told me no, he didn't want them lil niggas getting too used to special treatment. While in the store, I heard my cash app ding and shook my head. Reign sent me over three bands even though I ignored his question about payment. I'd put it aside to pay him for the plumbing services since he said it would start next week after he wrapped his camp up.

***

Reign had a group of fifteen high school aged boys who were interested in becoming barbers. I pulled up around 11:30 and started pulling the hot wing containers into my cart and walked into his shop where he had one man in the chair, with the boys gathered in a semi-circle around him watching him demonstrate. I walked in and everyone's head snapped towards me.

"Aye! She not in this chair so don't pay attention to her. Pay attention to me!" Reign snapped.

I smirked. This nigga was so rude. He pointed where I could set the food up and I quietly made my way over there, making as little noise as possible.For the next thirty minutes, I set up the styrofoam containers and the punch bowl and cups for them to drink out of. After ensuring everything was ready, I made my way to the door before Reign called out to me.

"Aye Chef. Come here for a minute."

In bewilderment, I walked over to where he was standing in front of the group.

"Listen up lil' niggas. This is Chef Rae. She is the one that's feeding y'all this week, so make sure you tell her thank you. She is opening up a restaurant real soon too, so make sure y'all tell the whole hood."

"THANK YOU CHEF RAEEEEE!" they called out in unison. I smiled and thanked them and then Reign dismissed them to eat.

"You got that bread I sent you right?"

"Yes, Reign. I don't know why though, since I told you that we're good."

"Look, this yo' business. I wouldn't even feel right taking yo' hard earned time."

"Is plumbing and construction not your business as well?" I cocked my head to the side.

He smirked. "Yeah.... But still... I appreciate you comin' through for me. So consider it even."

I waved him off. "Whatever, Reign. Thanks again, I'll see you tomorrow."

"What you on for the rest of the day?" he asked. I was a little surprised, this was the most conversation that Reign had ever given me. I shrugged. "I think Imma see what your twin is doing and now that I have some down time, I may finally go check out the bookstore across the street."

"Aight... thank you again. Them lil niggas tore that food up as you can see," and I followed his eyes towards the lil' niggas in question, indeed clearing that whole table and asking if it was seconds. I made a mental note to bring extra wraps for the next day. I underestimated how much teenage boys eat.

"No problem, Reign. See you tomorrow."

Chapter Fourteen

Desiraè

After dropping off day three's lunch, I made my way to Vibes and Lines for the first time and I honestly wished I'd gotten over here sooner. It was the most beautiful place I'd ever seen. What made Vibes and Lines special wasn't that it was just a black-owned bookstore – it was also a wine bar where they exclusively sold wines created by Black people. The books they showcased were in full support of Black indie authors along with the mainstream ones. With soft colors of burnt orange and emerald green, they had a built-in sunken couch in the middle of the store where patrons could relax, read, and sip wine. The store was owned by identical twin sisters Cherrice & Joyy St. Howard. The only way I was able to tell them apart was that Cherrice had ginger colored hair, while Joyy had dark green colored hair. They were around twenty-five and had been open for the last two years.

"Welcome to Vibes and Lines. Feel free to browse around or have a seat at the bar if you'd like to sip," I was greeted immediately by the one who I assumed was Joyy. Her forest green hair was in a cute middle-part layered style that had Reina's name written all over it.

I smiled. Her energy was warm and attentive, as she watched me browse through shelves and pick out a few books for my mama. She was really into Jahquel J, Ashley Antoinette, and Grey Huffington these days and always called to tell me about what she was reading. I made my way to the six person bar and asked for a tasting. The other twin, Cherrice came out to do that.

"Wait. I think I know of you," she started. I smiled shyly. "You're the girl that sells plates right? And you're about to open a restaurant soon?"

"Yup, that's me," I giggled. She pulled out a brown iridescent wine glass and a bottle of Love Corkscrew Rosè and poured me up.

"It's so nice to meet you! Joyy! I told you that was her!" she turned and yelled to her sister. Joyy popped back out from the inventory she was stocking and smiled at me. "Reina and Reign speak so highly of you. Next time you sell plates, please don't forget about us over here," she chuckled.

"Agreed. We like to eat too," Cherrice chimed in. I learned that Reina started doing their hair when they first opened their store and that they had an older sister who was a doctor and that their grandma grew up over here so that's why they decided to pick this area and go into business. I was surprised, people always had negative things to say about Englewood but they assured me that aside from the accident that happened a month ago, Englewood was much more chill than what the media portrayed.

Messy Ass Reina:

Raeeeee. WYD tomorrow? ⊠

I looked down at my phone and smirked.

Me

> What do you want, lady?

Messy Ass Reina:

> Don't you wanna go outside tomorrow night? It's a new spot I wanna scope out, and you need to have some fun. Plus, its this new style I wanna try on you

Me

> Do I look like your damn Barbie Doll hoe?

> Send the details

Locking my phone, I smirked at whatever shenanigans Reina was going to get us into.

***

I walked into Reign's shop on day four of the camp, and to my surprise, he had his students present me this jumbo card and they all signed it. It was the sweetest thing, and he really didn't have to. I wrapped him in a hug, electricity jolting between our bodies, once again reminding me that it had been way too long since I felt a man's body against mine. He smelled like Dior Sauvage, a hint of weed, and the shea butter and warm vanilla scent of Dove Body Wash. An interesting combination but it fit him perfectly. I'm pretty sure I looked like a fool showing him all 32 of my teeth but I really was so grateful.

"Reign... yall gone have my ass crying," I smiled, wiping away some tears.

"It really ain't shit." he smiled, which was a rarity in itself because this nigga was so stoic all the time. I wanted to take a picture of his smile and make it my screensaver. Maybe his twin was right. Maybe we did have it bad for each other.

After saying my goodbyes, I walked down to Reina's shop and just plopped in her chair. No hair with me, just vibes. If nothing else, I was going to get my hair done and since Reina thought I was her Barbie Doll, it was even easier to get my hair done. If the girl could, she would have me trying a new style every week. I don't know what she was gonna do when the summer came and she learned that I only kept my hair in braids or faux locs.

"So where are we going tonight?" I asked after she washed and blow dried me. It had been so long since I stepped out and it was my first stepping out as an adult in Chicago. Reina started parting and braiding my hair down for what I assumed was a quick weave.

"Ok, so boom. There's this new spot opening, real lowkey like that has hookah, food, and a bomb ass DJ. Reign grabbed us a section and is sending us a black truck since I don't drive drunk," she explained. "It's called The Palace. Supposedly celebrities and shit be sliding through there but I wanna go and support my homegirl Ca$hera that's spinning tonight."

"It's just gonna be us?"

"Nope. Reign is actually coming outside and I think a couple niggas from the barbershop are coming too. I invited Cherrice and Joyy too. All in all, it should be a good time. I used to talk to the promoter and he's trying to get back on my good side, so everything on him!" she winked.

I laughed. Reina was a mess.

"So what's the attire? What kinda vibes you going for?"

Reina smirked. "Put that shit on, that's the vibe."

I started thinking about what I could pull out my closet. It would all depend on whatever hairstyle Reina did. A couple hours later, she spinned me around to a very cutesy, shoulder length side part quick-weave that had a heart-shaped swoop and flipped ends. The color of the weave was a bomb mix of chocolate brown and honey blonde.

"Yeah. I ate that up," Reina admired her work while snapping pictures and videos of me. "When you get in the shower, Make sure you put a scarf, shower cap, and this large bonnet on." She rolled my ends with some rollers.

"If you want to, y'all can come pregame at my house. Y'all can either bring your own bottle or I can make us some drinks," I suggested. "Plus, Imma need help with my outfit."

"I got you! Send me the addy, we'll slide around ten or eleven."

***

A few hours later, I was showered and dressed. I decided on an mushroom beige colored corset from Fashion Nova with some brown snake-skin straight leg pants and a pair of satin, pointy toe heels the same color as my top. Gold necklaces, earrings, rings, and bracelets adorned my body and I sprayed a mix of my Venus Vs. Mars perfume and Fin'ery's Pistachio Please as the scent of the night. The bag of the night was a Mini Kobi in brown by Brandon Blackwood.

"Okayyyyy! The look is givingggg!" Reina screamed as soon as I opened the door. I thanked her and complimented her fit too. Reina was clearly GD to the bone. She had on black leather Dior shorts, a blue and black criss-cross halter top, and blue Givenchy shark ankle boots. Dark shades adorned her eyes and her diamonds were dancing – literally. She gave herself a curly flip-over quick weave and she smelled like Chanel perfume. The twins arrived shortly after she did and they looked so cute. Cherrice had on an all black romper with snakeskin Steve Madden thigh high boots that had touches of blue and yellow in it. Joyy had on a white leather mini skirt and a matching cropped jacket with a lace black bra underneath that showed off her toned stomach and belly button ring that was a book stack charm. On her feet were a pair of sky blue, satin Sali pumps by Brandon Blackwood. I had the same pair in hot pink.

"Whew. I'm so glad y'all ain't no bitches that I gotta ask what else you got in that closet!" Reina snickered. We all laughed.

"So you saying you wouldn't be friends with people who can't dress?" Cherrice asked.

"No, I'm not saying that. I'd help... but it would be annoying," she laughed.

I made them drinks and passed them out. "Okay, so we doing tequila tonight. I made cucumber margaritas with a tajin rim."

The girls oohed and ahhed, sipping and singing my praises.

"You can cook yo ass off and you can make a bomb ass drink. Yeah, my brother needs to wife you up!" Reina's messy ass hollered. I cut my eyes at her. The twins stared at us curiously, grins adorning their faces.

"Wait... you and Reign talk?" Cherrice asked.

I shook my head. "No! Reina is just being messy per usual. I'm 'bout to put her out!"

The girls just laughed. "D here is in so much denial. My brother likes her, but he's in denial too," Reina continued. I pinched her thigh, and she fell back on the couch, cackling.

"Well... I for one think y'all would make the cutest couple. He speaks so highly of you," Joyy chimed in.

"He does?" This was the second time I heard that today.

"Yeah. He hit all the business owners in the neighborhood like "Make sure yall support Chef Desiraè. She can cook good and she good peoples" Cherrice said, imitating Reign's gravelly voice. We all laughed, because she had his voice spot on.

"Well... that's sweet of him," I turned to Reina sipping my drink. "Did you know that his students presented me with a big ass card and had them all sign it when I dropped the lunches off today?"

"See! I told you that he likes you!" she hollered and we laughed at her antics. She got up looking for the bluetooth speaker to turn on some music. Juke Me From The Back filled the space and we all got up, moving our asses and taking shots. The twins rolled up and stepped on the balcony to smoke, while me and Reina took a few more shots. She looked down at her phone.

"My brother is outside with the black truck. You mind if he and a few of the guys from the shop come upstairs? Imma make them take a couple shots and then we can go."

I told her to let them up and then ran to the bathroom to pee and check my outfit. I was feeling nice, those three shots and two drinks I had made me feel buzzed yet still coherent. Joyy and Cherrice came back mellow as hell, and I could tell that the weed they were smoking was high quality.

Reign swaggered in with three of his guys and my mouth went a little dry. He had on a two piece, short sleeve black button down, matching loose fit pants, and a pair of black and white Dunks. On his neck was a simple cuban link chain that made the crown tattoo on his throat pop, and he smelled like his signature scent of Dove, Dior Sauvage and weed. He came in first and swept his eyes over me appreciatively, then introduced me to the guys, Chewy, Domo, and Linx. They all worked at the shop with him.

"Alright niggas. Y'all gotta catch up on the shots since y'all wanted to be late and shit!" Reina walked around with the <u>Jon Basil</u> bottle and the shot cups, pouring full amounts into theirs.

"Reina, you know damn well this a double shot!" Chewy groaned. "I hate drinking with yo' ass." Reina shrugged and laughed at him, holding her cup up to toast. I noticed that Reign had nothing in his cup.

"You don't drink?" I asked.

"Not really. Somebody gotta be alert though, these niggas overdo it," he nodded towards the rest of the group.

"Oh, well if you want some water, I'll get you some," I said and stood, feeling the liquor while walking to the kitchen and brought him an ice cold bottle of alkaline water. He accepted it, watching me while I watched him, his Adam's apple bobbing up and down as he drank.

"Why you staring, shorty?" he smirked. I blushed and busied myself with putting my heels back on, thrusting my ankle on his lap so he could fasten the strap for me. The feel of his rugged yet soft hands on my ankle made me feel something I hadn't felt in a while and I internally begged myself to keep it together. I looked over and found everybody staring at us, Reina and the twins whispering and giggling like some damn kindergarteners. I was embarrassed, meanwhile Reign was as cool as a cucumber as he secured my straps and stood up.

"Aight y'all. Let's go turn up some mo'," he said and grabbed my hand and pulled us out the door.

***

Y'all know that opening scene in Belly when the main characters are walking into the club in slow motion and the blue light illuminates their whole body? That's how it felt walking in with everybody. Reign was in the front, Reina was to his right, I was in the middle of them and the twins were in the second row with the guys behind them. We didn't have to wait in line, which I appreciated. The Palace was beautiful with gold and black decor all over and two levels with a stage. Reina led us right to the DJ booth where her friend Ca$hera was DJing, and gave her a hug and introduced us. Then the bottle girl came and led us to VIP on the second floor, decked out in gold couches, glass tables, and hookah set ups. The DJ had that bitch rocking, and the food was good too. Reign ordered us jerk wings, hot wings, tacos, and lamb chops and lobster tails. The promoter that Reina said was trying to get back in her good graces, ordered us two bottles of 1942 and two bottles of Dom Pèrignon, because apparently, it was Chewy's birthday too.

A-Ass so fat need a lap dance
Make a nigga eat it up like Pac-Man

I don't want him if the trap ain't trapping
Wouldn't be me if the mack ain't macking

Us girls rapped, smoked hookah, and shook our asses to Ken The Man's song, feeling the liquor entirely. Before we left, I passed out liquid IV and some lemon flavored BC powder because I just knew we would be hung over in the morning. Every so often, I'd look behind me at Reign who was coolly chilling on the couch, nursing a glass of cranberry juice. He had a blunt rolled behind his ear and I wondered when he would smoke it, since the smell of weed permeated the air up here.

I felt eyes on me and searched around until I spotted the culprit. In the section across from us, there LaTrice was, giving me the stank eye, pointing at me with the gaggle of bitches she was with. I couldn't recognize them, but I would bet my entire restaurant on those hoes being the same ones that helped her jump me when we were in high school.

Ay, bitches couldn't see me from the clouds
These bitches talk I can't hear 'em from the clout
Why is you here?
How you hating from the couch?

I stood straight up and rapped those lyrics with all my heart, pointing at them just like they were pointing at me.

"TRACKSTAR, I'LL RUN IN BITCHES MOUTH!" I yelled belligerently and pointed right at her.

"Aye, come sit down shorty," Reign came behind me, leaned down and said in my ear.

"I'm straight Reign," I turned and looked up at him, admiring how he looked under these club lights. Reign was so fine. Real chill. He grabbed my hand and gently pulled me towards the couch, handing me a cup of water to chug on. Three cups later, I was back up, bent over and shaking my ass when *Back That Ass Up* came on.

***

"Twins, when y'all start hanging with opp ass hoes?" LaTrice was now in our section, arms crossed, mean mugging me while Reina stood in between us. I whipped around so fast, because I just knew her bean head ass wasn't talking about me.

"Trice, go head on, because if she knocks you out, I don't wanna hear nothing about how we ain't help you. You keep fucking with this girl and for what?!" Reina yelled.

LaTrice ignored her, while I stared straight at her, wishing she would do something. See, people like LaTrice lived for the drama and I knew that. Maybe when I beat her up in high school, I knocked a few screws loose. Maybe when I popped her in the face at the hospital, she lost even more screws. Whatever the case may have been, I was so sick of her.

Shouldn't she have been at home mourning her dead husband?

Didn't she have three kids and an outside baby to take care of?

Why was she so concerned with me and who I hung with?

"Fuck you, LaReina! I told you I ain't like that bitch and you out here getting drunk and turning up with her ass! We supposed to be family!" LaTrice yelled.

LaReina laughed, looked back at me and her brother and got real close to her.

"Bitch, fuck you! *Family?* Family my ass! Mufuckas ain't hear from you before he died and damn sure ain't heard from you since the funeral wrapped. You only come around to start some fuckin' drama or when you want something. Maybe this raggedy ass wig on yo' head is too tight, but my cousin wasn't even fuckin' with you for real! He stayed cheating on you and wanted to divorce you but you always wanted to play the helpless act! Bitch, get the fuck out our section before you don't make it home to yo kids tonight!"

Well damn. I turned around back towards Reign who had that zoned out, stoic look on his face while I grabbed another cup of water. I was done with the liquor for the night. I wanted to finish turning up and then go make love to my bed. I was glad I didn't have to –

"BITCH! SECURITY GET THIS BITCH!" I heard Reina yell, as I felt watered down liquor drip down my hair, neck, and shirt. This bitch threw her drink on me. Reign moved me out the way to hold his sister back but he wasn't quicker than me. I grabbed the entire hookah, snatched off the hose, and ran up and whacked Trice in the face with it over and over.

"BITCH!" ***WHACK!***

"I!" ***WHACK!***

"TOLD YOU!" ***WHACK***

"ABOUT FUCKING WITH ME!"

WHACK! WHACK! WHACK!

I whacked her until I saw blood spill on my shoes and then I heard Reign yell to security, "IF YOU TOUCH HER, I'M AIRING THIS BITCH OUT!" He flashed a gun in the waistband of his pants and then I felt him snatch me up, pulling me to the stairs so we could exit the club. Chewy

211

and Linx held Reina back, while LaTrice's friends scattered. Scurrying out the club, we saw police everywhere and tried to act as normal as possible. The black truck was parked on the corner. My vision was so blurry and we were walking so fast, I needed to slow down before I threw up.

"Reignnnnn....." I slurred. "Slow down *please.*"

"Shut the fuck up and get in the car, Desirae" he huffed out.

He sounded so pissed and if I wasn't so drunk, I would have felt bad. I climbed in the back seat and laid my head back on the head rest. Shortly after, the guys, Reina, and the twins ambled into the truck, animated as fuck. Reign stood outside and lit his blunt, I guess trying to calm down but I wondered why he was so mad? She didn't come for him, she came for m e.

"You see how my bitch dog walked her stupid ass? That's exactly what her ass gets! Don't let D's cute face and demeanor fool you!" Reina slurred, re-enacting with her hands how I hit her with the hookah.

"Girlllll what the fuck was that about? One minute everything's cool, the next minute that bitch is throwing drinks and on the floor. What the fuck happened?" Cherrice wondered out loud. I said nothing, because my head was pounding. I let Reina tell the story, because I was too out of it to care.

The passenger door opened, and Reign climbed in, mean mugging all of us, but especially me. "Aight. I'm finna have the driver drop everybody to they crib. You first, Mike Tyson." The rest of the ride was quiet, and soon I heard light snores from the girls. Fifteen minutes later, we pulled up in front of my building and Reign came from his seat to open my door. Climbing out, I paused when I felt him walking behind me in my building.

"What are you doing?" I slurred, standing on wobbly legs.

"What the fuck it look like? Making sure yo' drunk ass makes it in the crib."

"You don't...you don't gotta be so rude, Reign. I don't even understand why you mad at me," I slurred, crossing my arms.

He said nothing, as he followed me to the elevator and pressed the 75th floor. The ride up was silent, him on one end of the elevator and me on the other. We made it to my floor and I pressed the keypad to let myself in.

"Desiraè?" he called out.

"Hmmm?"

"I want this to be the last conversation we have about this. You raw as fuck shorty. You got way too much going for you to be fighting in the club over a bitch who ain't got shit to lose. I understand that she came for you first, but you gotta control yo' anger. One wrong move could have you behind bars and I don't want my favorite chef being reduced to cooking prison slop. Now I gotta go talk some sense in her dumb ass, 'cuz I know that police ass bitch gone try to press charges."

My heart swelled at his words. In his own ghetto ass way, Reign's mean ass was so affirming.

"Reign?"

"Wassup shorty?"

"Shut the fuck up and kiss me."

He stared at me for a few seconds then got closer, cupping my chin in his hand. I closed my eyes and puckered my lips slightly, feeling all the liquid courage tonight.

"Nah shorty... I can't," he whispered and my eyes popped open, mortified. I stepped back and watched him disappear towards the elevator, feeling embarrassed as fuck.

Chapter Fifteen

Desiraè

I was never drinking again. Not only was a migraine footworking on my brain, but the dread I felt about the night before left me feeling extremely embarrassed. I didn't care one bit about taking that hookah and beating Trice's ass – she deserved it. But why would I ask that man to kiss me? Now he probably thinks I'm a hoe and that I be going around fucking on the friends and family members of the dead homies. I grabbed my phone and responded to some catering inquiries and then put all the girls in a group chat to check in on them.

> Y'all good?

One by one, they all started responding and recapping the night.

Cherrice:

> Hanging on by a thread… But I'm here.

Messy Ass Reina:

> Quiet as its kept, I'm glad I don't have any clients til 5 today. I been shitting all morning ⊠

Joyy:

> Did we take shots or did the shots take us?

Messy Ass Reina:

⬚ so…

Reina, don't you start⬚

Joyy:

We kinda wanna know too…

Cherrice:

Because, wtf was that about? How you go from hostess with the mostest to hitting a hoe with hookah?

Messy Ass Reina:

I told y'all don't underestimate my bitch! Trice raggedy ass deserved that! All she gone do is try to bash you on the internet or try to press charges

Cherrice:

⬚ press chargessss?

Joyy:

Wait, you talking 'bout LaTrice? The bitch that was married to LaShawn?

Messy Ass Reina:

Mmhmm. That hoe. ⬚

Cherrice:

Girllll. ⬚

What y'all getting at twins?

Joyy:

girl… not much, but when we first opened, Shawn came into the store to welcome us. He shouted us out on his Instagram, cool. The very next day, we wake up to her up and down our pages bashing us, accusing us of fucking her husband.

Cherrice:

Mind you, that wasn't true at all.

Joyy:

Bitch used to leave negative reviews on Google and Yelp before we paid to remove them. I been wanting to drag that hoe ever since but she's never even visited the store.

I was stunned. LaTrice really was a messy, miserable ass bitch.

Damn… sorry that happened to y'all. ⊠

And I really *was* sorry. The twins were cool and seemed down for a good time and as a fellow business owner, I knew how hard it was to build up your reputation and maintain a positive image. They didn't deserve the wrath of LaTrice nor her pettiness.

Cherrice:

Girl, its cool. As you can see, her bean head ass ain't stop shit ⊠

Joyy:

Needless to say, we glad you beat her ass. Reina told us that wasn't y'all first time getting into it.

> Nah… it wasn't. But that's another story for another day.

> Reign is gonna pull up on her to try and talk some sense into her. He doesn't want her pressing charges on you for a fight she started.

> and her ugly ass friends scattered like roaches. The security guard had to help her up ⊠

I remembered me and Reign's conversation last night and my cheeks warmed. What he said was true as fuck and here I went ruining the moment. I sighed, running my fingers through my hair. I texted Reina on the side and told her that I needed to come and get it touched up because it smelled like liquor. I actually really liked this style and wanted to wear it for a couple weeks before I got it loc'd or braided up. Falling back on my pillows, we chatted for a minute and then I sent a text to Reign.

> Hey Reign… thank you for walking me to my door last night.

He didn't respond, he just liked it with the thumbs up emoji.
Okay. Weird.

But then I figured that he was probably busy and would respond later. I also wanted to apologize for my forwardness but then I thought about it. Reign was giving me the vibes all night. Not like he wanted to fuck per se, but like he...likes me. From helping me put my shoes on, sitting me down to drink water, and letting me dance on him – maybe I was just reading too deeply into things because it had been a minute since I had male attention. I knew I was an attractive woman but I was engrossed in opening my restaurant. I rarely posted myself on social media, but when I did, my comments and DMs went up. And, when we were in the club last night, niggas was definitely eyeing me. When Chewy made a comment about me being fine, Reign shot him a nasty, silent look that he didn't think I peeped, and Chewy fell back and started paying more attention to Reina and the twins.

I felt a little confused, because I couldn't tell if he was just being nice or if he liked me but I knew I wasn't imagining shit.

***

"Reina... Imma ask you something. But if you make it a big deal, I'm not asking you shit else again," I spun around in her chair as she curled the end of my hair. Reina chuckled, feigning innocence.

"Me? Make something a big deal? That don't even sound like me. Wassup though?"

I rolled my eyes and took a deep breath. "Does your brother have a girlfriend or something?"

Reina grinned and when she saw me cut my eyes at her, she wiped the grin off her face quickly.

"Nah.. not a girlfriend per se. Bitches he fucks? Yeah. Bitches who think they're his girlfriend? Maybe a couple. But he isn't taking nobody serious."

I rolled my eyes. I couldn't understand the twinge of jealousy that surged through my body. Reign was a single, attractive man. Why wouldn't he be free to fuck and do whatever he wanted?

"One thing you gotta know about us is that we some weird ass Aquarius's girl. Commitment ain't really our thing but for the right ones we will. Why you think I keep a couple in rotation?" she laughed and stuck her tongue out. Reina was right. So many niggas vied for Reina's attention but she dealt with them only when she felt like it, which was rare because she said most nigga's were nothing but liabilities and headaches.

I sighed. A part of me felt conflicted because of the dead ex-boyfriend thing and the other part of me felt like I should say fuck it. I wanted to know what it was like to be liked, to be looked out for with no ulterior motives, and eventually...to be loved again. I missed the intimacy of having someone be *my* person. And I wasn't sure if Reign could or would be all that for me, but a part of me was willing to explore the attraction. But I refused to be the only adventurous and fearless one in whatever *this* is.

And, it could just be nothing.

Like, maybe I *was* tweaking.

But then, I thought about his actions when we all went out that night and I just – yeah... I didn't know about Mr. King.

But I was determined to find out.

***

One thing I could say about Reign is that he was a man of his word. Turns out, he also owned a construction company called Krowned Construction and a plumbing/HVAC system company as well. He built his shop and Reina's. He helped Vibes and Lines with their electrical and plumbing needs. And he serviced other business owners in the neighborhoods. In addition, he hosted an annual block party and back-to-school festival for the community, hosted barber camps for teens, and mostly kept out of trouble.

Not bad for a former street nigga.

He had a small team of four working day in and day out in my restaurant, and the plumbing issue was almost rectified. He refused to let me pay him and when I tried to send the three stacks he sent me back to him, he sent it back with a *"Stop fuckin' playing with me"* message attached to it.

Rude.

He still wasn't very responsive to me so I did the next best thing I knew how to do: I would cook him some of his favorites, put on one of my best outfits, and drop it off to him. It very much gave Molly The Maid but I needed him to tell me to my face that I was tweaking or that I was imagining a spark between us.

I made some jerk wings, a side of six-cheese baked macaroni, and some cabbage with andouille sausage in it. Reina had touched up my hair and it was a rare day that the weather in Chicago wasn't being bipolar, so I dressed in a short, black bubble skirt, a white Diesel tank with blue accents, and black Dior sandals. I had a fresh all white pedicure on display, and I smelled divine, like crisp green apples and honey. After I was done here, I was going to go sip wine and listen to R&B across the street because every month, Vibes and Lines hosted a very intimate show for poets and R&B singers to showcase their talent.

After dropping some food off to the workers, I sauntered down to the barbershop and immediately, all eyes were glued to me. Smiling at Goldyn, I promised that I would bring a plate for her and her son the next time I cooked.

"Aye! Chef Mike Tyson just walked in the building!" Chewy's ignorant ass called out and I flipped him the bird. Every time the guys who went out with us that night saw me now, they always joked about how I laid Trice's ass out.

"Shut up Chewy! Is ya boy back there?" I asked, already making my way towards the back.

"Chef Rae, I got a hundred dollars and my mama's link card. Is that enough to have yo' fine ass in my kitchen cooking every night? I heard you gets down," some ogre looking guy with the most yellow looking teeth I'd ever seen cheesed at me. His teeth reminded me of the nacho cheese you poured over meat and Doritos. I was disgusted.

"A hundred dollars?"

"Yes."

"*And* yo mama's link card?" I rubbed my chin as if I was contemplating it.

"Yup. And her shit come on at midnight," he leaned up as Chewy just muttered and shook his head, snatching the cape off him.

"Not a chance in hell, Shrek." I quipped, and the whole shop fell out, clowning ole boy. I left them to laugh and continued my way to Reign's office. I knocked twice and he yelled for me to come in.

"Here. I brought you some food," I put the container of food on his desk and took a seat in the chair across from it, crossing my legs. He eyed me curiously, opened it and inhaled the smell, a satisfied look on his face.

"Good looks. What you on?"

"I got a question," I started, feeling nervous all of a sudden.

"Wassup?"

"Why you been avoiding me?"

"I'm a busy man, love… I'm not avoiding you."

"Yes you have. So are we really not gonna talk about that night? I picked up on some vibes, I just wanna make sure I'm not tweaking."

He pushed a forkful of mac in his mouth and sighed. I stared at him, taking in his features and reminded myself to stay focused. Reign was the type of man that made a bitch wanna cook, clean, and wash everything. He was never the loudest in the room, but definitely the most impactful. More than anything, I liked his energy. It was calming and alluring, and very safe.

"You mean before or after you asked me to kiss you?"

My face warmed and for a split second, I diverted my gaze.

"About that…"

"Nah shorty. Don't renege now. Stand on yo' shit."

"Alright then. It may have been all the liquor I had, but it is what it is," I shrugged. "But I'm really talking about the vibes before. Do you like me Reign?"

His expression was unreadable at first and then he broke out into a rare grin.

"You been listening to my messy ass sister again?" he deflected.

"Reign!"

"Aight, look… I think you fine as fuck Desiraè. You got a good head on yo' shoulders. You about yo' business and I think that shit is sexy as fuck. But a nigga is conflicted, because Shawn was my right hand. Not just my lil cuz, but my silent partner in a lot of things… he talked about you a lot, especially before he died. He always mentioned how he fumbled you and all that shit. So as sexy, cool, and as ambitious I think you are, that's just a line I can't see myself crossing. My nigga is in the ground but loyalty lasts forever."

We stared at each other and I chewed my bottom lip, contemplating what I wanted to say next.

"My bad then. Take care Reign," I stood up and walked towards the door. Walking through the barbershop, all eyes were glued on me once again and I walked across the street, to drown my feelings in wine. I wasn't one to beg a nigga to fuck with me. And honestly? Reign wasn't wrong for feeling how he felt on the matter because it *was* taboo, in a sense. I felt a little stupid, but also understood that hey – its life.

***

"So how did his admission make you feel?" Doc asked, kicking off the start of our session.

"Salty, but understanding at the same time."

"Why salty?"

"Because... I like him. And I really wish I didn't, but I do. At the same time, I understand his hesitancy, so I won't push for it. There's always other niggas right?"

Doc nodded. "Yes, there are... and it's okay to feel what you feel too. Have you thought about how you're going to navigate being around him? From our last conversation, you explained how you and his sister were getting close. How do you think the conversation between you two will impact the relationship between you and her?"

I shrugged. "I haven't really thought of that. I'm just going to be normal. We didn't have sex or even kiss, so no need to be weird about it you know? Now if he starts acting weird or avoidant then that's on him."

"Do you think she will insert herself in between you all?"

I shook my head. We jokingly called Reina messy but she was actually really chill and minded her business. "No. But if she did, I don't mind setting a boundary. She's honest, so she told me that he already has women he entertains but she didn't offer any other information. I think she would respect my wishes if I expressed any discomfort."

"Well, that's good. Sometimes connections can get complicated and since you are building new friendships, I'd hate for them to get messy due to unspoken expectations or boundaries being crossed." We chatted some more and then Doc decided to poke at my feelings a bit more. The people were not lying when they said grief comes in waves. I was still coming to terms with the fact that Shawn wasn't here anymore and it felt weird.

"Do you think this attraction that you have to his cousin is powered by grief?"

I paused, thinking really hard about it. "I don't know. I don't think so, because I didn't even know him before everything happened. The first time I ever saw him was when I pulled up on my old block and while I took note of how cute he was, at the time I wasn't aware of his relation to Shawn. The couple times we did have conversations, it was about business. I actually didn't know they were related until I...I pulled up to the hospital." My voice cracked on the last part and I squeezed my eyes shut. As much as I wanted to wipe my memory clean, I don't think I would ever forget seeing Shawn's body laying on the ground like that.

"If anything, the attraction is rooted in how he supports my dreams. I don't think I've ever had that before. Sure, Dre paid for culinary school but when I started really making plans to open my restaurant, that's when his weird behavior started. Reign didn't know me from a can of paint, but told me I could come sell plates at his shop whenever I wanted, booked me to cater his camp, and even put other business owners in the neighborhood on to me. He heard me complaining about my plumbing issue and not only is handling it, but refuses to let me pay him for it. Or maybe he did it off the strength of what Shawn meant to him and wanted to extend that same grace to me."

Now I was feeling confused.

"It's hard to tell. Maybe it's not so binary and a combination of both." Doc countered.

"I would ask him but I'm not willing to have a conversation about it with him. He already told me that exploring the attraction goes against his principles and I don't want to do that to him. I'm not pressed. It's just a crush and I'll get over it soon."

"Understood. Emotionally, what are you looking for right now?"

"Nothing." I lied and Doc knew I was lying.

"Desiraè..." she warned.

I smirked.

"I don't know Doc. I get lonely. I *do* desire companionship and I miss having someone I can call *my* person you know? I ain't had sex since sex had me, and I *do* want to experience love in a way that's healthy. Maturity has helped me realize that I don't want to be someone's beginning or end...that's way too much pressure. I think I became that to Dre, and perhaps that was the root of his weird ass behavior. If the relationship has run its course, I think we should all have the right to move around without fearing harm. I want someone to choose me fully, not out of guilt or obligation. I don't want nobody feeling sorry for me because of what I've been through because I am past it. I want somebody who sees love as a choice and respect as a non-negotiable. That's what I want. That's what I need. That's what I *know* I deserve. So yeah... I wanna be a lover girl and all that shit, but I'm not in the mood to compromise myself *ever* again to get it."

It took a long time for me to realize that. I fell in love with the idea of loving myself and actually practicing it. I also knew that there was a big difference between self-love and desiring romantic love and neither cancels out the other. Doc taught me that self-love goes hand-in-hand with romantic love because loving yourself doesn't stop once you get in a relationship. For whatever reason, us women tended to lose ourselves when we got with somebody, giving them too much power to destroy us. I didn't want to experience that ever again in life.

"Desiraè, I have to say that I'm truly proud of you at this moment. You have come a long way and I am confident that with this newfound mindset, you will find what you are looking for in a partner...this isn't to say that it won't be difficult but, I know you are up for the challenge," Doc winked. We chatted a bit more and I walked away from that session feeling more confident.

Reign's stance on not exploring us was valid and I was comfortable enough with myself to be okay with that. I was young, turnt, fine as hell, and had a restaurant on the way. Sometimes the answers to life was fifty bands, not a nigga. And with my restaurant opening soon, who knew if I would even have time for love anyway?

Chapter Sixteen

Reign

Two months later...

Desiraè Thomas was gonna be a muthafuckin problem. Ever since she pulled up that day on Sangamon and then started coming around the shops, I was intrigued by her. My messy ass sister was convinced that we would end up together, but I couldn't do that to my cousin Shawn.

I sighed, sparked my blunt and inhaled as I thought about my fallen nigga. First cousins through our fathers, we lost touch for a while when my OG sent me and my twin to live with our Nana, but reconnected once we were some older young niggas. By that time, Shawn was married to Trice and on baby number two, but he always talked about a bitch that he regretted getting away. She was his first love, and he admitted that he used to do her dirty. I side-eyed the fuck outta him when he told me that he had four years on her and started fucking with her when she was fourteen, but the shit was so normalized in the hood, that what could I say? As conflicted as Shawn was, he was my blood.... And niggas thought it was okay to take him from me. From us.

Shawn wasn't all the way clean, but he wasn't all the way dirty either. He was co-owner of my barbershop and a silent partner in my construction company. The nigga also had a trucking business, a grocery store, and even coached little league football for the lil' niggas in the neighborhood. And niggas hated him. Since a lil nigga he had the streets on lock, selling everything from weed, to white girl, to pills that had gotten popular over the years. He took care of his entire family, put his siblings through school, and tried to retire his hoe ass mama from running the streets, even when she gave him her ass to kiss. Shawn was thorough like that. If he ever complained about his load, I never heard it.

I exhaled the potent weed as it traveled through my lungs. Thinking about Shawn made me feel everything and nothing at once but today, I didn't have time to dwell – I needed to get up and head out the door since today was the annual start of the summer block party that my shop sponsored every year. We closed down the street and offered free hair cuts, had bouncy houses, petting zoos, barbecued, and had a vendor fair for different business owners to come and sell their shit. When the party for the kids had run its course, we brought out live music performers and poetry artists sponsored by Vibes and Lines. It was a good, safe time that everybody needed. Though born in Englewood, my teenage years weren't spent in this area, so as an adult I moved back and gave back whenever I could. I used to be a fuckin' menace to society – now I just chilled, cut a few select niggas hair, and stayed out the way.

Unless it had something to do with my favorite chef.

Her and my messy ass sister were building a friendship and I already knew she was a solid ass woman. Yeah, she was beautiful, had a nice 'lil shape, but it was her hustle and ambition that got me. In a world where some women her age were trying to attach themselves to any nigga with money, Rae was on a mission to get it herself. She also just had good energy, and I knew it from the first time me and her ever exchanged words. She was what I'd like to call whimsical – curious about the world and going with the flow of life, but locked in and determined to make her dreams come true. When she talked, she made you want to hang on to every word. She ain't even know that every time she spoke on her restaurant, it made me wanna go harder with all my businesses. I could definitely see her becoming a widely-known chef and having people from all over the world come dine with her.

And I wanted to do everything in my power to make sure that happened.

***

Pulling off my block, I needed to handle something that had been bothering me for a couple months now. LaTrice was a thorn in my side. I wanted to dig Cuz up and ask him why the fuck he would stick his dick in this bird brain bitch? She was messy, miserable, and a fuckin' loser. She walked around causing drama wherever she went and it took the strength of a hundred angels not to let my sister knock her the fuck out. Granted, more often than not, Shawn was on some fuck shit with other bitches. It was nothing for Trice to pop up on him raising hell.

One time she pulled up to Reina's shop because she got word that one of her clients was fucking him. Okay, address that man or that bitch on your own time. We couldn't understand why she would bring that bullshit to Reina's shop. It was so embarrassing how Trice tore up her shop, knocking windows out and all, and what's worse is that she didn't even apologize to

Reina or offer to pay for her window to be replaced. So, Reina banned her from stepping foot on the premises and I didn't blame her.

I always thought cheating was some wild ass shit to do, especially on your wife. Trice thought she should receive a jersey or some type of trophy for being stupid enough to stick around while Shawn did his thing. Trice used to be real bad, like the type of bad where if you brought her around to your family reunion, there would be an uncle somewhere dapping you up, saying some *"I see you nephew."*

Over the years, she was still attractive but I could tell that the stress and drama that came from dealing with Shawn was taking a toll on her physically and mentally, which meant her appearance was getting impacted too. Quiet as its kept, niggas didn't respect women who were stupid for them. Niggas like Shawn needed to be left alone the first time and *maybe* he would tighten up. But Trice never listened and now look at her: mourning her dead husband who barely wanted to be married to her ass, who was pining over his ex-bitch.

I should stop calling Desiraè a bitch. I actually respect her, because I can tell she don't play. I tried to get some info outta Reina about her, but all she told me was that Cuz was her first love and that their relationship was toxic at best and that they haven't seen each other since she was like eighteen or nineteen. Otherwise, my sister was mute. Told me that if I wanted to know something about her, that I needed to stop being pussy and ask myself. What the fuck was the point of having a twin if they ain't gone give you the info that you want to know?

I couldn't do anything but respect it though.

Pulling on Trice's block, I sighed and looked around the quiet tree-lined street that her two-story brick home sat on. Shawn had his family ducked off all the way in Winnetka, famous for the house in the movie Home Alone. They actually lived two blocks over. Walking up the porch and ringing the doorbell, it took her a minute to come open the door, and when she did, she had a look of disgust painted all over her face.

"What the fuck is you doing here Reign? Shouldn't you be playing captain save a hoe with my opps?"

I scoffed. "Trice, she wasn't the one who needed saving."

Trice tried to slam the door in my face, but my size twelve foot stopped her from doing so. Pushing the door open, I crossed her threshold, and she backed into a wall, arms crossed and the meanest mug across her face.

"Why the fuck are you here, Reign?"

"I need to holla at you. I thought we agreed that you wouldn't press no charges against that girl?"

I had gotten word from one of my police homies that LaTrice was trying to build a case against Desiraè for that fight at the club a couple months back even though she started it. Trice had to go to the hospital to get stitches and found out her nose was broken in two different places, but I didn't have no sympathy for that girl because I watched her start shit with Desiraè because she was insecure. I could see if Rae was a hot head and just went around beating bitches up, but she wasn't like that. Very similar to me, she was laid back until she had to lean up. And when she leaned up, she wasn't one to do too much talking. She was hitting you in your shit and then done with the situation.

My type of bitch – I mean, lady. I mean, not *my* lady.

Fuck.

"You fucking her or something Reign? Why are you this concerned? This has nothing to do with you," Trice spat. I glared at her. Trice was so damn hateful and evaded accountability at every turn.

"Trice, you don't know me well enough to be in my fuckin' business like that. It don't matter if I'm fucking her or not, what matters is that you started shit with that girl and she finished it. Take yo' L like a grown ass woman and stop writing checks that yo' ass can't cash. It's pitiful."

Trice looked me up and down with disgust. "I know that dick well enough though."

The air in the room got thicker and if I was into putting my hands on women, I would choke the shit out of this bird brain bitch. Running my tongue across my teeth, I invaded her space and leaned down real close to her ear.

"Bitch, all you're good for is sucking dick and you can barely do that right. You over here a fuckin' widow getting beat up by his ex-bitch from when he was a young nigga, and can't seem to focus long enough to stop starting shit yo' ass can't finish. Speak on me again, and I can promise you, you can join your husband."

"Oh fuck you Reign! Stop trying to act like you a fuckin' saint. You're not! I'm only good for sucking dick but you were sliding in me like what, two, three times a week? Nigga please," she scoffed and walked down the hallway to her kitchen.

Okay, I was a flawed nigga. Fucking my cousin's wife was some shit that just happened, and it wasn't a moment that I was proud of. One day she was on a rampage trying to pop up on Shawn and I tried to console her since I knew where he was, but I wasn't going to tell her. Over a couple drinks, she started pushing up on me and since it had been a minute since

I slid in some pussy, I let her suck my dick. We fucked a couple times after that – the pussy was okay. I definitely had better, so I cut her off. I couldn't look my cheating ass cousin in the face knowing that I had crossed the line with his wife. Plus, I just ain't do drama, and Trice was a dramatic ass bitch. Imagine a bitch crying about how her husband doesn't love and respect her, while she has his cousin's dick hitting the back of her throat. That was over a year ago, way before he died and Trice's hoe ass knew it. Thank God I never hit the bitch raw.

"I ain't no saint shorty, but you heard what the fuck I said. If I find out that you're trying to press charges on her or bash her on the internet, Imma make sure you join your husband and yo' kids will be raised by foster parents."

Her eyes glowered with rage and then defeat. Trice knew I wasn't one to be fucked with and even if her intentions for having children were fucked up, she did love and care for those lil' niggas.

"Alright, Reign…you got it. Now can you please get the fuck out my house?"

I was already walking down the hall by the time she said that and hopped in my blacked out Range Rover.

Desiraè Thomas was a muthafuckin problem. But for her, I'd solve every single one.

***

The block party was in full swing when I pulled up. Parking in the back, I walked through the shop to dap some niggas up and observe what was going on outside. In our parking lot was where the food was, and smack dab in the middle was Desiraè's fine ass. She had on a pair of light wash, denim shorts, some raw ass sky blue retro Jordan 4's, a white tank top and a sky blue baseball jersey that said *Mz. Earline's Kitchen* on the back. She had these long ass box braids in, both light brown and chocolate brown colored that brought out her eyes. I wasn't close to her, but I knew she smelled good – Rae always smelled good, like something floral or fruity. She had a table set up out there and it looked like she had her people's with her. Her OG was out there, a big nigga on the grill, and a younger nigga and two other women I never saw before helping her set up and pass things ou t.

"That bitch bad as fuck ain't she?" Chewy's voice interrupted my observation of Rae, and I shot him a steely look. When we all went out that night, I peeped that Chewy was trying to get on that with her, but in so many words, I told his ass to chill. Selfish, I know, but I ain't give a fuck. Desiraè wasn't mine... but she for sure wouldn't be with that nigga either. Chewy was a hoe in every sense of the word. He had like five kids by four different women and hoes stayed busting out the windows of his car or flattening the tires on it. I grilled his ass so hard that night that he had no choice but to harass my sister and the twins since they didn't take his ass seriously.

It was something about Desiraè that made me want to shield her from all the fuck shit these niggas had to offer – even if that nigga was me. I had already betrayed my cousin once by sliding with LaTrice's dumb ass. I couldn't betray him again by getting with his first love.

But I'd be a liar if I said that in a perfect world, I wouldn't be willing to explore that attraction with her. Her body felt so right up against mine when she danced on me at the club. She smelled good as fuck, and she had that shit on too. I could appreciate a fly ass woman, since I was a pretty fly nigga myself.

"My fault, folk. I forgot yo' ass likes her," Chewy chuckled as he looked over at her. I mugged his ass, walking over to get a plate of food. Chewy followed behind me, laughing and talking shit. The line was long but I didn't mind waiting. The burly nigga was grilling hot dogs, jerk wings, salmon, steak, and veggies and she had sides of her infamous mac and cheese, baked beans, and pasta salad. My stomach grumbled, as I realized that nothing touched my stomach today. I loved this girl's cooking man. I was decent in the kitchen but Desiraè cooked like somebody's big armed g ranny.

I wondered if her pussy tasted just as good as her food did.

We moved up in line and I dropped a hundred dollars in her lil tip jar, just to irritate her.

"Wassup Reign?" She spoke coolly. Ever since that day she popped up on me at the shop and I told her that I couldn't pursue nothing with her, we didn't talk or see each other much. Her and Reina were still tight, and they saw each other often. I had my employees wrap up her plumbing work and now her restaurant was almost ready to open.

I nodded to her and then watched as she swept her eyes towards Chewy and saw them brighten.

"Hey Chewy!" She perked up and came from behind the table to give Chewy a hug. My brows furrowed slightly before I changed my face to my signature stoic look. Showing all thirty-two of her teeth, I listened as her and Chewy joked and talked shit to each other.

If Chewy wasn't my nigga, I'd shoot him.

Well, maybe shooting him was a bit extreme, but I was pissed. What the fuck was so special about Chewy that she was letting her dimples pop out and giving him hugs? If she was my bitch, I would be snatching her little ass up.

I walked off on them before I did something out of character, until I heard my name get called in a sugary sweet voice. I spotted Karma, my bitch who wasn't my bitch and swaggered over to her. She was there with two of her home girls that worked in her shop.

Karma was a girl that I had known for a while. She was a lash tech and owned a shop over on the next block. She was exactly how I liked them: brown-skinned, big lips, thick, and could suck a mean dick. If I was interested in settling down, she *might* be the woman who would fill the position. She was relatively chill, always answered when I called, and most importantly – not messy. She didn't require silly shit like dates or anything, and I suspected that was because she had a nigga in her life who already played that position.

Rumor had it that she had some old ass nigga funding her lifestyle and that was fine, because that meant that she wasn't really in my pockets. Don't get me wrong, I wasn't a stingy nigga. I didn't mind spending a lil' bread and buying shit for a bitch's birthday or something, but I wasn't no pull up on you with flowers, send you good morning texts, fly you out type of nigga. And I damn sure wasn't spending no bread if I ain't least know what the bottom of a bitch pussy felt like.

Except, I did a ten thousand dollar plumbing job for Desiraè's restaurant for free and paid her three bands to cater my barber camp. She tried to send that shit back to me but I told her to stop fuckin' playing with me.

Conflicted, is what I was. Maybe a little bit of a hypocrite too.

"Wassup Karm? Wassup ladies?" I gave Karma a side hug and then nodded at the ladies. They greeted me back and then walked in line to grab them food.

"Not much...I missed you this week," she batted her long ass lashes and discreetly felt on my dick, and I instantly bricked up. I stepped back a little because secret or not, I didn't do all that PDA shit.

"My bad about that. Just been hella busy."

"Mmmhmm. I hear you. Well, holla if you need me," she gave me another side hug and I admired her thick ass switching away in her denim skirt. Biting my bottom lip, I made a mental note to hit her fine ass up later when the block party ended.

"You know she's fucking an old ass man, right?" Reina's messy ass appeared out of thin air beside me. I looked at my twin and grilled her.

"Reina, stay out of people's business," I retorted. Karma's business was her business, as long as she ain't bring me nothing back. But it wasn't like I was sliding in her raw anyway. For whatever reason, most niggas didn't believe in using condoms which was astonishing, because most niggas I knew had kids they ain't even plan for or more trips to the clinic than they cared to admit.

I could never fold for that and prided myself on getting tested every other month or whenever I got a new sex partner.

Reina's eyes landed on Desiraè's table and she stared back at me, eyes burning a hole in the side of my face.

"When you gone stop being pussy and tell her that you wanna date her?"

"Reina..." I sighed.

"Nah, twin. Don't deflect. You gone let Chewy of all niggas try and snatch her up?"

"*Reina*!" I stressed.

My twin and I were close. She knew all about me and LaTrice because one night that bitch was blowing my phone up, sending nasty videos and Reina happened to see it. She cursed me out so bad and didn't talk to me for a week straight. What was funny about that is that we shared a two-flat apartment building, me living upstairs while she lived downstairs. She walked past me as if I was just some nigga on the streets and wouldn't talk to me again until I cut her off.

"I'm just saying. Though, I don't think she takes him seriously."

Sure didn't look like it to me. After Chewy finished his food, Desiraè had him behind her table passing out plates to customers and the nigga looked like he enjoyed it. Desiraè was the type of woman where you'd do anything just to be in her presence. So I really couldn't blame my nigga, even if I did think he ain't deserve to breathe the same air she breathed. If he kept this bullshit up, he wouldn't be breathing at all.

I sighed once again, pulling my phone out and told Karma that I was sliding to her crib after this.

Desiraè Thomas was a muthafuckin' problem, and I wanted her to be mine to solve.

Chapter Seventeen

Dre

I remember the first time I fell in love with Desiraè. It was fourth period in high school, and we had a couple honors classes together. The teacher called on her to answer a question about the reading, and she answered it correctly, impressing everyone in the class because our teacher assigned us a hard ass book to read. I think it was Sula, by Toni Morrison. English wasn't my favorite class, I was more of a math and science nigga. Desiraè was somebody you just took notice of. Not because she went out her way to command attention, but because she just had this aura about her that made you want to know who she was and what she was about.

So I put myself in her line of vision and for a while, I thought she wasn't fucking with me. I would leave her notes in her locker, buy her small things for her birthday, and even call her Gramz's house phone for her when we got assigned a group project together. I quickly found out she had a boyfriend though, and instantly knew that nigga was a fuckin' therm. I hated his ass, not just for the chokehold he had on my baby, but also because he was the reason that my OG wasn't amongst the living. My OG was a drug addict and LaShawn Davis's bitch ass was her supplier. It's because of him, I had to go from foster care to foster care, until I was able to emancipate myself at sixteen. I remember when I first realized that my mama was on drugs. It's like she changed overnight. She went from having a thriving career as a nurse to becoming thin and cracked out. I'm not sure what led her to go from full-time nurse to full-time crackhead but it fucked my life up.

Desiraè reminded me a lot of my mama. Not the crackhead part – but the good parts I remembered about my mama. The sad parts too. My OG was sad a lot and when I first met Desiraè, she was too. Her beautiful brown eyes were filled with so much sadness and I just wanted to make her feel better all the time. I wanted to save her in ways that I couldn't save my OG. So, I made myself available. When she arrived on my doorstep that day, battered, bloodied, and broken, I knew I finally had my chance to save her.

But with a woman like Desiraè, you couldn't put too much on her at once, or she would run. I knew I had to be her friend first. Not let my desire to have her, hold her, *possess* her overshadow the need to make her feel safe.

To tear her walls down.

To show her that I was all she needed in this world.

I would play whatever role she needed me to, as long as it ended with her being mine.

I loved her. I loved everything about her, even the parts I couldn't figure out.

But in due time, I figured her out. And even her ugly parts, I still loved.

Desiraè was a woman who needed taming.

Except, she wasn't a woman who desired to be possessed. I remember when we broke up at her grandmother's funeral. Murderous thoughts plagued my mind and I wanted to end her and LaShawn right then and there. But I wasn't a street nigga. And, I could never hurt my baby. So as much as it broke me, I had to let her go.

But something told me that she would run to her Gramz's house and when I found her unresponsive on that bathroom floor, I knew I had to call Ms. Nicole and save her. And let her go. It took two years for us to reconnect. I went to school, got a degree, and purposely stayed in touch with her mama until I could make my move. During our separation, I fucked plenty of hoes and paid for plenty of abortions. There was only one woman that I wanted to have my kids and rock my last name. When we finally reconnected, it was rocky at first. A part of me felt like a bitch for how petty I was being towards her. But it was all a part of my plan. I even entertained going to see lame ass Dr. Love if that's what it meant to get my baby back. Dr. Love made me uncomfortable though, because I think she was able to see right through my facade. She asked me plenty of hard questions, and a couple times, my mask slipped.

Right when D and I got on the same footing, I played the role of doting and supportive boyfriend.

She told me she wanted to go to culinary school, so I paid for it as long as we could move in together. She acquiesced and we started living together again. I came home to home cooked meals and in house pussy almost daily. Desirae didn't have to work, or go to school if she didn't want to. She didn't pay bills in the apartment that we shared.

But she wanted more.

Always wanted more, and I hated it.

She started going harder in culinary school. Then she got head chef-in-training at her job. Then she started talking about how she wanted to pause on trying to have kids. She went and got birth control in her arm and I was pissed, because that meant that I couldn't fuck with it. She no longer depended on or needed me, and I was the type of nigga who *needed* to feel needed.

I loved Desirae with everything in me and that night when we argued, my mask slipped again. So I left, before she realized who I truly was. I figured that I would give her some space for a few days and then we would come to a compromise. I figured that proposing at her graduation would have her overlook how I moved towards her and the fact that I broke the promise we made.

Imagine my surprise when I realized that not only did my baby not want to hear me out, but she also wasn't going to take me back either. Desiraè was done with me and from there, my world began to crumble.

***

I walked up to Mama Nicole's front door and squared my shoulders. What I was about to do was crazy, but I was a man in love. I fucked up, and I just wanted an opportunity to make things right. I was hurt that she turned down my proposal, but figured that all she needed was a bit of time and space.

I wanted to go to the next level with Desiraè. I rang the doorbell and replayed what I was going to say over and over in my mind. I would get on my knees in one hundred-degree weather wearing a leather outfit, if that's what it took to get my baby back. She opened the door with a puzzled look on her face.

"Ummm.... can I help you?" she asked, like a fucking customer service agent. Ever since she started therapy and worked hard not to curse people out anymore, whenever she was mad or annoyed, she talked to us like she was an HR professional or something.

I'd rather be cursed out. At least then, I knew she still actually gave a fuck. Desiraè was so cold when she didn't give a fuck about something, and I was never on the receiving end of it until recently. I wanted her to still give a fuck about me even though I fucked up.

"DeAndre? Why are you here?" she asked again, her hand on her hip and a scowl across her pretty face. She was dressed down this day, and I heard loud chatter from the living room. Mama Nicole and Jamaal loved to host, so it didn't surprise me that there was some type of kickback or barbecue going on. If you were blessed to be in their tight-knit circle, then you knew your belly and heart would be full because Desiraè and her family were genuinely good people.

I wasn't too prideful to admit that I missed them. My mama was dead, I never knew my sperm donor, and I was an only child as far as I knew. Sometimes, I felt like Desiraè didn't know how blessed she was, especially during the years she was estranged from her family.

"I... I came to talk to you. I miss you, bae. And I want you to hear me out," I replied earnestly. Her eyes turned colder, and she pressed her lips together in a thin line.

"No thanks," she replied flatly and went to slam the door in my face. Before she could, I snatched her close to me and in one swift motion, I tossed her over my shoulder. She screeched loudly and started beating on my back as I took three long strides to get to my car. Before I could fully reach it, I felt another body slam into us, sending us both flying against the lawn. Desiraè screamed, and I heard Jamaal ask if she was okay.

I sat up in the grass and immediately felt Dayvon's fist fly into my face. He uppercut me so hard that my neck snapped back. Dayvon was really quiet, usually played the background, and didn't say too much. He loved his sister, though, and was her silent protector. We didn't talk too much, but that was because he didn't talk too much to anyone. I never heard him raise his voice, let alone ever saw him fight.

But because he shared the same blood as Desiraè, I should've known that he wasn't no hoe when it came to fighting, because his sister wasn't either. Jamaal came over and snatched me to my feet, then gave me quick body shots that had my knees buckling. I couldn't even put my hands up to defend myself. To be honest, I wasn't much of a fighter. I knew how to defend myself, but these two niggas were animals.

Mayhem ensued, and all I felt were fists and feet on various parts of my body. I swear I felt my ribs crack.

"Bitch ass nigga! Why the fuck did you pop yo ass up over here and think you was leaving with her?"

Before I could answer Dayvon, he popped me dead in the mouth and pummeled my face repeatedly, while Jamaal kicked me in my stomach. It was chaos around us, and only the sounds of sirens and a few people pulling them off me made them stop.

I refused to go to the hospital and limped my sorry ass to my car and drove off, feeling defeated. My pride was shattered because not once did I hear Rae scream for them to stop. Jamaal was plugged with the police in Bloomington so I couldn't even press charges, especially since I showed up on their property unprovoked. They had ring cameras for their front door, so I know they wouldn't hesitate to turn over the footage and get me locked up.

I had to bow out gracefully and give everybody time to cool off. That's all they needed, some time.

Well, that time never came, because a couple of days later, not only was I blocked on every app and number in their circle, but I got served a restraining order the same day, too.

***

I stopped going down memory lane and peered over at a snoring Kamira. My fiancèe was almost eight months pregnant and bad as fuck. I liked her. I had love for her. I pretended like I was in love with her.

But she was no Desiraè.

I came across Kamira Clarke when I was on some fuck shit the first night me and Desiraè argued. She was a bartender at this hole-in-the-wall spot I sometimes frequented with co-workers and we got to chatting. She was a welcomed distraction, something to take my mind off the fact that I almost put my hands on Desiraè, something I promised that I would never do. I knew all about how her and that bitch ass nigga she used to be with always fought, and that was something I didn't want to bring in our relationship. D worked hard to control her anger and her words. Dr. Love may have been a lame to me, but that therapy shit seemed to be working for Desirae. I just think that I was a lost cause.

Although I wasn't in love with her, Kamira was like a breath of fresh air. She looked like a taller version of Keri Hilson, with the seductive eyes and all. I didn't lie to Desiraè when I told her that I didn't cheat on her. I didn't – but I did always return to the bar, especially after D turned down my proposal. The day that she turned down my proposal, I tucked my tail and went to the bar. Seven drinks of Hennessy on the rocks later, I shot my shot at Kamira. She was hesitant at first, but I convinced her. Once she got off, I was too drunk to drive home so we went to her place – a modest apartment not far from her job.

We didn't fuck that night, but the next night we did. When she asked about the anniversary date on my back and the initials on my chest, I lied and said it was in honor of my mama.

And for a moment, I had a new addiction. Kamira's pussy was good – so good that I didn't bother strapping up, asking for test results, or anything responsible. I wanted kids more than I wanted anything in this world, and at that point, it didn't matter who they would be by. If Kamira didn't want to be a mama, I'd kill her and raise our kids as a single dad, then eventually find them a new mama.

Wait. I couldn't kill Kamira, she was too sweet. And unlike Desiraè, she didn't have this craving for independence. She would make the perfect trophy wife. Once she told me that she was eight weeks pregnant, I made her quit her job at the bar and move into me and D's old place. One day I came home from work and she was curled up on the couch, watching reels on Instagram. Sometimes, she would send me some throughout the day, shit she thought would make me laugh or meals she wanted to try.

Kamira was okay in the kitchen. She came second place to Desiraè, so sometimes I cooked or we would order out a lot. If I didn't have a vigorous gym routine, I'd be fat as hell with how much we ate out. I never told Kamira about Desiraè and from the video she showed me, I was glad I didn't. When I watched those videos, my blood began to boil. I was blocked from everything and had a restraining order put in place all because I popped up to Ms. Nicole's crib and tried to kidnap her. I was walking with a slight limp with the way that her brother Dayvon and her step daddy Jamaal beat my ass.

In the video, she was talking about her taking over as head chef for a restaurant in Chicago and how she would be participating in something called The Black Excellence Ball. From there, I set a plan in motion. Me and Kamira would be going to that ball. And, even if I didn't get to talk to her, I was going to see my baby up close. What I didn't expect was for her to see me in the audience. I didn't expect Kamira to go up and talk to her either, like she was some celebrity. The thing about being with someone for so long is that you were able to pick up on all their non-verbal expressions. I knew the many faces of Desiraè Janelle Thomas like the back of my hand. When her eyes swept over me, I couldn't read her expression. She seemed present, yet her mind was elsewhere too. Kamira had to pee, so that gave me enough time to slip in the crowd and make myself incognito.

I saw the slap.

I heard the argument.

And my blood began to boil once again.

You see, Desiraè didn't know that I knew all about him messaging her on Instagram.

I could understand it though, because she just had that effect on niggas. Long after she exited your life, she would still remain impactful. A scent, a show, a song – a lot of things reminded me of her. She took up space in my dreams at night and crowded my thoughts during the day.

So, though I thought LaShawn was a bitch, I understood why he kept sniffing after her because here I was engaged with a baby on the way, doing the same thing.

The difference between me and him though?

Desiraè belonged to me. Whether she wanted to or not.

I stayed tucked in the shadows that night.

Me and Kamira eventually moved up to Chicago.

And finally, Shawn was out the way.

Now, I just had to put the next part of my plan in motion.

Chapter Eighteen

Desiraè

Time was flying and I was now a month away from my restaurant opening. The interior construction was almost complete, kitchen equipment ordered, furniture delivered, and plumbing job complete. I passed all my building and state board inspections and now all I had to do was interview and hire some people. Deciding to push the soft opening back was actually the right idea. Instead of a soft opening, I decided to just continue to cater and give out samples and sell plates at the different community events that happened throughout the summer. That proved to be more impactful than I thought. Reign may have been an asshole, but he was right about people in the neighborhood not caring about my social media popularity, or if I graduated from culinary school or that I worked at La Reaux downtown. They wanted someone they could relate to and because of my age, I got underestimated a lot.

Until they tasted my food.

Then, they began singing their praises, trying to book me, and hounding me for plates whenever I would announce that I was selling. When I started out the social media roll out of announcing that the restaurant was opening soon and that I was hiring, there was a line of hundreds of people out the door who wanted a chance to work with me. I was overwhelmed and humbled. To work for me, you had to go through three rounds of interviews. I wanted quality people who had knowledge of the food industry, excellent customer service skills, and could take direction well. I planned to be very hands on, and didn't mind rolling up my sleeves to put in work. If you were applying to work in the kitchen, your interview was for me to show you how to make a dish and then you recreate it in your own way. Regardless if you had formal training or not, Gramz taught me that a real cook knew how to make any dish into their own. From the hostess down to the janitors, Mz. Earline's Kitchen would be a place that exuded excellence.

"Whew girl, you know I love you because it is early as shit," Reina yawned, making her way to the table I had set up for interviews.

It was Sunday morning, and it was round three of interviews and about fifty people stood outside waiting for me to open the doors. Reina had come to help me and keep me company, because in her words, "Ain't nobody gone be making my fave chef look bad – or I'd beat them up." I smirked at the thought. It was nice to make a new friend and you realize that they don't play about you. Dressed down in a pair of black pants and a Mz. Earline's tee, I slid her a mango smoothie and a breakfast sandwich I made for her.

For the next couple of hours, we held interviews with hella people. Reina was so seriously unserious the whole time. One question she asked was "Can you fight?" and can you believe that people had the nerve to answer her if they could or not? When I told her to chill, she told me that she needed to make sure I had people in here who could defend themselves and me if need be, because she wasn't always going to be available to run down from the shop and jump in.

I have no idea why I am friends with this lady y'all.

"We got anybody else? We need to go over the notes so you can call people back and start training them in the next week or so," Reina said. I shook my head, looking at my list and seeing all the names but one crossed out.

"Somebody named Kamira Clarke is on the list, but she didn't show up. I wanna go home and look over this list. And probably eat something too."

"Well, Imma grab some stuff from the shop and then trail you to your crib. You feel like cooking or you wanna order in?" she asked, and we discussed our plans for the evening. The closer I got to opening day, the less I felt like cooking. I would be getting back in my foodie bag and going to visit different restaurants throughout the city to satisfy my hunger. People thought chefs wanted to cook 24/7 and it's like no... There's no energy left after we service so many people. After putting up the tables and chairs, I looked around the progress of the restaurant and smiled. The white marble floors got laid last week, the furniture would be getting placed later in the week and my sign and door decals would be set up next week. I got a bit emotional and smiled. I was so proud of me and couldn't believe some nights that –

KNOCK!

KNOCK!

KNOCK!

KNOCK!

Four loud knocks or rather bangs on the door sounded off from the front as I came from the back. A tall, hooded man dressed in all black had his back turned and I furrowed my brows. Interviews were over an hour ago, and why was this man dressed in a hoodie in ninety degree weather? Walking slowly to the front, I unlocked the door and cracked it halfway.

"I'm sorry, if you're here for interviews, they were over an hour ago. If you follow the restaurant's social media pages, I'll post any hiring opportunities as they come up." I pulled my hand to close the door and lock it, but as soon as I did so, the man turned around suddenly and yanked the door back. Upon looking in his face, all the breath left my body as I stared at who I knew to be DeAndre.

***

"Wh-what the fuck are you doing here DeAndre?!"

Time froze as we stared at each other for a moment. I tried to back up but he pushed me roughly, forcing me further into the space as he locked the door behind him.

"It's been quite a long time Rae-Rae," he answered, a wild look in his eyes and his voice sounding ominous. Like he was here, but not really present. I blinked at his ass, and noticed that this goofy had shaved his head bald so now he was looking like a milk dud. He had always been tall and put on some muscle over the years, but his muscles looked a little flabby from what I could see in his hoodie. I rolled my eyes and walked off on him, picking up my phone and running into Reina and Reign as they came through the back.

"Why you looking like that?" Reign asked. I sighed.

"My stupid ass ex is in the front and I don't know what he wants but I'm irritated. I have a restraining order on him!"

Reign and Reina's eyes turned dark, almost black and both of them wore identical mean mugs on their faces as Reign pulled me behind him and walked towards the front.

"Who the fuck is you nigga? Get the fuck outta her establishment!" Reign yelled, the unmistakable sound of him taking the safety off his gun echoing throughout the space. I gulped and looked at Reina.

"D, I need you to relax and let my twin handle it. That nigga not gone make it out here alive," she said while patting her purse.

If I know Reina like I think I do, no matter what small designer bag she has for the day, she is also carrying something that will have yo' mama pulling out a black dress. In her infamous words, find you something safe to do.

I see exactly why I'm friends with her now.

Dre narrowed his eyes and sneered at me, the setting sunlight shining off his bald head and curled the corners of his lips up. He looked so fucking stupid!

"Damn, Desiraè, I see you ain't waste no time." My eyes bucked and my jaw dropped, because is this not the same nigga who is engaged with a damn kid on the way? One thing about a nigga, he will he have the audacity!

I peeked from behind Reign. "Boy, if you don't get the fuck out of my establishment!"

"I'm just here to make good on my promise baby. I made sure that bitch ass nigga Shawn couldn't bother you no more. I promised myself that when I got rid of him, I would come to collect you so that we could be a family once and for all.... Whether it's in this life or the afterlife my love."

I reared my head back and stepped fully around Reign who gently pushed me back behind him.

"A family? Nigga, you are either engaged or married with a fuckin' baby on the way! We broke up over a year ago! You have your family! Why the fuck are you here and bothering me stupid?!"

"Nah, you got it all wrong you see... you wanted LaShawn dead and I made sure it would happen. Kamira just gone have to understand that when she drops my baby, I'm gonna take it and raise it with you."

"I did not want LaShawn dead!"

"Bitch what?!"

"What the fuck is he talking about D?!"

All three of our voices yelled out in unison and we snapped our heads back in Dre's direction.

"Yes you did. You said, and I quote that you hope he and his bitch drop dead," and he pulled out his phone, pressed a button, and a recording from my argument with Shawn at the Black Excellence Ball filled the room.

"...In fact, I hope you and that stupid bitch die tonight just so I can make sure you don't say shit to me and you better not contact me from the afterlife either."

POW!

POW!

Reign fired his gun twice and it hit Dre in the right knee, dropping him instantly. But his weak ass villain monologue didn't stop there. This fool laughed maniacally, and clutched his bleeding knee, gritting through the pain. I looked at the twins and their expressions were unreadable and that scared me. Cause bitch, was I next?!

"You know Rae, I gotta give it to you. You surprised me. I thought I could get you in line and make you see things my way when I left you. You were never satisfied with the life I tried to give you, always wanted to be independent and do shit on your own, ignoring the fact that I saved yo dumb ass all them years ago when you tried to take yourself out on your Gramz's bathroom floor. I should've followed my first mind and left you for dead."

POW!

POW!

I ducked as Reign shot his gun twice in the other knee, cutting Dre's monologue short. My eyes stung at his words, but I refused to let those tears drop. I was more pissed that there was blood all over my new floors. It was baffling that Dre turned out to be this crazy... like had he always been this way and I just ignored the signs? And what the fuck did he mean that he made sure to get rid of Shawn? What in the crime show is this?

Reign turned around to look at me with murder in his eyes. Dre was groaning and Reina was eerily quiet.

"Call clean-up," he told Reina and walked towards the back of the restaurant, out the door.

Reina pulled her phone out and talked for three seconds and then confirmed that someone was on the way. About seven minutes later, three brown-skinned men pulled up and grabbed a groaning Dre who seemed to be in delirium from the pain. They took him through the back and dropped him in an non-descriptive white van and pulled off.

"Lock up," Reina called over her shoulder and I stood there frozen. Snapping out of it, I locked the restaurant up and Reina walked me to my car.

"Reina, I –"

She held her hand up. "Not right now G....We need some time to process and tie up this loose end but when I'm ready, Imma slide on you. I'm not sure about my brother though.... It's a good thing them cameras ain't get installed yet huh?" and she gave me a wry smile as she walked away to her car. I paused for a moment, then started my car to go home and wash the day off of me. This day had tweaked me out, but I doubted that sleep would come easy.

***

I tossed and turned all night. So much so that I got in my car and drove all the way down to Bloomington and laid on my mother's couch until they got up for breakfast in the morning. My mother took one look at me and bolted to the couch, putting my head in her lap as she stroked my hair. Jamaal came and sat on the opposite end of the couch, putting my sock covered feet in his lap.

"What the hell happened Baby Girl?" he asked, and the levees broke. My face crumpled in pain from recounting the words and actions of Dre. I didn't know if he was dead or alive and I was scared to death that his bullshit would fall back on me. It was astonishing to me that someone I shared my life with turned out to be such a looney toon. To think so lowly of me and throw my darkest time in my face. What did I ever do to deserve that? I never asked that nigga to save me. Doc and my parents were right, that nigga *was* jealous of me.

My mama was .38 hot, cussing and fussing as she paced around the living room.

"I'm so sorry baby! And you say your friends took care of it? Maybe we should call a lawyer... When did you say people were coming to install cameras in your spot? You need cameras on at all times Rae-Rae.... Jesus, I can't believe that bean head ass nigga! Jamaal, what can we do?"

"Nicki, we gotta relax. Rae baby, answer your phone. This the third time they done called," Jamaal said, looking down at my phone. It started up again and I noticed that it was Reina calling.

"I'm outside," she announced and then ended the call abruptly. I looked at my phone in bewilderment and remembered that me and her shared locations, so that's why she knew where I was. Walking to the front door, I opened to find Reina standing there with her arms folded. She was dressed in leggings, a white cropped shirt, and Crocs with hair stylist charms all over the top of the shoe. Ushering her in, I watched as she walked towards the living room and spoke to my parents. They had already met a couple times before.

"Should we give y'all some privacy?" Nicole asked. Reina shook her head.

"No, I think that what I have to say should be heard by all parties," and she pulled her gun out and set it on the coffee table. Nicole's eyes bucked, but me and Jamaal didn't look surprised at all. He just pulled his gun out the back of his waistband and sat it on the table too.

"Alright.... Yesterday was... a lot. I came over here to temperature check. I understand that you and my cousin had y'all issues, but be straight up with me.... Did you ask that crazy nigga to handle my cousin?"

I vehemently shook my head. "No! It's been over a year since I've spoken to him. I saw him briefly at the Black Excellence ball back in February, but we didn't cross paths. Instead, I ran into the girl I saw him with. She's apparently his fiancèe and pregnant by him."

"She got a restraining order on him after he called himself trying to pop up on her last summer," Jamaal added. "Her brother and I handled that though."

"Ok... so what happened? You wished death on my cousin and a little over a month later, he's dead?"

I sighed. At the time, emotions were high and my anger was warranted. As much as I couldn't stand Shawn, I didn't really want him dead. Nor would I do anything to hurt him. I needed Reina and Reign to understand that. I wasn't a malicious woman.

"I cussed him out after LaTrice tried to embarrass me at the event. He followed me to the bathroom and was waiting for me after I finished using it. I spazzed Reina, I can't lie... Trice's bitch ass really tried me and I couldn't knock her out like I wanted to. I had no idea that Dre was up there or was recording me. Shawn was trying to apologize but when I'm mad, I don't be trying to hear shit. I slapped him and you heard what I said in the recording but... I would never do anything t-t-to take...take him away from his loved ones," my voice cracked. The guilt I carried behind what I said to him weighed on me more and more each day.

Reina stared intensely at me, her expression unreadable and lips in a thin line. She was usually so playful and unserious, but none of that was happening today. The air was thick with uncertainty. Looking at it from her perspective, I could see why she had her doubts. It looked sus as hell, but I needed her to believe me. Her and her brother had been nothing but good to me, so I didn't want to lose her friendship. Being doubted like this hurt.

"So what happened the day of the accident? You were the only one out there... came to the hospital..."

"Look, what you trynna say girl? My daughter didn't have shit to do with Shawn getting killed!" my mama erupted and jumped up. Reina grabbed her gun and swiftly switched the safety off, pointing it at my mama. I jumped in the middle of them and Jamaal pulled her on the other side of the living room.

"Mrs. Nicole, I don't want to disrespect you or your home but this conversation is between me and Rae. I don't pull my shit out unless I plan on using it... please don't make me have to," Reina calmly said. Almost too calmly. She didn't raise her voice, change her facial expressions, nothing. Stunned, my mother fell into a quick silence then snapped her head towards Jamaal and let him lead her out the living room, mumbling and cursing under her breath. *"Can't believe this damn girl pulled her shit out on me in my own damn house..."*

I turned my attention back to Reina and watched her, watching me.

"The day of the accident," I started slowly. I hated thinking about, let alone talking about that day. Seeing your first love die in front of you was traumatizing. "I was leaving your shop. Shawn pulled up behind me and started trying to apologize again. I didn't curse him out, didn't give him much conversation at all and he started spazzing. I drove off on him. That's when that big black truck came out of nowhere and...cr-crashed into him." I tried to keep the tears at bay, but I couldn't. Reina's look softened and she sighed deeply. She made no moves to console me and honestly, I didn't blame her.

"I...I feel guilty for saying that shit to him, Reina. I feel like if I would have never said that, he would have never gotten hurt. I'm...I'm sorry" I was sobbing at this point. Admitting my guilt and now knowing that DeAndre had something to do with his death really fucked with me.

Reina sighed again and then grabbed her gun, placing it back in her purse. She stood up and looked me over once again. We stared at each other, the tears on my face drying and the look on her face was identical to the stoic one that her brother usually wore. Wordlessly, she walked out the living room and down the foyer to the front door. Seconds later, I heard the door slam and her car start up. Mama and Jamaal came back in the living room and I fell into my mother's arms.

"So... what now?" she asked. Another tear escaped my eye and slid down my cheek.

"I don't know," I whispered.

I just didn't know.

Chapter Nineteen

Desiraè

One week later

"It wasn't your fault Desiraè," Doc said softly.

Being back in Doc's office on her couch felt surreal. This was our first in-person session in months, but I needed to see her. I felt myself falling into the deeper end of my thoughts and I didn't like that for me. I was stressed and very anxious. Nothing helped me get a full night's sleep and it had been one week since me and Reina's conversation. I hadn't heard from Reign and couldn't bring myself to reach out. I was so discombobulated, that I hadn't even begun reaching out to people to let them know that they'd been hired or set a training date.

I couldn't focus on the restaurant right now.

I gave Doc a watery smile. I cried recalling everything that transpired over the last week and the look on her face was one of shock, worry, and concern.

"Then why do I feel like it is?" I whispered.

"Because a part of you feels like you can control someone's actions and you can't. You can only control your own. It isn't your fault that Dre violated you in the way that he did. It isn't your fault that he came up with a plan to harm Shawn, as an attempt to get you back. Though affected, you weren't the cause for any of those events. I understand that through their grief, your friends Reina and Reign may be looking for someone to place blame on... it's natural. And you are an easy target right now. While I don't think you should be held responsible for the actions of another, I do think that it's necessary to give them their space and not force them to speak with you or even believe you. This isn't your first time being the villain in someone's story and it likely won't be your last... but this situation here? It's not your fault."

I slumped my shoulders. I did think that I could control someone's actions and understood it was an unhealthy way to move about life. I figured that if I was a good big sister and granddaughter, that it would make my mom come back. Then, when I got with Shawn, I figured that if I held him down and turned a blind eye to his cheating, then that would make him do right by me. Then, when I got with Dre, I did everything I could to make him forgive me, not knowing that he was jealous of me this whole time. With Reina and Reign, I own up to what I said to Shawn but at the end of the day, I wasn't responsible for whatever Dre orchestrated. Dre wanted to blame me and save me at the same time and that wasn't fair. From his weak ass villain monologue, it sounded like he wanted to control me more than anything and I just couldn't understand why.

What about me gave that I wanted to be controlled? I would be respectful, but I needed a mate to understand that I also needed to be free – free to explore and live out my dreams, free to be my full self, free to fall, free to soar.

I needed freedom. So often, we as women made being in a relationship our entire identity. I didn't want that for myself. I wanted a good partner to enhance who I already was, not take credit for creating me. And make me raise a baby with him after we weren't even together? I wondered if his dead mama did crack with him still in her womb. None of that shit made sense, and I felt bad for his baby mama – wherever and whoever she was.

"It wasn't…It's not my fault," I stammered.

Doc nodded. "Say it more confidently, like you mean it."

I straightened up on the couch, squared my shoulders, and looked her directly in the eyes and repeated myself. She had me repeat it seven times and by the time our session was over, I was starting to believe it.

I knew I had a long road ahead of me, but at the end of the day, Dre's actions were his own. I missed talking to Reina, but I had to respect her and her brother's grieving process. I was responsible for my own process and honestly felt like whatever happened to Dre was his own doing.... Speaking of which, I wondered what happened to him?

Maybe it was just best that I didn't know.

Chapter Twenty

LaTrice

Ten years.

I'd given the man I loved more than anything ten years of my life and what did I have to show for it? Sure, I had a house, cars, jewelry, and birthed his children... but none of it seemed to be enough. LaShawn Davis didn't love me the same way I loved him and it showed by the way he constantly cheated on me and disrespected our union.

I sighed, sipping my concoction of red wine and the sleeping pills I had my doctor prescribe me.

I was miserable, and it was all that bitch Desiraè's fault. I hated her ever since her freshman year, but honestly before that. When Shawn started parading her through the hood as if he wasn't my man first pissed me off to no end. He got me pregnant and made me get an abortion after I got kicked out of my mama's house for getting pregnant. Then he turned around and got her pregnant, as if I was supposed to let that ride.

I *hated* that bitch! She thought she was better than me because she had Shawn doing shit he never did for me and tried to play the humble role. He had her laced in the latest name brands and diamonds and wanted to build a life with her but... not on my watch!

Like, I was here first.

I was there even when we would break up and he would fuck other hoes.

I'm the bitch who ended up with his last name and pushed out three of his big headed ass kids. Although, the paternity of that last one was questionable, because I was fucking Reign and Shawn around the time I got pregnant.

That bitch Desiraè still had a chokehold on him, even after she left Chicago for five years. The bitch moved on, had a boyfriend, and last I saw graduated from fucking culinary school. Yet the wind blew him in her Instagram DM's faithfully. He was enamored with Desiraè, wanting to apologize to her for how he treated her... the nigga never gave me no apologies.

In fact, he told me he hated me constantly and thought that getting our lawyer to draw up divorce papers would actually make me sign them. For a nigga that was super smart when it came to the streets, Shawn sure was dumb.

There was no me without him.

My whole life revolved around making sure he wasn't embarrassing me and raising our kids. I didn't work. I didn't have anything I was passionate about. I never even graduated high school, let alone thought about going to college. I was meant to be a kept woman and LaShawn eventually conceded and kept me up well. I wore the title of Mrs. Davis happily, unless I had to check a bitch. But I was getting too old to be out here fighting.

When DeAndre from high school slid in my inbox with a proposition to take out Desiraè once and for all, I was immediately on board. He said he had evidence that they were cheating on us with each other and then she left him after she graduated from culinary school. He said that Shawn was giving her money to fund her weak ass restaurant and that he was planning to make me sign those papers he drew up two years ago. I checked his bank statements and the only thing I saw was him sending her two bands via CashApp, once. Shawn also had offshore accounts that I knew about but didn't have access to, so I wasn't sure if Dre was telling the truth or not, but I saw red. I wanted that bitch to be put to sleep permanently and Dre would be just the person to do it.

So how did I, LaTrice Greene-Davis end up as a widow at age the tender age of twenty-six?

Because Dre was a dumb ass. And a liar. And by the time I realized what had *really* taken place, I got word that my husband was dead, while little miss Desiraè was walking around untouched. That was *never* a part of the plan.

A lump formed in my throat as I thought about Shawn. Regardless of our tumultuous past, I loved him. I just wished he loved me more than he loved Desiraè. He was going on apology tours to her left and right, meanwhile I *never* got an apology. He spent the last few years of our marriage resenting me but I couldn't say that I didn't know why.

I ruined his life. But a girl had to do, what a girl had to do. And I don't regret any of it. When I switched past him that day on Morgan, he could've left me alone. He didn't have to follow me to BaBa's. He didn't have to pay for my food. He didn't have to take my virginity on my mother's bathroom floor while she was at work two weeks later.

How could he not think that we went together after all that? Why would he think that after getting me pregnant, and then getting kicked out of my mama's house, and *then* getting forced to have an abortion would ever make me come up off him?

***

"Shawn... I have something to tell you," I breathed over the phone, whispering so I wouldn't wake my two little sisters, who were sleeping on the bunk beds across from me in the bedroom we shared. His background was loud, and he sighed impatiently, not saying anything until he got to a quieter place.

"Wassup Trice? I ain't got a lotta time right now, I'm handling business," he said coldly. Shawn was always so hot and cold with me. One minute, he would act like he really liked me. He'd spend time with me, buy me food, and we would fuck whenever my mama wasn't home. The next minute, he would act like he didn't know who I was, ignoring my calls, walking past me in public. It made me feel so confused. I loved Shawn. I gave him my virginity and wanted to be his girl, his number one. I always answered his calls and tried my best to hold him down. Nothing seemed to work though. He couldn't stay out of hoes faces and I was getting tired of beefing with bitches over my man. I hoped that the news I had to tell him would make him have a change of heart. Maybe he would move me in with him and we could be a family.

"Trice? Say what you gotta say man, you holding up my line."

I swallowed and took another deep breath. "I'm... I'm pregnant Shawn. My period didn't come this month and I...I took a test and it came back positive." My stomach lurched and it felt like my lunch was about to come up after I revealed that. I didn't know how to feel. My mama preached to me endlessly about keeping my legs closed and not becoming a teen mother like her. She always complained that she was never able to live out her dreams and do whatever it is that she wanted to do because she decided to have us. Our daddies wasn't no help and I couldn't even tell you who mine was even

272

if I walked past him on the street. I didn't see myself having kids, but I loved Shawn.

"Pregnant? And how the fuck I'm 'sposed to believe that baby is mine?" his tone harshly cut through my thoughts. I looked at the phone in disbelief. He knew he took my virginity and I never fucked with anyone else before, regardless of what bitches and niggas in the hood said about me.

"Shawn... don't fuckin' play with me G! You the only nigga I ever been with! We never used no fucking condoms! You —"

"Man, get the fuck off my line with this lame ass shit! I pull out every time and my homie told me that pussy for everybody, Trice. Ion know why you think I'm some type of goofy."

Tears pricked my eyes but I refused to let them fall. Rumor had it that there was some new lil bitch that had his attention and that was what had him acting different but I hadn't seen it for myself.

"Shawn, fuck you and yo' lying ass homie! I'm only fucking you, can you say the same?"

There was nothing worse than sharing your body with a nigga who wanted to share his body with any and everyone else. Shawn was embarassing, yet nothing would make me come up off him.

"Nah, I can't Trice. So what the fuck you trynna do? You called for some bread or what?"

I scoffed when I realized what he was insinuating. "What do you want me to do, Shawn? My mama is gone flip out when she finds out I'm pregnant!"

"Get rid of it," he said coldly and hung up on me.

A few weeks later, I did end up getting rid of it, going to a non-descript building up north to get my baby sucked out of me alone. The nurse practitioners looked at me with so much pity. They offered to call me a cab home but I declined, opting to take the bus home. I called Shawn every day for two weeks straight after that but he never answered. That same day, my mama found the after care medication they prescribed me and kicked me out the same day after I confessed.

That's when my Auntie took me in and my life went downhill fast.

***

I scoffed at the memory. My sisters and my friends thought I was so stupid. And, maybe I was.

But Trice always got the last laugh. When I got word from him that Desiraè was pregnant, I saw red. I remember when he sat me down and told me that he couldn't fuck me anymore because she was pregant with his baby and he had to focus on being a family man. I wasn't trying to hear none of that, and I sucked his dick the same night he told me. Shawn was slipping away from me. She wasn't the first girl he fucked around on me with, just the one who seemed to have that most impact. He actually *wanted her* to have his baby. Meanwhile, I got mine sucked outta me *alone*. I knew then that every chance I got, I would make the bitch's life a living hell. Just like I did all the other girls who thought they lil weak ass pussies could snatch Shawn from me.

Admittedly though, Desiraè wasn't a punk. We were around the same height and though skinnier than me, she packed a punch. The bitch was one of those people who you didn't expect could fight, because she minded her business and mostly kept to herself when we were in school. Because everyone thought she was Shawn's main bitch, people naturally gravitated towards her and tried to be her friend, but the weird bitch kept to herself.

I was the real popular one. I was the ringleader of my crew and all the ugly ass bitches who wanted to fuck Shawn, wanted to be my friend. Hoes would report to me like the morning news on the days that I would come to school.

The rumors were getting to be a bit much, so I observed her for a week straight and that was probably the first time I had perfect attendance. Once I confirmed what I already knew, I looked at my crew and told them that we were jumping her after school. After making sure that brick was smashed repeatedly in her stomach, we got ghost. I was surprised that she didn't snitch to the police. But fuck her.

After I fought her on King Drive, I went to stay with my auntie because my mama wouldn't let me back in her house. She said I was a terrible influence on my younger sisters all because all I wanted to do was smoke, drink, fuck, skip school, and chase after Shawn all day. As if she ain't have me at sixteen. My auntie welcomed me in her home but I had to work to earn my keep if I wasn't gonna go to school. I repaid my auntie for her kindness by fucking my step-uncle every chance I got. When me and Shawn would be on the outs, me and Uncle Skeeter's ass would be in their bedroom tearing it up between the sheets and for a couple years, my auntie was none the wiser.

Until one day, she caught us and tried to kill me.

I ran out of their house and took a cab all the way to Shawn's house and let myself in with the key I had stolen from him. I walked in to find this nigga groaning and moaning, naked as the day he was born with blood all over him. It looked like he got in a fight with a bear and when I asked what happened, he said that Desiraè had done that to him. I was already nineteen by then and needed to have a stable place to stay. I didn't want to end up on the streets so I did what any woman would do in my situation:

I played the role of supportive girlfriend and nursed that nigga back to health. The doctors were able to attach his balls back to his nut suck and after it took him about six weeks to heal, I was riding that dick into oblivion. The goal was to get pregnant and then feed him a sob story about how I had nowhere else to go – which wasn't totally a lie. My auntie was not fucking with me and my mama had washed her hands with me. My sisters were still young teens living in the house and I knew that once my cousins and grandma caught wind of what I did, they wouldn't fuck with me either.

When Shawn got caught on a drug charge, I drew up some fake marriage documents so that I wouldn't have to testify and surprisingly, he got off. I did end up getting pregnant again, but I purposely waited until I was about twelve weeks until I told him, so that he wouldn't force me to get another abortion. As the icing on the cake, I made us go to the courthouse and get married, or I was going to snitch on him. I didn't *want* to send Shawn to jail, but *something* had to give. He had too much freedom, was too callous and cocky to give a fuck about me. I didn't really give a fuck about who he messed with.

I just didn't want him messing with Desiraè.

For a while, my plan worked. I had my daughter. He still hustled. And my family and I made amends. I knew they didn't trust me, but I needed babysitters. Shawn was never home, and his mama was raggedy and still in the streets. When I got pregnant again, she said she was too young to be a grandmother and that we shouldn't expect her to be a babysitter. The gag is – I wouldn't trust LaShawnda to watch a pot of water boil.

So with my family, I played my role. I told them that me and Shawn were now married and that I had even found God. I told them that I'd gotten my GED and just wanted to be close to my sisters and mother again. I told them that I didn't mean to have sex with Auntie Terri's husband and that he had just come on to me — now that part wasn't totally a lie. I may or may not have seduced that nigga but he was the adult, not me. He was the married one, not me. I was just doing what I had to do, since Shawn wasn't really giving me money like he used to when he was still sniffing behind Desiraè. My little McDonald's job wasn't paying shit but Unk would break me off some of that truck driver money when Auntie Terri wasn't looking. Who forces a teenager to pay rent anyway?

And then that girl's grandmother died, and my world came crashing down again.

I knew she died because the whole hood knew. Kidney failure or some shit but I didn't give a fuck, because I hated that old bitch too. Nevermind that my mama would get plates from her all the time when we were low on food because my mama had to choose between the lights being on or food filling the fridge. Ms. Earline never charged my mama either, but so what. My mama shoulda learned how to work her pussy like I did. I hated Ms. Earline because if Desiraè wasn't her granddaughter, she would've never come to live with her. If Desiraè didn't come to stay with her old ass granny, then she and Shawn would have never met. And if she and Shawn would have never met, me and Shawn would be living in our happily ever after by now.

I guess the universe had other plans.

***

DING-DONG!
DING-DONG!

My door bell sounded but I was feeling lethargic on the couch. My wine glass and sleeping pills were scrawled across the table, with only a swig of wine left in the bottle. Luckily, my kids were with my sister for the weekend because ever since Shawn died, I wasn't in the mood to deal with them. Hell, whoever was at my door should've called first.

I heard my locks turn followed by heavy footsteps and my eyes glanced up at Reign entering my living room with his usual unreadable expression on his face. I licked my lips. Fucking Reign was enjoyable but he cut it off quicker than I expected. Maybe it was his guilty conscience eating him up, I don't know. Now that Shawn was dead, maybe he would at least let me taste that big, pretty ass dick of his again.

I was mourning after all.

"What are you doing in my house, Reign? And where did you get a key to get in?" I asked, slightly slurring my words.

Wordlessly, he walked over to the chairs across from the couch as sat in one of them, his eyes looking like bottomless pits of blackness. Reign was handsome, but not in your usual way. He almost always had a mean mug on his face and he rarely smiled or laughed. Even when fucking, he never let his facial expressions portray any type of joy.

Regardless of what his mean ass said, I *knew* my pussy was good.

"Let me ask you something Trice and don't you fucking lie to me bro," he said coldly. Goosebumps raised on my arms and I looked at him, trying to sober up but the combination of the pills and the wine had my heart beating too fast.

"What is it, Reign? You got some nerve coming up in here, questioning me about shit in my own fuckin' house."

"Does the name Dre ring a bell to you?" and you could have heard a pin drop at how quiet it got, only the sound of the clocks on the wall and my central air blowing.

I swallowed and quickly weighed my options. I could lie and pretend that I didn't know him or I could... Well, I didn't know what Plan B would be. I just knew that I couldn't admit to Reign's menacing ass that I conspired with him to get Desiraè killed. I didn't know what it was about that damn girl, but she had these niggas wrapped around her fingers. Reign was probably fucking her and that's why he felt the need to press me about that bitch last month. I never saw him look so angry or possessive over any woman and that pissed me off.

What is it that this bitch had that I didn't?

I snapped my head up in what felt like slow motion and glared at him.

"DeAndre who? No, I don't know no fuckin' Dre," I popped. My heart rate was increasing and I diverted my eyes from Reign's glare.

"I never said DeAndre, Trice. So yo ass do know him."

Shit.

Fuck.

Damn.

"I meant to say... I only know of one person by that name. Is his full name DeAndre?" I feigned confusion.

Reign gave me a rare smirk and I got scared. This nigga never, and I mean *never* smiled or smirked at my ass.

"Nah, shorty... You know exactly who I'm talking about. Which means you know he tried to kill Desiraè and that you ordered him to take care of Shawn instead. Gave his ass twenty bands to do it, too."

My face paled.

"No! I did not order him to take care of Shawn! I only wanted *that bitch* dead!"

No matter what, I loved Shawn. I would never line him up to get killed. Now that bitch Desiraè? She could join all those miscarriages and her grandmother for all I cared.

I *hated* that bitch.

"Yet, he would never try and take out the love of his life....nigga had it out for Shawn since we was shorties. His mama was a cluck and Shawn used to serve her. That nigga plotted on my cousin...and you led him right to him," Reign was looking at me but it seemed like he was talking to himself. I gulped. And forced myself to think about something that would make me cry. Maybe tears would sway him from doing something to me. Hell, I would suck his dick, let him fuck me in all my holes, move out the state – anything to live to see another day.

I sat up, slowly. The cocktail of wine and sleeping pills had me drowsy.

"Reign..." and my voice caught in my throat watching his twin slip into the living room, dressed in all black with gloves to match. Reina had been wanting to beat my ass for a minute now and this was the perfect time. She glared at me and stalked towards my kitchen, and started turning knobs on the stove.

"I gotta give it to you, Trice. You slick as fuck. You hate Desiraè that much over a nigga who didn't even want to marry you. You were just something to do when it was nothing to do. I hate my nigga got caught up and I hate that even my dumb ass slipped up with you but," he looked me up and down disapprovingly. "Maybe you can try and be a better person in your next life."

He stood abruptly and I smelled the gas from the stove leaking but couldn't move. My eyes got lower and lower and the sounds of their footsteps and voices sounded muffled. For the life of me, I couldn't even stand up. I knew I overdid it on those sleeping pills and the wine made it no better. My heart felt like it would explode at any moment.

A loud BOOM sounded off from the kitchen and I watched through lowered lids a fire start on top of my stove and catch onto the curtain that was over the windows above the sink.

I was going to join my husband finally.

I guess I took it literal when I said til death do us part when we exchanged vows all those years ago.

There was no point in screaming for help. I couldn't even cry as the flames spread from the kitchen to the living room. As they crept closer, prickling my skin, I inhaled once more and prepared for my final place in hell.

Girls like me weren't going to heaven anyway.

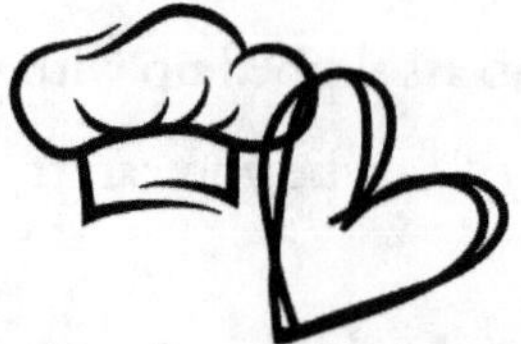

Chapter Twenty-One

Reign

"Hi, my name is Dorissa White with Channel 7 News. We are here at the scene of a gruesome house fire, claiming the life of one victim. The fire seems to have started due to an unattended grease explosion and the victim's remains were claimed by the fire. No further details have been released. Back to you, Bob."

What Tupac say? I ain't no killer but don't push me. As I watched the pretty, brown-skinned news anchor run down more news, I smirked. It wasn't often that I played God but before taking out that bitch ass nigga, I made sure to get some information out of his ass first. It took three days, but his ass ended up singing like a canary. I questioned what type of pussy Desiraè had to make a nigga get out of his body like that but also realized that good pussy or not – she ain't deserve to get lined up like that. Reina already told me that she pulled up on her to do a temp check and that her story added up. She also told me how she upped the pole on her OG and I just shook my head at my twin.

She could be so fuckin' ghetto at times... not at all the lady that our Grandma raised her to be.

***

After calling clean up, we had this bitch ass nigga in one of the warehouses that Shawn had for his trucking business. Since he was gone now, the responsibility of it fell on me. I had the crew suspend his ass from one of the exposed beams in the ceiling and pulled up a chair. I considered myself a reformed street nigga, but some shit you couldn't shake. I had seen and done things that kept me up at night. I got out the game when I was twenty-three and that's when I opened my barbershop. Niggas needed something constructive to do and I never planned to hug the block forever. I lost too many homies to the grave or to the cell and even after a couple stints in juvie, I knew I didn't want that for myself. I wasn't an outwardly violent nigga and I wasn't overly flashy. I got my money and minded my business. The only times niggas had to see me was when it was time for them to get sent to hell.

"LET ME THE FUCK GO! BITCH ASS NIGGA!" Dre's therm ass yelled out. I took a pull of my blunt, and exhaled. This nigga was a trip and I ain't have much conversation for his ass. I watched his body writhe and shake, as blood stained his dark sweats.

This nigga deserved a slow death. It was what I specialized in, which is why more often than not, I kept that side of me tucked.

"You the bitch ass nigga. The fuck you pop up into her restaurant like that for?" I had to ask. Something was clearly off about his ass and before I sent him to his eternal resting place, I needed to know.

"He took everything from me!"

"Who did, goofy?"

"I don't gotta tell you shit!" he opened his mouth to push out a glob of spit, but it didn't land on me. I looked where it landed near my feet and looked back up at him, unimpressed with the dramatics.

"Imma give yo ass one more time. You not getting up outta here alive, so you might as well speak your peace. Or we can gone head and get it over with. The choice is yours, but I ain't got all night." I pulled out a lawn chair and rested my hands behind my head.

He remained silent, and after about ten minutes, he was still saying nothing, so I motioned for one of the workers to start chopping off toes and fingers.

"AARGHHHHH! OKAY! OKAY! I'LL TALK! I'LL TALK! THAT BITCH ASS NIGGA TOOK EVERYTHING FROM ME! MY MAMA! MY GIRL! HE TOOK EVERYTHING!"

I furrowed my brows. "What do you mean he took yo' mama?"

His eyes fluttered with tears as he floated in and out of consciousness. The thing about being a methodical killer is that you had to have patience. You had to be precise. The blood loss alone was wearing him down and I contemplated on just letting him bleed out.

"My-my-mama....she was on drugs. She died when I was thirteen... that b-bitch ass nigga fed her drugs!" he hollered as he watched his ligaments fall one by one in a tub filled with acid.

"And just how the fuck do you know that dummy?"

Shawn jumped off the porch hella young as a dealer. Hand over fist, the game was taught to us by our daddies before they both had an untimely demise. Our daddies didn't teach us to ride bikes or how to tie our shoes. They taught us how to cook dope and shoot to protect ourselves and our family. We weren't taught to have a moral compass when it came to a cluck, so holding on to something like that for so long was blasphemous for me. A cluck don't care where they get their next hit from so the more I thought about it, the more I felt that this nigga's anger was misplaced. And more than anything, what did that have to do with Desiraè?

That's why the fuck I was here. Messing with my Rae of Sunshine was a sure way to awaken the beast.

"I DID MY FUCKING RESEARCH!" he winced. "I HIT UP LA-TRICE AND PUT THIS PLAN IN MOTION TO MAKE HER THINK I WOULD KILL DESIRAÈ. I TOLD HER THAT THEY WERE CHEATING WITH EACH OTHER AND THAT SHE LEFT ME AFTER SHE FINISHED CULINARY SCHOOL. I TRAILED HIM FOR MONTHS, THEN MADE MY MOVE. HE WAS DEAD AND I WAS THOUSANDS OF DOLLARS RICHER! RAE BELONGS TO ME!"

I had heard enough. Anger coursed through my veins and I sliced that rope to dissolve his body in the tub of acid. Hearing his blood curdling screams and seeing his skin bubble up and then dissolve satisfied me in a way I couldn't explain. For months, I wondered who got at Shawn. How they were able to pull up on him like that and speed away unscathed. He had no known beefs. Niggas hated in the city but we we were grown now, getting money and taking care of our families. I moved silently, calculated, and precise yet had no information.

In a way, killing this nigga was vengeance for Shawn and Desiraè.

I couldn't act like I grew up with Desiraè or even knew much about her, but from what I observed over the past few months, I knew she was a stand up woman. Not perfect, but she did right by people. She ain't deserve to have a hating ass nigga in her corner. She ain't deserve to have a nigga who wanted to do nothing but dim her light in her corner. She needed a nigga who would let her be free – within reason of course. But Rae was so solid, she wouldn't cheat on a nigga in the name of freedom. She needed to be free to dream, to explore, to love, to fail forward, to just... be. Since a shorty, she took so much on the chin. I ain't wanna place her strength on a pedestal but it was equal parts admirable and sad as fuck. She had more heart than most niggas but as young as she was, as sweet as she was, she didn't deserve to go through any of that. I didn't want to save her, I just wanted to give her a soft place to land. But before I stepped to her, I had to get my shit together. I just hoped she would want to accept a nigga when it was all said and done.

***

"So what's yo' plan when you just pop yo crazy ass up over there?" I asked Reina, who was currently driving to Rae's crib. I was along for the ride. Surprisingly, Rae didn't stop sharing her location with Reina, but neither of us heard a peep from her. She hadn't been by her space in two weeks and as far as we knew, the restaurant was still set to open in two weeks. Reina had this idea to pop up and force her to talk to us.

"Well, Imma make her come to the door and if she don't answer, Imma shoot the door handles off. Then we gone talk, you gone profess your undying love for her and then she gone cook us something to eat, cuz I've been starving," Reina shrugged. I stared at my twin, and made a mental note to call our mama and ask if she stood in front of the microwave while pregnant with us. Reina wasn't wrapped too tight. I wasn't either, but we ain't talking about me right now.

"Something's wrong with yo ass bro," I shook my head at her. "And confess my what? I'm not in love with her ass."

Reina looked over at me. "You took out two people on her behalf. You're *something,* my nigga!"

I sucked my teeth in response and watched as she pulled into the guest parking in Rae's garage. Hopping out of her car, we bypassed the security and rode the elevator all the way up to the 75th floor. Even little shit like this – going from living in her Gramz's crib in Englewood to staying in a loft downtown was something I admired about her. Regardless of the hand that she was dealt, Rae made something out of nothing.

How could I not be in love with her ass?

Being courteous, Reina rang her doorbell three times and then pulled out her phone to check her location after she didn't answer. "It says she's here. Let me call her."

She called back to back three times and she didn't answer. Just when Reina cocked her gun to aim for the handle, Rae swung the door open and glared at the both of us, obviously looking like she just woke up.

"How can I help y'all?" she drawled, hand on her hip and mean mug permanently pressed on her face.

"Hey friend! I missed you!" Reina squealed, pushing past Rae and making her way to the living room. I offered Rae a sympathetic expression and followed behind my crazy ass twin. Rae looked good in a pair of black Hustle Honeyz biker shorts and a matching cut-off white crop top. She still had those long braids in and they were in a big bun on top of her head. Slamming the door behind us, Rae stomped into the living room and asked us again what we wanted.

"To talk to you. I miss you friend. Are you okay?" Reina asked. Rae's eyes bucked at her like she lost her mind, lips in a thin line. She closed her eyes briefly, counting to ten silently and opened her eyes, staring at both of us.

"Look... if y'all are worried about me saying anything, I won't. I got cameras installed and made sure the outside ones from the street didn't show anything. I'm giving y'all space to process whatever it is y'all feel towards me, but I'm not beat for conversation about much today... I'm tired," she sighed, sitting on the couch across from us.

Reina's crazy ass pouted. "Wow, I don't think I like your tone towards us for real. I'm sorry for almost shooting yo mama. I didn't mean to!"

"I'm not the one you owe an apology to about that, Reina. And my tone is fine... you're just not used to me being this way and that's okay. The thing is, I'm being cool, calm, and collected. I'm not mad at y'all. I'm just giving space where it's necessary," she replied.

I began to feel bad. Her mouth was saying one thing but the eyes... the eyes tell on you every time and Rae's eyes showed that she was more disappointed and hurt than anything. I never wanted to disappoint or hurt her.

"Aye. You disappointed in us?" "Did we hurt yo feelings?" I asked, just to make sure my spidey senses weren't sending me off. Rae looked me up and down and she opened her mouth and then closed it, thinking about what she wanted to say.

After a minute, she spoke again. "I guess I am, just a little bit. However, I see where you both were coming from. I'm an outsider. I had history with Shawn but not with either of you, so of course I'm the first person many look at when it comes to situations like this. I don't know what happened to Dre and I honestly don't wanna know… I just know that regardless of what he said, his actions were not my fault. Y'all don't know me well enough, but I'm not that type of person who would…would set someone up to get taken away from their family. Regardless of what transpired between us, I don't hold any malice in my heart. And in order to *know* that, you'd have to *know me and* my heart."

For once, Reina shut the fuck up and I was my usual quiet self. We all stared at each other and I searched Rae's eyes while trying not to look away myself. Her eyes could be intense sometimes. She had the kinda eyes that drew you in and made you want to spill all your secrets because you knew that she would hold them under lock and key. I cleared my throat.

"LaTrice is dead," I confessed. Reina snapped her head in my direction and glared at me.

"*Reign!*" she stressed, wanting me to shut up. But this girl made me have word vomit.

Rae's eyes widened then relaxed. "Again, not my business, but prayers to her family," she said emotionlessly. That's some real nigga shit. She could've made lewd comments and said some snarky shit, but that just wasn't who Rae was as a person. She wasn't a fake bitch either, so her eyes didn't fill with tears or anything.

"I'm telling you because Dre reached out to her and offered to take you out. But he really had intentions on taking Shawn out. That's how Shawn ended up dead and you're able to walk around untouched. He put it in her head that y'all was cheating with each other and that he gave you money to fund your restaurant. That girl had a deep hatred for you Rae. I'm sorry that nigga hated on you too."

Rae's face went through all the emotions until she settled on a stoic expression. She nodded once I finished talking and then stared straight past me and Reina.

I cleared my throat. "Dre is dead too, Rae." I felt bad as fuck for dropping a bomb like this on her. The room filled with an awkward silence but none of us made a move to leave from our spots. Reina was chewing on her bottom lip, looking at me and I was staring right at Rae.

"Did you...?" she started to ask but her voice got caught in her throat.

"Rae..." Reina started, but I glared at her to shut her up. Rae spaced out for a second and chewed on her bottom lip until she drew blood.

"Well," she snapped her eyes towards me and Reina, looking us directly in the face. "Thanks for telling me... so like... did y'all come to swear me to secrecy? I told y'all, I'm no snitch." She stood up. "Thanks for the visit... but I wanna finish taking my nap now."

Silence fell over the room again and finally, I stood up. Reina followed my lead and we walked towards the door. Rae followed behind us and allowed Reina to give her a side hug. I wanted to hug her too, but thought it was best that I not cross that line. As we made our way out the parking garage, Reina sighed deeply.

"So what do we do now, Reign? I miss my friend," she pouted. Truthfully, I didn't know.

"I guess we gotta do what she did.... Give it time."

Chapter Twenty-Two

Desiraè

Imagine spending years of your life with a nigga, just to find out that he hates you. I wouldn't wish this knowledge, nor the remnants of what it feels like to know, on my worst enemy. And according to Reign, that bitch is dead. After Reign and Reina left, I tried to fall back asleep, but my thoughts wouldn't let me.

Shawn's *dead.*

Dre is *dead.*

LaTrice is *dead.*

I know me and Doc went in depth on how none of this was my fault, but I couldn't help but think that if I never dated Shawn or Dre, LaTrice wouldn't hate me so much. Maybe, just maybe they would all still be alive. It wasn't my cross to bear, but it was still heavy. Sometimes, I wish I never met any of these people at all. Rolling out of bed, I walked into the kitchen and poured myself the biggest glass of wine. I needed something light to numb the pain, if only temporarily.

Walking to the balcony, I sat on the lounge chairs and overlooked the skyline. Three people I never expected to, are now dead. Sadly, I felt bad for their kids… yes, even the ones with LaTrice. I couldn't stand that girl, but no child deserved to live life without their mother and father. And then what about Dre's baby? Whoever his fiancèe was, was sure to be devastated if she ever found out. I wouldn't dare ask the twins for details on what they did with him though.

The twins.

I wasn't one to really get mad at people for being mad at me, but being seen in that light didn't override the sting, despite what logic told me. It made me wonder what was the point of building a friendship with them if they were still going to be suspicious of me? I didn't even carry myself as an opp ass bitch. Not only was I disappointed, but my feelings were hurt too. I had to shake it off though, and get ready to open this restaurant. I had stalled long enough, and that wasn't cool. Pulling out my iPad, I sent emails and text messages to the fifteen people I hired. I told them that training would start in two days and that they would receive uniform shirts on their first day. I also gave them until the end of the week to complete and submit background checks and sign NDA's. I anticipated some bumps in the road, but I wanted this grand opening to still happen on Gramz's birthday. Even if it was just a soft launch.

My phone buzzed at the same time my stomach started growling, so I ignored the phone and went to see what was in the fridge that I could cook. I came up with nothing, so I grabbed my phone to order something. A seafood trio plate from Provarè would do the trick. Swiping through the app, my phone dinged again with a text message. Seeing who it was, I sighed and rolled my eyes.

Reign ⬚

Rae…you ignoring me?

> How can I help you?

> I'm downstairs, come take a ride with me.

> No thank you.

> I don't believe I asked.

I rolled my eyes and slid my phone across the counter, because who was he talking to? Moments later, the doorbell rang and I just knew it wasn't my food getting delivered that fast. Opening the door, I looked right at Reign's mean mug with one of my own.

"Reign, you can't force me to come take a ride with you. I'm tired and don't feel like being bothered."

"You gone let me in or what?" he replied. My blood began to boil, cuz boy what?! I just said I was tired.

"Look, I don't know if what you doing impresses these other bitches you got out here, but I'm not them. I said I was tired and didn't feel like being bothered," and I slammed the door in his face. About thirty minutes later, I got the notification that my food was outside my door and when I opened it, Reign's smug ass was sitting criss-cross applesauce in the hallway, smashing my damn food.

"REIGN! I JUST KNOW YO GREEDY ASS AIN'T UP HERE EATING MY FOOD!" I stomped over to him, snatching the bag and lo and behold, this nigga was tearing my seafood pasta with the extra lump crab meat up! If he wasn't so much bigger than me, it would take Jesus and all twelve of his disciples to get me off of him.

But I didn't beat up niggas anymore.

He smirked, producing a toothpick out of nowhere and rose to his full height. "Why you slam the door in my face Rae? Come on. I already placed another order for you. I ain't know you fucked with Provarè, that's my second favorite restaurant."

I whipped around and just stared at him, then sighed and went in the crib to put on my shoes.

***

Reign was a certified asshole. Like, who steals my food and eats it but then opens my car door, buttons my seat belt, and turns on some Three Piece as we zoom down Lake Shore Drive to go get me the food he had already eaten?

Reign King, that's who.

The only noise in the car was the sound of the radio and his air conditioner blowing. I had nothing to say to this aggravating ass nigga. He pulled up in front, put his hazard lights on and rounded to my side of the car, opening my door again. When I glared at him, he reached across me and unbuckled my seat belt then grabbed my hand and pulled me towards the door.

I'd lie if you asked me, but secretly, I enjoyed it. My hand felt soft in his bigger hand and I liked this sudden feeling of security that fell over me. He chopped it up with the bartenders and the owners and then introduced me.

"This is Chef Rae. She's about to open up that new soul food spot down on 71st," he announced. I offered him a weak smile for putting me on the spot and then spoke to everyone else, feeling shy and underdressed. Once our food was done, he grabbed the bag with one hand and my hand with the other. Opening the door for me again, I slid in and waited on him to buckle my seatbelt again.

Hey, don't introduce me to a vibe you can't maintain.

Once he strapped me in, he walked over to the driver's side, hopped in and placed the bag gently on my lap. I tore into the food and all you heard was me chewing and smacking.

"You ain't gone say thank you?" he broke the silence.

I paused mid-chew. "No. Nobody told you to be ignorant and eat my food!"

"Should've come out with me... I wanted to take you out to eat, mean ass."

"Are you and your sister hard of hearing? I just told y'all earlier that I was tired and wanted to take a nap. No means, no Reign."

He nodded. "Fasho it do. But it wasn't a question Desiraè. Most girls just do what I say, I never gotta ask twice."

I paused and looked at him again. "That's the problem, Reign... I'm not most girls and you won't group me in as such. Understand that you're in the presence of something different, or get the fuck out my face G."

He chuckled, and I got back to my food. I needed to meet the chef at Provarè so I could hire them for my personal use. It was just *that* good.

After a while, I looked at him. He seemed zoned out while driving, drumming his fingers on the steering wheel while humming King Louie's *Bandz Up*. I would have never guessed that this stoic ass nigga to listened to R&B. But here he was, looking the most relaxed I've ever seen him.

"You gone quit staring?" he queried. I rolled my eyes.

"Why am I here, Reign?" dusk was settling over the city and he was pushing his truck south on LSD. I watched him pull into the Oakwood Beach parking lot and turn his truck off.

"Cuz I want you here. Is that cool wit' you?"

"No. But I don't have a choice huh?" I quipped sarcastically. He said nothing as he rounded the truck and opened the door for me again. As he unbuckled my seat belt, I inhaled his scent of cologne, shea butter scented Dove, and Tide laundry detergent. It made me want to snuggle with him for a few days and then get back to work.

And then I snapped out of it, cuz girl what the fuck? Not me wanting to snuggle with this crazy man. Nigga didn't even look like he *snuggled.*

He led me over to the rocks that overlooked the water and a sense of calm washed over me for the first time in weeks...well months, if I'm truly being honest. Chicago was a beautiful place and our summers were unmatched. We sat in silence, the sound of the waves providing the soundtrack for the evening. I closed my eyes to take it all in and quietly practiced some breathing exercises that Doc taught me.

"I like you, D." Reign said out of nowhere. I popped my eyes open and regarded him carefully.

"I want to be your man one day... but it's a lot going on right now and I respect that. I'm just putting how I feel out there," he continued.

"And what is it that you feel? You just made statements, Reign. Lots of niggas like me...doesn't mean anything though." I learned over the years that I was a very literal person who valued clear and concise communication. I didn't like ambiguity or mixed signals. Unless you came right out and told me you liked me and a plethora of reasons why, I was one to take nice gestures, compliments, and all that other shit as just a nigga being nice.

At the mention of other niggas, Reign's eyes flashed with something along the lines of possessiveness and I stared right back at him with defiance. What I said wasn't a lie, nor was I purposely trying to make him jealous. I was just stating facts, per usual.

He sighed. "You not finna make this easy on a nigga, are you?"

I smiled and shook my head. "Not a chance, boo. So wassup? Use your words."

He smirked at me and looked at the water.

"Aight Desiraè, I like you. Probably since the first day I ever saw you but outta respect for my cousin and his feelings, I couldn't be bogus and shoot my shot. Over the last few months, we've all gotten to know each other and I realized I really *liked* you. Like, I wanna wake up with you a few days out of the week. I wanna go on stupid baecations and let you turn yo' brain off for a few days cuz you deserve that. I want to keep you safe and let nothing else ever hurt you. I wanna see that dimple pop out when you smile, and eat your food every day if I could. I wanna help all your dreams come true and if I can't help, I at least wanna support them. And I wanna see you free... free to be you and do you and give you all the things you want and even shit you didn't even know you wanted. I ain't never really had a girlfriend but I think it's cuz I was waiting for you."

And maybe, just *maybe* I was getting soft out here, but my eyes watered and when I turned to him, he engulfed me in a hug and gave me the sweetest kiss on the forehead. For girls like me, I don't think I ever envisioned myself having a "soft life" like the girls online chat about. I knew I'd rather be respected than loved because after two failed relationships, I wasn't sure that what was left of my heart could handle anymore pain or heartbreak.

Yet... There was a side of me that was very optimistic.

Could I be the girl who had it all in terms of thriving business, a husband, a kid or two, a dog, and a house with a white picket fence? I felt like Michelle Obama was the only woman on earth with a good nigga, but then I thought of Reign... he obviously wasn't perfect, but I felt so... *safe* with him. And finally feeling safe with a man after experiencing so much hell with them was a foreign experience for me.

Reign was different. Because, his natural kindness wasn't just extended to me. He extended it to his family, his friends, and even the little niggas on the block. He was a protector in the physical sense... I just was unsure if I could trust him to protect my heart, too. We stayed hugged up, my ears listening to the rhythm of his heartbeat. I fit perfectly in his arms and I never wanted to let go.

My body was on fire.

I hadn't been kissed, touched, cuddled, or loved on by a man in so long. It felt equal parts foreign and equal parts comfortable. He kissed the top of my head repeatedly, and at one point I leaned in and kissed his lips.

Pillow soft, is how I would describe them.

Warm and inviting.

A cold pop on a ninety-five degree day.

That first sip of water after running a mile.

I can't believe he let me kiss him, because now I never wanted to stop.

But, I did. An inquisitive bitch like me had questions.

"Why you stop?" he groaned.

"Is this the part you ask me to be your girlfriend?" I needed to know. He regarded me carefully before he answered.

"Not yet..." his voice trailed off. I raised an eyebrow and waited on him to finish.

"I'm saying not yet because when I secure you Rae, I don't want nothing distracting you. Even though yo' last nigga turnt out to be a bitch, I'm not crazy enough to think that you ain't mourning him. To be truthful too, I gotta cut my hoes off if Imma approach you for real. I would never give no bitch a reason to try and come to you as a woman and –"

"So you're not ready to cut your hoes off? Okay, thanks for the honesty," I cut him off and then stood up, brushing the debris from the rocks off my biker shorts. I wouldn't speak about my grieving process because I was *tired* of talking about it. Tired of feeling so many things at once. Tired of blaming myself too, even though Doc and the sticky notes around my house reminded me that it's not my fault.

"Rae, listen –"

"No, Reign. It's really okay. I get it. You like me. You know I like you. And even though I have my reservations, you're really not ready because you need to tie up... "loose ends"" I air quoted the last part.

Reign sighed. "That's not all I'm saying –"

"Then what is it, Reign?" I cut him off again.

"Let me finish, Rae." He didn't raise his voice. He didn't puff out his chest. He spoke firmly, yet gently to me and *that's* what made me shut up.

"I like you. You like me. But I need to get my shit together. When I come for you, I don't want you to have any reservations about being with me. So yes, that includes cutting hoes off and preparing myself to be *your* man." His tone was earnest and he held me captive with his direct eye contact.

I stared at him for a moment and then nodded my head. "Okay."

"Okay?" he questioned.

"Yeah. Seriously, thank you for the honesty. I appreciate it, but I won't be waiting on you, Reign."

"What you mean? I wasn't really asking you to wait…" and I clocked that he wasn't being truthful.

"Reign, I didn't take you for a liar G." I crossed my arms and cocked my head to the side. "The expectation is for me to do what while you get your shit together? How long does it take to get your shit together? You said that you want me to be free right? Well… then that's what I am going to continue to do. And while I'm being free, living my life, and running my business, if another man comes around and wants to be with me, I owe it to myself to see what's to him…. No matter how much I may like you, I'm not putting myself on hold for no nigga."

Reign was too stunned to speak, so after a while he stood up and walked towards his truck. I followed behind him, the night air thick with tension but I didn't care. I wasn't lying when I said that I appreciated his honesty. It now let me know where we stood and gave me the freedom to focus on myself. I liked Reign, but the idea of being anyone's girlfriend after everything that happened, kinda repulsed me at the moment. I'd never been this intentionally single in my life. And while I desired to find my person, I wasn't willing to make room for it in my life right now. Besides, I clearly needed to do a better job at vetting niggas. The shit with Dre still blew my mind.

That being said, I still wasn't gonna turn down any dates or anyone's objects of affection. We drove in silence and Reign pulled up to the loft and looked over at me.

"Rae?"

"Yeah?"

"I wanna be yo' friend."

"We *are* friends Reign. And I'm grateful for you," I replied earnestly.

"Nah... you really my sister friend, but I wanna be yo' friend too. And not cuz I wanna change yo' mind about waiting for me. You right, life *is* too short to be on hold for anybody. But you cool as fuck and I want us to build our own friendship."

I searched his eyes and the sincerity shone through his orbs.

"Okay, Reign. We can be friends," I obliged and leaned over and kissed his cheek. Without giving him a chance to get out and open my door, I undid my seatbelt and walked into the building.

***

The next afternoon, I walked into Reina's shop with some food for her, a peace offering if you will. I wouldn't say that we were beefing, but there was space that was needed. My mom told me how she called to apologize for upping her heat on her, and surprisingly, my mama said she forgave her. Nicole Thomas had surely grown a lot because I don't know if I could forgive my daughter's friend for pulling a gun out on me in my own house.

"Raeeeee! Ugh, I'm so happy to see you!" she gushed, stopping mid curl on her client to give me a hug. I sat in her sitting area and scrolled through my phone until she finished. Once she was done, she strolled over and plopped into the chair, looking exhausted.

"Whew! Girl I'm so glad that was my last client. I had *five* heads today since six this morning. I missed you though friend. What brings you by?" she asked.

I handed her the container of jerked turkey wings with a side of dirty rice and my mac and cheese and she swooned.

"How did you know that I didn't even stop to eat today?"

"Cuz I know you girl," I smirked. Reina was a hard worker. Even though she technically didn't *have* to do hair, she still did it because she genuinely enjoyed it. Her days were long and she often didn't stop long enough to eat, which is why I took it upon myself to feed her and her brother often.

"Once you finish eating, let's go across the street and talk over a glass of wine," I suggested. She nodded and tore that food up. Inwardly, I smiled. I loved when people enjoyed my food. After washing her hands, Reina linked her arm through mine and we walked into Vibes and Lines and took a seat at the bar. Joyy nor Cherrice were in today, so one of their employees poured us up.

"So, what's been up? We good now?" Reina sipped her glass of ViaRae.

"Yeah... but I wanted to talk it out first. I'm not here to offer apologies and I don't expect one from you. However, I don't like not talking either," I started. "Friendship is important to me, Rei. Loyalty is too. I spent a lot of time in my past life trying to prove myself to people and in this stage of my life, I don't wanna do that. It didn't feel good to have my character questioned, so yes, I was disappointed with y'all. However, I understand completely where you all were coming from so it didn't feel right taking it *too* personal. With that being said, understand that you ain't gotta question me like that. I'm as solid as they come and over time, you'll see it. I just hope you appreciate me enough to see it through."

Reina's eyes got glossy as she took in what I said. I gave her a slight smile as I watched her gather her words.

"Rae.... I know you said you didn't expect apologies, but I still want to offer one. I am sorry for questioning your character... emotions were high and this grief, man –" her voice cracked and she paused. "My cousin was not perfect but I miss him every day. And some days are better than others...but this shit is *hard*, Rae. Even though we've only known each other a short time, you've taught me that friendship is important to me too. So I *am* sorry. I called yo mama and apologized too. You don't have to prove nothing to me, Rae. Just... bare with me. Okay?"

I nodded and we clinked our glasses together, cheering to friendship and starting over.

"Also, there's one more thing," I started as I sipped on my wine. Reina looked at me expectantly, so I took a deep breath. "I like your brother. Your brother likes me. However, he isn't ready to be in a relationship right now and truthfully, I'm not either. We decided to be friends. I'm telling you because I know you like to make jokes about us being together, but that's just not in the cards for us right now so respectfully... no more jokes, G. Ion' wanna hear that. I actually wanna be his friend."

"*Damnnnn.* Is this what grown women friendships is like? It's like you checking me but surprisingly, I'm not offended at all. I gotchu Rae. Don't you wait around on him neither!" she said.

I laughed. "Do I look like the type of bitch who will wait around on a nigga?"

"Not at all, my girl!" and we clinked glasses again, finishing up the night.

Chapter Twenty-Three

Desiraè

Everyone wants to run a business. Nobody ever talks about how hard the shit is though. I started my day at 5AM, feeling a mix between groggy, nervous, and excited. I had fifteen people to train and the soft grand opening was a few weeks away. Time was of the essence and I didn't have any extra to spare. After getting myself together, I threw on my chef jacket, a pair of jeans and my Crocs to head straight to my restaurant.

My phone dinged, and I saw I had a few missed texts from my family, Reina, and... Reign. I sighed when I thought about Reign. Our conversation from the other night was heavy on my mind but I had to stand on business. But what people failed to tell you about standing on business is that it didn't always feel good.

Especially when your coochie was crying out for attention. Taking a moment to respond to everyone, my eyes lingered over Reign's message and my breath caught in my throat.

Simple, but impactful. So impactful that all thirty-two of my teeth started showing with my dimple popping out to match. I shook my head and parked, some pep in my step after receiving that message.

I marveled at the sight of my restaurant. The marble textured, black and white abstract flooring contrasted greatly with the deep red walls. We had a bar area, twelve tables and booths for dining, and a space for people to order carry-out. On the walls, I had a large gold frame that housed a black and white photo of Gramz handing out plates on her back porch with a small plaque underneath that said *In Loving Memory of Earline Thomas.* On the other walls were black and white and a few color photos of my family and I over the years. I wanted the feel of the restaurant to be like stepping into your Granny's crib, so me and Nicole spent hours poring over old family albums and getting them printed at Walgreens. We also had the black people holy trinity – a picture of Barack Obama, Martin Luther King, and Malcolm X. We also had a picture of Black Jesus because are you really at a Black owned restaurant if you don't see Black Jesus on the wall?

The booths were big enough to seat eight comfortably and in the middle of the space sat a long wooden table perfect for large parties. My restaurant was medium sized, only around 2,500 square feet and *all mine.*

I was proud.

Ecstatic.

And so damn nervous!

But I had to mask it. I couldn't let my nerves trick me into believing that I wasn't worthy of opening up a restaurant. I could do this. And it would become a staple in Chicago just like so many of my other favorite restaurants.

Squaring my shoulders, I headed towards the back room that would be used as my office and grabbed the employee handbook that Nicole and I made. In there, it had expectations of how I wanted this restaurant to be ran, how I wanted my employees to conduct themselves, and how I wanted them to treat one another. From what I learned, a restaurant was only as good as its management team and the environment it created. I wanted to foster a positive one where people looked forward to coming to work. Where customers would leave with raving reviews and full bellies.

I had big dreams. And it felt like... I could actually accomplish them.

My phone beeped and my ring camera alerted me that my first five employees were starting to arrive, my kitchen crew. Shortly after them were my five servers, all women who ranged in experience. Finally, my three bartenders and two cashiers arrived, looking eager. Out of the hundreds of people who applied, these were the fifteen that made the cut and I couldn't wait to work with them. After exchanging greetings, I led a brief orientation and midway through, I received another alert from my ring camera that someone wanted access into the space. Looking at the camera, I noticed it was a taller, honey colored woman who favored Keri Hilson. She had a messy bun, a plain white tee and some grey joggers on while holding a carseat with a sleeping newborn in it. Frowning, I excused myself and wondered why she looked oddly familiar.

"I'm sorry – we're not open yet," I started, staring up in her eyes and then glancing down at the cutest little boy who was in lala land.

"I know. I came to see if you were still hiring... my name is Kamira Clarke and I was supposed to be here the day that you had open interviews but... something came up," she said breathlessly, glancing down at her son.

"I'm sorry…. All positions have been filled. However, if or when I need to look for help again, I'll be sure to contact you." I started to close and lock the door, but she stuck her foot in it.

"Please… listen…. I just had a baby almost two months ago, but his daddy – my fiance has been missing for weeks without a trace," her lip began to tremble, no doubt the weight of being a new mother and an ain't shit baby daddy taking a toll on her. "I *really* need this job. I'm not from here but I moved here to be with my fiance. I've followed you for years and finally tasted your food at the Black Excellence Ball a few months back."

I squinted and that's when it hit me.

That face.

The voice.

Pregnant.

Missing fiance.

Her name.

Kamira Clarke was Dre's fiance… I gulped, wondering what kinda trick was God trying to play on me.

I closed my phone and put it in my pocket. Training for the day was over and I sighed while sitting down behind my desk. I couldn't believe how ironic life was. I thought long and hard about it and thought that her child shouldn't have to suffer because its daddy made poor decisions. So, I hired her.

And that's when I realized that I probably should have talked to Reign and Reina about it. Because the situation doesn't just affect me, it affects everyone around me. Later that night, Reign and Reina pulled up and looked at me expectantly.

"So... um... okay. Dre's fiancèe came to the restaurant today." I blurted, trying to read their facial expressions. "She came looking for a job. She had the baby a couple months ago and she looked so distraught. So... I... ummm.... Ummmm... I hired her." I averted my eyes and the room fell silent for what seemed like an eternity.

Glancing up, I looked at the twins exchanging silent glances. Then they looked at me.

Reign rubbed his hand behind the nape of his neck and then stroked his beard. Reina chewed on her bottom lip, a telltale sign of her trying to form her words together instead of blurting out whatever came to mind.

"Rae... you good G. We gone keep an eye on her. If anything funny comes up on her background check, we gone take care of it." Reign finally said. He glanced at his sister and they held another silent conversation with their eyes. My mind began to wander around the ways that they would *"take care of it"* but I ultimately decided to mind my own business. The less I knew, the better and though the idea of being friends with people who would kill for me scared me, it strangely made me feel safe as well.

I blew out a breath. "So y'all not mad at me?"

Reina shook her head. "A little annoyed that she popped up and you had to make a hasty decision... but no, not mad at *you*, Rae. At the end of the day, you have to make the best decisions for your business to thrive. Don't be afraid to fire no hoe that ain't pulling their weight. And if miss fake ass Keri Hilson turns out to move funny, I won't hesitate to slice her thro–"

"Reina!" Reign cut her off, but I heard her loud and clear. I also sighed a sigh of relief.

"You solid Rae. And we'll never question you again. Shit is weird, but we gone protect you," Reign expressed seriously. His eyes showed so much sincerity and I felt very... safe.

This was different.
Different than I ever experienced before.

I wasn't sure what the universe was conspiring but I did know that with the twins on my side, I had nothing to worry about.

Chapter Twenty-Four

Desiraè

"You ever heard of nervous system recalibration?" Doc asked. Here it was another week and I found myself able to snag an in person session. Life was getting hectic with the grand opening date getting closer and closer, but I wanted to find time to center myself and a part of me doing that was sitting on Dr. Love's couch.

My brows furrowed and I shook my head. "No... what is that?"

"Think of it this way. For a while, your nervous system was in disarray. You were always anxious, always expecting something to go wrong, and couldn't find peace. Life may always ebb and flow like that because nothing is perfect. So to recalibrate means to readjust, reexamine, or to correct. Tell me, how does your nervous system feel now? Especially in regards to certain people, places, or things?"

I tilted my head in deep thought. I never thought about how my nervous system *felt*.

It was just constant moving on.

Constantly having to get over something.

Constantly having to accept things I couldn't change.

Constantly changing things I couldn't accept.

As I thought about it, Doc continued. "Even if you don't know how to describe it, one thing I want you to realize is that you've done the work. You're continuing to do the work. And you're not defined by your past mistakes. We as humans tend to focus so much on the work we have left to do that we forget to pause and acknowledge the work we've done."

I gave her a meek smile. I was definitely apart of that group of humans she spoke about. Learning to be present and acknowledge my progress would probably be something I had to work on for the rest of my life. Doc waited patiently, the hum of soft R&B instrumentals playing softly while the smell of her lavender and sea salt jasmine candles permeated the air.

"I think...my nervous system feels... kinda okay now...," I started slowly. "Like... nothing is perfect. I am stressed with the grand opening getting closer and closer...love life is non-existent. Death has been all around...guilt and grief still plagues me from time to time... yet at the same time, my family is good. I have good friends around me. I get to do what I love. I'm making my dreams come true. I am... proud of myself. I can face myself in the mirror now. For a long time, I wasn't able to do that, you know? But now I can... and my nervous system feels... stable. I never felt so stable before."

Doc nodded, smiling warmly at me. "Stable. I like that."

"I do too. I think it's something I've always wanted to experience. A long time ago, you told me that life ain't no cake walk... and while that's true, I realized that there is stability that can be achieved in the midst of the chaos."

"You are correct. In the midst of chaos, your internal world can still find peace on shaky ground. While challenging, you have proved that you can withstand the storms that life throws at you. Now I want you to bask in your stability. You deserve that."

I was getting softer and softer these days because upon hearing that, my eyes welled up with tears and came spilling out on my cheeks in droves.

I would try my hardest because Doc was right – I *deserved* to bask in my stability.

***

A few days later, I stood inside my restaurant concluding another day of training. My front and back of the house employees were training hard and I was confident that by the time the grand opening day arrived, they would be equipped and ready to go. A knock on my office door caused me to look up from my computer screen where I noticed Kamira standing, looking slightly distraught.

"Hey Kamira. What's up?" I probed.

She sighed. "I gotta check out a little early today. My baby apparently has diarrhea and the daycare he goes to is calling me to pick him up. He was fine this morning!"

Pulling my bottom lip into my mouth, I nodded. "It's fine. You worked hard today so go take care of your son. I hope he feels better."

She walked further in my office and I watched her plop down in my chair, looking exhausted. I imagine trying to work while raising a newborn was hard as fuck.

"I'm sorry to dump this on you. But I just need a minute. This shit is *hard*," her voice cracked and my eyes slightly widened as tears threatened to spill out her eyes. I felt so bad and I didn't know how to comfort her.

"My life is so different now and I hate it. My stupid ass fiance is nowhere to be found, my baby won't sleep through the night, and I'm trying to navigate a new city and a new job…. I feel like I'm drowning and there isn't a life jacket in sight. I love my son but… nobody told me that motherhood would be the trenches like this." she angrily wiped a tear coming down her eye.

I just nodded, letting her get it all out. I didn't have much to add to the conversation because I wasn't a mother and the guilt of kinda-sorta knowing what happened to DeAndre made my throat feel like it was closing up.

"I left small ass Bloomington and while it *is* home, I don't wanna go back there. I…*I can't* go back there. I need to make this shit work for me and my son," she continued. One thing I noticed immediately about Kamira was her optimism. She came to training every day with a smile on her face and was super helpful towards her co-workers. She wasn't a slacker and she was the best bartender that I had on staff.

I needed to figure out a way to help her, especially since I was connected to the reason why her life was unfolding the way that it was.

And her son was innocent. He would never grow up knowing what his father was like, never know what he sounded like, and as a person who lost her father young, that type of shit sticks with you….even though I never acknowledged it.

She was crying silently now and I just stared at her. After a few moments, she abruptly stood up, squared her shoulders and wiped her face. "Thanks for listening. I'm sorry I started crying all over your office…. Let me go get my baby." and with that, she offered me a weak smile and walked out the door.

I was silent for a while after she left, just rubbing my temples and hoping that I didn't get a migraine later. I pulled out my phone and dialed a number that I was starting to learn by heart.

"You good Rae?" he answered on the first ring. I heard the buzz of barbershop clippers in the background and the chatter of voices.

"Reign... I need your help," I started and proceeded to tell him my plan.

Chapter Twenty-Five

Desiraè

T he date on the calendar read August 8th. Gramz was now celebrating her day in heaven and while the grief I felt on her birthday ebbed and flowed, today I was feeling okay. The weather was gloomy and that irritated me but nonetheless....

It was grand opening day.

The culmination of my blood, sweat, and tears was coming to a head today and I was a jumble of nerves. If you would've asked me over a year ago if I saw any of this happening, I would have said yes... just not as quickly as it did. From graduating culinary school, to leading the team at Chef LaBreaux's restaurant to finally opening my own restaurant, I had to remember to stay present and not get swallowed by all the shit that was sent to distract me. The past few weeks were a blur, because between training my employees and making sure everything was in place for today, I was exhausted.

But today? Oh today we celebrated.

I had a ribbon cutting scheduled and needed to get dressed and out the door. I showered and then Reina came barreling in my bathroom with her flat irons and edge control. For whatever reason, I let her convince me to take my braids down and let her do a short sew-in bob that was jet black and asymmetrical. My mom, Angie, Bri, and Robin all spent the night with me last night so I wouldn't have to be running all over the city to get my hair and makeup done.

"How you feeling baby?" my mama asked, handing me a green apple smoothie and a granola bar to munch on while Reina flat ironed my hair and slightly bumped the ends. I met my mother's gaze in the mirror and she had a melancholy look on her face. With it being Gramz's birthday, I knew that her grief ebbed and flowed too. Over the years, she shared with me how much guilt she still carried surrounding the years she was absent. She still worked with Dr. Love to manage and navigate those feelings and the intensity of them when days like Gramz's birthday popped up.

"Nervous," I admitted. "But proud."

My mama beamed. "You *should* be proud, baby. You overcame so many challenges to get to this point. I do believe that this is the part where God will allow you to thrive as you walk deeper in your purpose. When you get too overwhelmed, remember that God, myself, and the rest of your friends and family have your back." On the friend's part, she looked at Reina and offered her a small smile. They weren't on bad terms, but they of course weren't buddy-buddy either. My mother forgave Reina but that didn't mean that she would overlook what she did. Reina accepted that, and treaded lightly after worrying for a bit that my mama didn't like her.

Once she finished my hair, Robin did my face with the Fenty skin tint, some lash extensions, and a bomb eyeshadow look that gave the corners of my eyes a pop of red to represent my brand colors. It was rainy and humid, so I wasn't in the mood for a full face today.

Getting dressed was fun. Bri made everybody custom Mz. Earline's tees that they all styled in their own way. Reina cut hers in a crop top, Angie made hers into a one shoulder shirt, my mama even tied hers up to show off her shape and I just knew Jamaal was gonna be on her ass. I had on flowy white linen pants and another custom chef jacket. It had my name stitched on the left breast pocket and on the back was my favorite picture of Gramz – holding me as a baby. On top of the picture in intricate script, it said Mz. Earline's Kitchen. Along with my charm bracelets and a diamond one that my brother gifted me, I sprayed my scent of the day, slid on some Crocs and we were out the door.

Reign sent a Mercedes-Benz Sprinter for all of us because he said that there will be no drinking and driving tonight. The restaurant would be open for about four hours today but we were closed on Mondays. I was hosting an after party at Vibes and Lines and we planned to get tore down. I wasn't even a huge drinker but after the stress of the past year, I deserved it. As the sprinter turned on 71st, my stomach dropped to my toes when I saw the growing crowd of people outside my restaurant.

My restaurant.

It was finally here.

Finally happening.

On Gramz's birthday like I intended.

When I woke up this morning, the weather was gloomy. Now, as the sprinter rolled to a stop, the sun was shining and the skies were clear. The girls and my mama got out of the van first and Reign poked his head in, looking handsome in his own Mz. Earline's tee and some black Amiri basketball shorts that clung to his waist nicely.

"You ready Rae? The big day you've been waiting on is here," his voice was laced with mellow excitement and his eyes shined with pride. I touched up my lip gloss before answering and then turned to him. Taking a deep breath, I nodded. He reached for my hand and we walked towards the crowd of people and the flashes from multiple cameras and cheers from the crowd overwhelmed me immediately. I squeezed Reign's hand tighter and he slightly pulled me into him, leaning down so he could whisper in my ear.

"You got this. Head up Rae. You have nothing to be afraid of. We got you." and he gently dropped my hand and nudged me towards the crowd while he blended in the crowd, keeping watch.

As I walked closer, my friends and family held bouquets of red and white roses and handed them to me. I walked closer to the entrance and there was a large red bow on it. I marveled at my sign and door decals on the glass.

Reign and I... were getting closer as the months went by. He was solid just like his sister, protective, and I felt at peace whenever I was around him. I liked that he started coming out of his shell more and always had an encouraging word or helping hand for me. It was evident that we still liked each other, but I was firm about not waiting around on him. Instead of focusing on the potential of what could be, we nourished our budding friendship. Even if we didn't end up together, I was content with having him in my life as a friend.

And that was growth. I was evolving over night and I liked when I was able to peep it.

I held my head up and sauntered to the entrance. To my left and my right stood my friends, my family, and supporters. To my surprise, Dr. Love and

Chef LaBreaux were there too. I gave them both a huge hug, genuinely surprised to see them.

My mama handed me a giant pair of scissors and I closed my eyes and went into a quick prayer.

God, thank you for blessing me with multiple chances at starting a new life. Thank you for never taking your hands off me, even in seasons where I wasn't even speaking to you. Thank you for blessing me with the people around me that you did and removing the ones who meant harm. May the success of this restaurant exceed my wildest dreams.

Amen.

On the count of three, I snipped the ribbon and the cheers almost made me temporarily go deaf. I felt my mom hugging me first, crying and praising God. I hugged her tighter and shed a few tears myself. The next person to hug me was Reina. I melted into her frame, thankful for new friendships that could stand the test of time. I remember being so against having female friendships, now I had a few women I could count on.

Loved that for me.

The next person to hug me was surprisingly Kamira. Guilt still twinged through my body, but she was a hard worker and would be a good mother. She loved her baby boy and I took it upon myself to set up a trust fund for him that he could touch when he became an adult. She also got monthly checks deposited to her account from Dre's life insurance policy. No one knew what happened to Dre's body and Kamira gave up on continuing the search for him, instead focusing on raising her son. I could see her becoming Assistant Manager for me one day but by no means were we close.

Chef LaBreaux hugged me next then pulled back to show her dazzling smile. "I knew you could do it Desiraè.... Much success to you!"

What a woman.

Someone who believed in me, gave me an opportunity, and nurtured my gifts and talent. I used to call her so much whenever I would get frustrated with running Le Reaux and she would pour into me with so much encouragement, firmness, and wisdom. Oftentimes, she reminded me that just because I was young did not mean that I was under qualified. She said being young gave me more time to make and learn from my mistakes. I felt like I could do anything,

Dr. Love hugged me next. "I am so proud of you. You have not only overcome so much but you've *grown* into yourself as well. Don't tell no-body, but you are my favorite client," she winked. I chuckled and hugged her tightly. I remember being so against going to therapy even though I knew that I needed help. Over the years, Dr. Love and I built a healthy rapport. She never took credit for healing me but I have no idea where I'd be if I didn't get under her care.

Getting to this space in my life was always in me though, even when I doubted myself.

The doors to the restaurant opened and those who had reservations were seated as quickly as they could. My hostess and waitresses were doing good so far and the bar was packed with people. My family had me take thousands of pictures and I even got an interview with The Triibe again. A few business owners in the area came out to congratulate me and we posed for pictures. Starting a business can often feel lonely and some people feel like they're in competition with each other. I was happy that people were so welcoming towards me and seemed genuine in connecting.

Cherrice and Joyy came up with a huge bouquet of white roses and a gift bag filled with samples of their wine they were working on releasing next year. "Hope you ready to get *drunk* tonight!" Joyy exclaimed, busting out a small little twerk. Cherrice egged her sister on and smirked at me.

"We are so proud of you, Rae. Can't wait to celebrate you later!" Cherrice hugged me once again, then walked over to speak to my family.

I was getting overwhelmed with the love and my hands were getting heavy with all the bouquets I was holding so I started walking to my office and stopped to check on the kitchen. My employees were hard at work, making sure every dish was prepared with love and efficiency.

"You don't need to worry about that today," Reign's voice called out behind me and I whipped around to face him. I started to object but he gave me a piercing look that shut me up. Instead of responding, I handed him my bouquets and he followed me to my office. To my surprise, there were already empty vases all over my desk and on the shelves.

"How did? When did..." I was about to be a blubbering mess today and my makeup was going to have to be redone if they kept this up.

"I told you... I got you shorty. You don't even have to ask 'cuz Imma gladly do it." I ran into his arms and gave him a hug. He tensed up at first but then he relaxed and brought me closer to him, resting his head on my shoulder while awkwardly patting my back.

Reign was... the simplest shit made me speechless.

"Reign... do you not hug nigga?" I pulled back and laughed at his slight discomfort. He was patting my back like I was a baby and I found that hilarious. He sucked his teeth, shaking his head.

"I do man... it's just...." his voice trailed off and I noticed him adjusting himself. I raised my brow and stepped back.

"Friends don't do that," I teased. He cut his eyes at me and stood up.

"They don't, that's why you can't be hugging me like that, while looking like that, while smelling that damn good," he stressed.

I smirked and rolled my eyes. "My bad Reign... anyways... Thank you for getting me vases for my roses. I appreciate you more than you know."

It wasn't just about the vases. It was the way he showed up for me yet never took credit or threw anything in my face. Reign was solid, and that was one of the things I loved most about him.

"It ain't shit Rae... you know that though," he called over his shoulder as he walked out.

After he walked out, I took a moment to myself and just took in the silence. I remember when I hated silence, but these days I welcomed it. Silence helped me center myself and stay present. It was easy to get lost in the moment and forget to breathe.

Even with shaky breaths, I was breathing easier these days.

***

After walking around the restaurant and greeting the patrons, getting pulled aside for interviews and pictures, and making sure my staff was doing okay, the day was finally over and I was ready to turn up with my loved ones. I changed into a pair of black shorts, a custom Mz. Earline's tee that was made into a corset and a pair of red platform heels. My mama and Jamaal made sure that the staff would clean up and stock everything that ran out while we operated today while I was across the street. Reina, Bri, Angie, and Robin walked with me with new matching shirts that said

CONGRATS CHEF RAE! On the front and dammit, if I didn't start crying again.

"Girlllllll. You don't even cry this much, please pull it together!" Bri playfully quipped, pulling me into her side.

"I'm just overwhelmed with the love," I blubbered. The girls huddled around me, giving the sweetest group hug. Reign, Chewy, and Linx walked up and immediately, Chewy began to play.

"Aw shit we hugging?" he joked, pulling Bri into a hug.

"Unt uh girl, don't hug him. His ass is fertile," Reina teased.

The way Bri jumped out his arms as if he had the cooties was comical to say the least. Under no circumstances, did she do men with multiple kids or multiple baby mamas. Chewy was cool to me, a fun guy to hang out with but our flirting was harmless and I would never take him seriously. He definitely had too many kids, too many baby mamas, and too much drama.

Reign eyed me and blurted, "The fuck you change into those little ass shorts for?"

All eyes were on us as I smirked at him. "Cuz it's time to turn up. Now tell me I look cute and let's go take some shots!" He rolled his eyes and followed behind us as we entered Vibes and Lines.

I was floored once again. There was a balloon arch in the shape of me with my Mz. Earline's tee on and a chef hat. Whoever the artist was managed to get the long braids I had in too. To the left was a black photo backdrop and a 360 photo booth that had neon lights spelling out *Congrats Chef Rae.* About one hundred shots were lined along the bar and I saw DJ Ca$hera in the corner starting to play music that had Reina and the girls popping their asses already. I screamed and wiped my tears, overwhelmed with the love already. We took shot after shot and at one point I found myself bopping on the bar like I was from out west.

My knees would pay for that in the morning.

But I didn't care.

I earned it.

Earned this peace.

Earned this forthcoming success.

"Aye... don't get too drunk. I got a surprise for you," Reign reached up and helped me off the bar and pushed a cup of water in my hand with some Liquid IV powder.

"A surprise?" My brows furrowed as I gulped the mixture of water and electrolytes down.

He walked off towards the DJ booth and grabbed the mic. His eyes were low and tinged with red, and I knew he was slightly buzzed because we convinced him to take three shots with us before he stuck to smoking with Dayvon and the twins.

Ca$hera lowered the music and all eyes were on him.

"Desiraè." he commanded me and my feet immediately moved to him.

"You sure that's not her new boyfriend?" I heard Jamaal's messy ass loudly whisper to my mama as I walked past them.

"Aight. Ion do all this talking shit but had to get on the mic one time for the lady of the hour. Desiraè, when I first met you, I ain't gone lie... I thought you were just some Instagram chef. You was snooping around here late at night, then again early in the day, recording yourself. I told you that yo' ass had to get in the field if you wanted people to take you serious... you was offended... but the next day, you walked into my shop with your head held high and some bomb ass food in your cart. Between my shop and my sister's you sold out. Over these last few months, I watched you hustle hard in spite of a whole lotta shit going on. You never folded. You never stopped dreaming. You never stopped getting in the field. We had a conversation recently and I told you I wanted to support your dreams as much as humanly possible. My sister has a solid woman in her corner and I have a new friend in mine too. So follow me..." he said, taking my hand.

Everybody filed out behind us. We stood in front of the store and Reign continued his speech.

"I think your name, your restaurant deserves to be known not just in Chicago, but all over the world and one day it will be. For now, let's get the whole city hipped to you. Look over there," he pointed. I turned my head and gasped. There in the distance was a huge digital billboard. It had a picture of me posing on one side in my Chef's coat and on the other side it had the words *Mz. Earline's Kitchen Now Open* with my business hours and the address.

"Reign...." I crumpled my face in my hands and cried *again*.

"It ain't shit Rae. I'm proud of you shorty" he replied, engulfing me in a hug.

My friends and family cheered and pulled out their phones, snapping pictures and videos of the billboard.

I couldn't believe this was my life now. One filled with love, support, and success. And like my girl Jhene Aiko said, life wasn't perfect...but everything was indeed beautiful here.

The End

Book Club Questions

1. If you and your partner were not aligned on having children, would you break up with them?

2. If your ex was contacting you on social media, would you tell your current partner? Or keep it to yourself? Discuss why.

3. What is your take on Dre's behavior after the argument he and Desiraè had? Was he wrong or justified for leaving?

4. How would you feel if your ex moved on not long after you broke up with them?

5. What is your opinion on LaTrice? Was she a victim or was she justified in her actions?

6. Should Reign and Desiraè pursue a relationship? Or should they remain friends?

7. What are your thoughts on LaReina and Reign?

8. Was Desiraè too harsh with LaShawn?

9. Is there a right way or a wrong way to grieve?

10. Do exes deserve our forgiveness?

11. Was Dre's hatred towards Shawn justified or misplaced?

12. If you were Desiraè, would you wait on Reign?

13. Is love enough to sustain a relationship?

Keeping Up With Kia

To keep up with all the vibes, lines, and a little bit of life in between, follow me on my socials:

Instagram.com/KiaSmithWrites

Join My Facebook Group

TikTok.com/KiaSmithWrites

Join the email list